WK DEC 2016
RU Sept A
RU June 18

LU JUN 2018
MI OCT 2018

D1792383

The Terminal City Saga

Terminal City

Winter's End

Reaper's Edge

BOOK ONE IN THE TERMINAL CITY SAGA

TERMINAL CITY

Trevor Melanson

EDGE SCIENCE FICTION AND FANTASY PUBLISHING
AN IMPRINT OF HADES PUBLICATIONS, INC.

CALGARY

Terminal City
Book One in the Terminal City Saga
Copyright © 2016 by Trevor Melanson

This is a work of fiction. Names, characters, places, and incidents are the products of the author's imagination or are used fictitiously and are not to be construed as real. Any resemblance to actual events, locales, organizations, or persons, living or dead, is entirely coincidental.

Edge Science Fiction and Fantasy Publishing
An Imprint of Hades Publications Inc.
P.O. Box 1714, Calgary, Alberta, T2P 2L7, Canada

In-house editing by Brian Hades
Interior design by Janice Blaine
Cover Illustration by Eran Fowler

ISBN: 978-1-77053-083-6

All rights reserved. No part of this book may be reproduced, scanned, or distributed in any printed or electronic form without written permission. Please do not participate in or encourage piracy of copyrighted materials in violation of the author's rights. Purchase only authorized editions.

EDGE Science Fiction and Fantasy Publishing and Hades Publications, Inc. acknowledges the ongoing support of the Alberta Foundation for the Arts and the Canada Council for the Arts for our publishing programme.

 Canada Council for the Arts   Conseil des Arts du Canada

Library and Archives Canada Cataloguing in Publication
CIP Data on file with the National Library of Canada

ISBN: 978-1-77053-083-6
(e-book ISBN: 978-1-77053-084-3)

FIRST EDITION
(J-20160628)
Printed in Canada
www.edgewebsite.com

Dedication

For Vancouver.
You're most beautiful in the rain, no matter what anyone says.

Heaven and hell suppose two distinct species of men, the good and the bad. But the greatest part of mankind float between vice and virtue.

—David Hume

Chapter 1

JACOB STOCKWELL NEVER *made himself the center of attention. Traveling from city to city one tavern at a time — befriending lonely strangers in the dim corners of America — Stockwell was, at first glance, a wholly unremarkable man. And perhaps that worked in his favour.*

For sooner or later, he would tell these strangers all the same tale. "Have you ever seen the devil?" he would ask. Because he had, he'd say. And not just through the deeds of wicked men — he had seen the devil's magic.

They called themselves necromancers, Stockwell would tell them, and he'd been tracking them all over this country to find out just how far the poison of necromancy had spread. They were possessed, he explained, made into Satan's minions. He'd seen them destroy a man's soul with only a thought, watched him drop dead.

"Now just imagine there were more of them," wrote Stockwell in a letter to one of his recruits. "Imagine they came after you or, worse, your children, setting them on the path to Hell. There's a sickness spreading under America's feet, in her soil, in her roots. If good men like you and I don't fight back soon, it will be too late."

And so some of them did. Thus, 1876 marks the birth of the modern inquisition.

The rest, as we know only too well, is history.
—Samuel Benedict, *The New Necromancer*

It was Friday night in Manhattan and people were traveling in packs, laughing, yelling, women's heels clamoring like hooves on cobblestone. Simon Paisley was middle-aged, overweight, and all but invisible to everyone around him. He caught a whiff of perfume as a group walked by, reminding him of the last time he'd been close enough to smell a woman. It had been a while.

In his mind, where Simon spent most of his life nowadays, he was planning the rest of his night in thirty-minute intervals. He figured he'd arrive home at about 10:30 — it had been another late night at the office — and that he would eat dinner until 11:00. Something microwavable. Then he'd take a half-hour bath. At 11:30, he would put on a movie, though he hadn't decided which one yet, and afterward he'd go to bed, assuming he didn't fall asleep on the couch. That was happening more and more.

Simon had grown increasingly fond of routines. He took pleasure in compartmentalizing his days, his life.

But there's a problem with plans, and it's that they have one hell of a natural enemy: chaos theory. A single moment in time, a single event— that's all it took to undo everything. Simon had learned that lesson the hard way.

The street light turned red.

Stepping briskly, Simon crossed the intersection, car engines humming on either side of him. He was already sweating through his dress shirt; fall was just around the corner, but summer had decided to go out with a bang. With his free hand, Simon loosened his tie and unfastened the top button of his shirt. Heat never used to bother him like this, but he'd put on some extra pounds over the last few years. Divorces could do that.

Simon turned the corner, his Upper East Side apartment popping into view. It was modest, all he could afford in Manhattan with the costs of child support. He didn't mind making the payments, though. He loved all three of his kids, more or less equally, and unlike their mother, they still reciprocated that love. It was too bad she didn't want them living with a necromancer.

He'd been a necromancer for twenty-six years now, Simon — a fact he regretted revealing to his ex-wife. It happened five years ago. He'd forgotten to lock the bottom drawer in his desk one day, and Sharon had bumped it open the next. Curiosity took care of the rest. She confronted him about the books she'd found, confused, and Simon, well, that's when he did something stupid. He told her the truth. He told her he was a necromancer. He explained that he used spirit energy to make things, to fix them, that he could communicate with the dead. He healed the paper cut on her index finger as proof, but proof made it worse. Proof made it unforgivable.

At least he got a good joke out of it. "How do you get a Catholic to file for divorce?" he'd say. "Ya tell her you're a necromancer."

Just then, Simon noticed a white, mostly windowless van idling out front of his apartment building. He wondered if someone was moving in. The van's back door slid open. A man stepped out. He was much taller than Simon and dressed in a black suit. His eyes were fixed on him, and then so was the rest of him.

"Can I help you?" asked Simon.

"You need to come with me," replied the tall man.

"Excuse me?"

"You need to get in the van." He grabbed Simon's shoulder. "Right now."

"Get your hands off me." Simon stepped back. "What do you think you're doing?"

The tall man, it turned out, was not a patient man. "No more warnings," he said. "Inside. Now."

Simon wasn't going to comply. If anything, he was going to run, but the tall man must have seen flight in his eyes. Before Simon could go anywhere, he was pinned against the passenger door, easily outmuscled. When it dawned on him to call for help, the tall man covered Simon's mouth with one large, rough hand. Simon made a muffled cry. Then he felt something sharp prick his neck. He bellowed another muted howl and tried to wriggle free, but his strength was diminishing. The world around him started to spin.

"See you soon, Mr. Paisley," said the tall man, removing an empty syringe from Simon's neck.

Simon hit the pavement.

The sound of a dripping pipe. Footsteps. Voices, but he couldn't make out the words.

Simon was coming to. He lifted his head and opened his eyes. He was indoors, someplace he didn't recognize. The lighting was dim. Cracked concrete comprised the floor; rusty copper pipes lined the low ceiling. He couldn't see the walls— lost, like he was, in the distant darkness.

Simon was sitting in a rickety wooden chair with his arms behind his back. His wrists were bound together with duct tape, his legs and torso tied to the chair. His head was pounding. He tried to recall what had just happened and it took him a minute to remember. The white van. The tall stranger. The needle. What had happened after that, Simon hadn't a clue. How much time had gone by, he couldn't say.

"Our friend is awake," said a man behind him.

Simon could hear two of them, but only one stepped into view. Simon didn't recognize him. He wore a black suit not unlike the tall man's.

"I hope you slept well," he said, an unlit cigarette dangling between his lips. He reached into his coat pocket and fetched a silver matchbox; it was embossed with a crucifix. "I'm Mr. Huxley." He swiped a match along the strike strip. "Behind you is Mr. Underwood. Do you know why you're here, Mr. Paisley?"

Mr. Huxley was an ugly man— a lived ugly, not born ugly. His dark brown hair was greasy and slicked back, exposing the corners of his receding hairline, and his hook nose looked like it had been broken more than once, probably for good reasons. Simon already hated him.

"No," replied Simon, "I don't." But he did. He knew exactly why he was here and who these men were too. It took him a second, but now there was no mistaking it. They were inquisitors. He'd never seen one before now, an inquisitor that is, but he'd heard about them. Every necromancer had, and every necromancer watched out for them. Like necromancers, they kept their existence secret, and thus the war between them remained all but invisible. For Simon Paisley, however, it had just come into plain sight.

"I said I don't know why I'm here," repeated Simon, even less convincingly this time. "I don't know what you want with me."

Mr. Huxley stared at him disapprovingly, sucking on his cigarette, listening to the pipe drip. Another minute passed.

"For God's sake, I don't know anything." Simon raised his voice, spit flying from his lips. "Whoever you're looking for, it isn't me." The grim reality of his situation was sinking in: they would torture him unless he confessed, and if he confessed, they would kill him.

"I hear you." Mr. Huxley was apparently back on speaking terms. "But I'm not sure I believe you. Do you, Mr. Underwood? Do you believe our friend here?"

"Can't say I do," said Mr. Underwood from somewhere behind Simon.

It all sounded very rehearsed.

"That's two against one." Mr. Huxley looked amused. "So what is it you're not telling us, Mr. Paisley?"

"How many times do you want me to say it?" asked Simon, shrugging, shaking his head. He leaned forward and whispered his words this time: "I don't know what the hell you're talking about."

"Interesting," replied Mr. Huxley, "because your ex-wife thinks otherwise." He was smiling victoriously, but like his words, Mr. Huxley's emotions felt practiced. "We inquired about you. She had lots to say, Sharon did, and it wasn't, well... particularly flattering. But she was quite helpful, a good God-fearing woman too. We liked her, didn't we, Mr. Underwood?"

"We did."

"She's a liar." Simon was now as furious as he was frightened. He wanted to kill these men almost as much as he wanted to save himself. Unlike his present company, however, he'd never killed anyone before, but he got thinking that he knew how, at least in theory.

"Seemed like an honest woman to me," said Mr. Huxley.

Simon had heard enough. He closed his eyes and dropped his head to his chest. Then, no louder than he breathed, he began to chant. Mr. Huxley didn't hear him, too busy listening to himself. Mr. Underwood, too deaf, listened to his partner as well, like an eager elementary school student.

"Would be a weird thing to lie about," said Mr. Huxley. "Still, we're thorough people. You're not here because of something your wife said. At least, it's not the only reason. We've scoured your apartment, Mr. Paisley. You're a man with many secrets, but you cannot hide them from us. We know who you are. We know *what* you are."

Simon's incantation was now a whisper, its words crystallizing with clarity. Though not comprehension: Only men and women who'd died could truly understand Deathspeak, the language of the dead— the language of necromancy.

Mr. Huxley, finally taking notice, furrowed his brow and took a step back. "What the hell do you think you're doing?"

Simon reopened his eyes. They were red — solid red — and aimed squarely at Mr. Huxley. The inquisitor fell to the ground choking, streams of blood pouring from his mouth and nose. But unfortunately for Simon, his attack ended as quickly as it had begun; a large, familiar hand covered Simon's mouth, silencing him and stopping the spell.

Mr. Huxley was on his hands and knees, moaning and grunting, spitting out mouthfuls of dark blood. "Son of a bitch!" A string of reddened saliva dangled from his bottom lip. Slowly, he picked himself back up. His face was whiter than heaven, but he managed to stand, if only barely. He wiped the blood from his mouth with the back of his hand, red seeping into his sleeve, then looked back toward Mr. Paisley, less confidently than before— but far more angrily, and that was worse.

"That was a very bad idea," he said, panting. "A very. Bad. Idea."

"Would that count as a confession?" asked Mr. Underwood.

"Yeah," said Mr. Huxley. "That would count as a confession."

Simon stared at Mr. Huxley with irreconcilable hatred in his eyes, but the red had faded from them.

"Any last words?" asked Mr. Huxley.

Mr. Underwood released his hand from Simon's mouth but kept it close, ready to mute him again.

"Fuck you," said Simon. "You'll get what you deserve. Sooner than you think, you bastards."

"You don't say," replied Mr. Huxley, unimpressed. "Care to elaborate?"

"Rowland— he's back. He will kill you, you know. You and your oversized partner. And there's nothing you can do to stop him."

"Rowland's dead." Mr. Huxley lit another cigarette and walked past Simon, who was still bound to his chair, unable to see either of his captors.

"You wish," uttered Simon.

"Not even necromancers are immortal, Mr. Paisley, as you're about to find out," said Mr. Huxley. "Rowland's no exception, and neither are you. I'd recommend asking God for forgiveness right about now, although I'm not sure God will believe you. I wouldn't blame him. He calls necromancy an 'abomination unto the Lord,' did you know that? Deuteronomy eighteen. Not that you would care." He stepped back into Simon's field of vision with a red gasoline jug in hand and a roll of duct tape around his wrist.

"You're not God," said Simon.

"Neither are you," replied Mr. Huxley, stepping forward. "But your kind, you have trouble understanding that." He pointed the jug at Simon; it made a swishing sound. "You act as if, well, you seem to think your magic makes you like *him*. But it doesn't, Mr. Paisley. You're not a god, certainly not the one true God. At best, you're a pebble with mountainous delusions. It's kind of funny, don't you think?"

No one laughed.

Mr. Huxley coughed, took another drag off his cigarette, and then looked like a man gathering his thoughts. "I'm sure you know the story of Adam and Eve," he said. "Even a necromancer like you. It's a... cultural touchstone. Now, my friend, what do you think the story of Adam and Eve is all about?"

"I'm not your fucking friend." Simon glared at him disdainfully. "And I don't care. It's a fairytale."

"Actually, it's a story about evil," said Mr. Huxley. "Evil is not a fairytale. On this, I hope we can both agree. Adam and Eve's story is about the form that evil takes here on Earth. As the story goes, Satan, disguised as a snake, tricks Eve into eating forbidden fruit from the tree of knowledge of good and evil, which angers God, who in turn kicks man and woman out of Eden— yada, yada, yada.

"But why did God forbid them from eating that fruit in the first place?" he asked. "God's a smart god, the smartest a god could be, so he must have had a good reason. Was he just toying with them, testing their obedience?

"No," said Mr. Huxley, crouching down so he and Simon were eye level. "God doesn't play games, Mr. Paisley.

"God wanted us to understand that evil knowledge is harmful. He hoped that, all by ourselves, through our wisdom and humility — the virtues he was gracious enough to give us — we would triumph over the temptation of evil knowledge. That's why he gave us the choice, necromancer. Because he believes in free will. But we made the wrong one, and we continue to make wrong choices. You especially, Mr. Paisley— you've made a lifetime of wrong choices."

Mr. Huxley finished his cigarette and flicked it to the floor.

"Evil knowledge is a plague," he said. "It pollutes your soul from the inside, destroys your goodness, your innocence, your faith, until all that's left is a shell, scraped clean like a hollowed clam. The man you were, the man made in God's image— gone.

Which is bad enough, but you're also contagious, Mr. Paisley. Your wonderful wife had the strength to resist, but what about your children— will they? Just how many more souls would you corrupt if we let you walk out of here tonight?

"That's what we're fighting against. Isn't that right, Mr. Underwood?" Mr. Huxley held his gaze on Simon.

Mr. Underwood stepped into view and nodded his big head. "Need to keep it contained," he said.

Simon forced a sharp laugh. "Justify it however you like," he replied. "At the end of the day, you just like killing people."

Mr. Huxley looked at him for a couple long seconds, swiping a drop of sweat from Simon's brow with his index finger as if to sample it. Simon was drenched in the stuff, his clothes clinging to his arms and legs.

"Ali Kazmi," said Mr. Huxley, staring over Simon's shoulder, staring as if there was something behind him worth staring at— though Simon suspected there wasn't. "Good kid. Lived in Toronto with his mom and dad and his older sister, Maryam. He liked hockey and video games." Mr. Huxley's tone had changed. "Ali was just twelve years old when Jared Snow paid him and his family a visit. But Jared didn't care about Ali. He didn't care about Maryam or Mom and Dad either. Jared only cared about two things: himself and necromancy. Everything else was... sustenance, a resource for the taking. Every person, every home. He would kill and steal and kill and steal— over, and over, and fucking over. He felt nothing. He couldn't. The necromancy had... numbed his humanity. It had consumed him, Mr. Paisley, and in doing so came to consume Ali. He was just twelve years old when Jared Snow murdered him and his family. Murdered him because that bastard needed a place to stay for a week."

Mr. Huxley bit off a piece of duct tape and slapped it over Simon's mouth, locking in his last words. "I've let you say your piece, my friend," he said in almost a whisper, "but you've got it all wrong. It's necromancers who like killing people. I've seen too many innocent men and women — children — die at the hands of your kind in ways you can't imagine." He spoke softly. "I'm sorry it's come to this. I don't want to kill you. I don't like killing people, Mr. Paisley." Then he stood back up. "But you give me no fucking choice."

Mr. Huxley stepped forward, lifting the jug of gasoline over Simon's head, and began to pour. He showered his hair, his shoulders, drops splashing Simon's face, and then the rest of him — his arms and legs, his fingers and feet — until the jug was empty and every part of Simon was slippery and smelled like gasoline. Then Mr. Huxley dropped the container, and it was time.

The gas was painfully pungent. Worse, some had seeped into Simon's mouth. It tasted like it smelled — like poison. He didn't want to die, but he knew this was the end. The thing was, deep down Simon had always figured he was immortal. He didn't think about it — he didn't *want* to think about it. He just felt it, and left it there. Now, for the first time in his life, his immortality had abandoned him, and he was left feeling like some animal meeting its inevitable end. Like he'd been so stupid for not seeing it sooner, for not believing in death even as he practiced in it.

Mr. Huxley reached into his pocket and pulled out his pack of cigarettes. He flicked the lid open and looked inside. "Last one," he said, fetching his matchbox, the silver one with the cross. Mr. Huxley lit the cigarette. But not Simon, not yet. "I know it might seem unnecessarily cruel," he said, "burning you alive." He took a long drag. "But they say if you don't burn a necromancer, if you don't get rid of the body, they might come back from the dead. Not sure I believe that myself, but I like to think the fire is… cleansing. That maybe it can burn the corruption out of you, give you hope for Purgatory. But I'm not God."

Then Mr. Huxley lit a second match and took a step backward. "Farewell, Simon." He flicked the small flame forward.

Simon watched the match spiral through the air, wondering if it might go out before it reached him, not that it mattered now. The rest happened so quickly. The fire landed on his lap then raced toward every trace of gasoline, engulfing every part of him, until the inferno was all he could see or smell or inhale, until fire was his universe and death his best friend.

They had taken everything from him: his world, his dignity, his life. Everything but his thoughts. Those were still his, at least for a while. Like everyone who dies and goes to the Spirit Realm, Simon would fade into nothingness, into less than a memory. He would fade, and he would fade alone. But for now, even as the fire scorched his flesh, even as he screamed unconsciously, he held onto his mind.

In the end, it was his ex-wife he thought about. Sharon, who had betrayed him. Sharon, for whose folly he was dying. Sharon, who was still the love of his life. And so he remembered the good times and forgave her for the rest.

Simon Paisley's body was no longer recognizable, melted into a black and red sculpture that could have been any human being. They all looked the same afterward, thought Mr. Huxley, standing five feet away with an empty bucket in hand. The fire had been put out, but the body was still sizzling. Still hot with life.

Mr. Huxley slid a cell phone out of his pants pocket and dialed the only number on the contact list.

After four rings, a woman answered. "He's dead, I hope."

"Simon Paisley's been taken care of," replied Mr. Huxley.

"Good, good. Glad to hear it. Keep up the good work, hun." She suddenly sounded pleasant, if not a bit condescending, exaggerating her Texas accent as she often did. "But our work never ends, now does it? Your next target is Lester Wright. Mr. Wright has been on our list for quite some time. We have reason to believe he's somewhere in Terminal City. An informant of ours claims she saw him on a bus."

"Terminal City," he said. "So, you're sending us to Canada, eh? It's been a while."

"Very funny, Mr. Huxley, but I wouldn't quit your day job. I'll email you the details."

"There's one more thing." Mr. Huxley hesitated.

"Spit it out, sugar," she replied.

"Well, it's probably nothing, just an empty threat, but Mr. Paisley, he said that Rowland had… returned or something."

"Rowland? You're sure he said Rowland?" She sounded concerned. Mr. Huxley was surprised. She never sounded concerned.

"I'm sure, yeah."

"That is… interesting. Well, don't worry your little head about it. Just focus on your job, Mr. Huxley." She hung up.

Mr. Huxley pocketed his phone a little too aggressively. "Between you and me, Mr. Underwood," he said, "Ms. Westcott really pisses me off sometimes."

"Why's that?" asked Mr. Underwood.

"She can be really disrespectful, you know? Not just with me but everyone. She always seems so — what's the word — dismissive, I guess."

"Oh."

Mr. Huxley rolled his eyes. "Never mind," he said. "Can you go fetch the bags? I'll wait here."

Mr. Underwood nodded before wandering off into the darkness. Mr. Huxley listened to his heavy footsteps clanking up the metal staircase at the far end of the room. He listened until he couldn't hear them anymore. And then Mr. Huxley keeled over, planting both hands on his knees, and began to dry heave.

Ooowack.

"Not again."

Ooowack.

"You're saving lives." His voice was low and raspy. "You're doing God's—"

Oooooowack.

Mr. Huxley burped, exhaled, then spat on the ground.

After a minute of slow, deep breaths, he stood back up, reaching into his coat for another cigarette. When he flipped open the pack, he remembered he was all out.

Mr. Huxley sighed.

"Goddamnit."

Chapter 2

I DON'T MIND *the rain. It comes down a lot in Terminal City, that's for sure, but let me ask you this: is there any city out there more beautiful than Terminal? When the sun comes out, and even when it doesn't, this city shines. The rain keeps it clean, keeps it shimmering, keeps our pocket of the world perfect. At the end of the day, even a rainy one like this, there's no place I'd rather call home.*
—Terminal City Mayor Sandeep Samra

Mason Cross was getting ready to leave. Or at least he should have been. He was lost in his head again, standing idly in his dad's old library, reading each bookshelf like a page, from left to right.

Throughout his twenty years on this planet, Mason had often been told that he was very much his father's son. He'd always hated hearing this, not wanting to be anyone but his own man. Lately, however, it bothered him less—ever since Dad's untimely death in a car accident.

That was nine months ago. It was early September now, and a lovely day according to his mother. But Mason was still inside, in a room where he'd spent much of his childhood, reading and writing, drawing and thinking—unraveling his creative ambitions, and there had been many. So while officially it was Dad's den, really, it had always been Mason's room. After all, the books here were mainly for show. There were no guilty pleasures or mass-market paperbacks—only unread classics, books fit for a man like John Cross, the brilliant professor, the great writer.

Soft beams of sunlight slipped past the windowpanes with perfect precision, dappling the floorboards and his father's oak desk with hues of gold, as if the room itself knew this was goodbye and wanted to look its best.

Someone knocked. Mason turned around.

"Mason." His mom stepped through the door with a book under her arm. She was dressed in a grey cardigan today, the same shade as her hair— she'd only recently stopped dyeing it. "I was rifling through some boxes in the garage.... It's such a mess in there." She sighed, shaking her head as if disappointed in herself or— who knows. "Most of it was your dad's, you know. Anyway, I found this and remembered he wanted you to have it." She handed her son the thick leather-bound book.

Mason flipped it over, examining both sides. The book looked old and its cover was plain. He tried to open it and discovered he couldn't.

"Oh, there's one of those, what are they called..." She pointed. "A combination lock."

He saw the lock along the fore edge, sealing the book shut. "Weird. What's the combination?"

"I don't know." She shrugged. "I thought maybe you would. I'm sure you'll figure it out. You two always did think alike."

"Thanks, I guess." Mason didn't even know where to begin.

She smiled at him, inhaling audibly, as if suddenly deprived of oxygen. "I just know he's so proud of you."

She did this a lot: spoke as if her late husband were still around. In her mind, he was. Sometimes she'd tell Mason that his dad had spoken to her in a dream the night before. Mason didn't believe in stuff like that, but it was her way of coping, so he kept his opinions to himself. Even when she started going to church. Before three months ago, he hadn't realized she considered herself a Christian. Occasionally, she would ask him to come, but he never did. Her husband, an unrepentant atheist until the end, would have been more outspoken were he not dead.

"Anyway," said Mason, "I'm all packed now."

"Is your stuff in the—"

"Yeah. Everything's in the car."

"Okay." She hesitated. "I'll get my keys." She walked out slowly.

While his mother fetched her car keys, Mason went to the bathroom for no other reason than to check his reflection. For a while, he tried to convince himself that the face staring back at him was an adult's. As usual, it was to no avail. He used to believe turning twenty would make him feel like a grown man. Now, with his twenty-first birthday just around the corner, he was hoping that moving out would do the trick.

Mason headed downstairs to his mom's car, the nicer of the two in the driveway. He wasn't taking his own vehicle, a boxy brown Volvo that once belonged to his dad, because he wouldn't need it where he was going.

Tomorrow, Mason would begin classes at Carwin University, Terminal City's premier institute of higher learning. Woo-wee. It was also where Mason's father had worked (as a tenured professor of Latin and linguistics). He'd often wondered if that had helped his application, if they had taken special pity on the son of a departed professor. In truth, up until about nine months ago, Mason hadn't been sure he would ever go to university. He'd successfully avoided it for three years, not wanting to follow in his father's footsteps, as if that would have been too easy or something. But Mason had grown tired of mundane jobs, and he missed his dad.

The heavy book in his hand stirred up memories of his father, but then so did most things. He glanced at its unassuming cover and wondered what he might find inside.

The book wasn't all his father had left him. In his will, John Cross had left his son a house— a rather conveniently located one, in fact, right at the edge of Carwin's campus. The home was old and big, and it might have been beautiful if not for the overgrown hedges and chipped paint. It had been passed down three generations now. His dad said it was a family heirloom. That seemed to be his excuse for keeping it. The truth was John had done most of his writing in that house— presumably in peace and quiet, away from his family. But now it belonged to Mason, and today it would become his new home.

"Are you sure you have everything you need?" his mother asked, locking the front door.

"Yeah," he replied. "I'm sure."

She had a bouquet of flowers tucked under her arm, purple lilies this time. Mason didn't need to ask why. His dad's grave was on the way.

They got into the car. She was driving. From the passenger seat, Mason reached into the back and dropped his new book into an open cardboard box packed full of dishes that didn't match. Scribbled on the box in messy black felt was the word *FRAGILE*. He should have heeded his own warning. The book landed with a crunch.

"Shit."

His mother looked at him, eyebrows furrowed, as if that shattered cup might be a sign of things to come now that he was on his own.

"It's fine," said Mason.

She shook her head and started the engine.

They took the highway. Terminal City was an hour's drive from Sanford, the town in which Mason had spent most of his life. Honestly, he couldn't believe it had taken him this long to finally escape. He was more excited than he let on.

Mason hung his arm out the window and watched trees go by— and occasionally, another car passing them. His mother had always been a slow driver, but after her husband drove himself into a tree, she became an even slower one.

As she turned off the highway, it began to rain. "I hope it doesn't rain all day." She switched on the windshield wipers. "It was so nice this morning."

"Rain can be nice too," replied Mason.

"Well, I prefer sunshine," she said.

"Ah." He continued staring out the window. Their conversations were never long.

It was pouring by the time they reached Terminal City. Mason liked coming here. He'd always felt he was a city person deep down, though he'd never actually lived in one. Terminal was a modern metropolis, its teal glass skyline clustered along the oceanfront like a crown of inverted icicles. And cranes— lots of cranes. It was a growing city, gentrification showing its polished fangs on every street corner— a café here, a brew pub there. If anything was going to stop Terminal City, it was nature, crammed as it was between two endless bodies: the blue-green mountains to the north and the ocean to the west.

"Do you see that?" his mother asked, pointing upward.

Mason turned his gaze downtown, just beyond the river that cut through the city's core. "The big tower?"

"I read in the paper that it's already the tallest in Terminal City," she said. "I think it's supposed to open next spring. I forget what they're calling it."

"The Apex." He'd read the story too. The skyscraper was a contemporary monolith, its glass body twisting upward like licorice.

"That's it. Must be quite the view up there." The car was slowing down. "I'll just be a second," she said, unsnapping her seat belt, "unless you want to join me."

They were idling outside his father's cemetery. Mason could see his grave through the window. "That's okay," he said.

His mother didn't press him on it. She grabbed her umbrella and the lilies from the back seat, and then she stepped outside. She was quick, like she said. Mason figured she just wanted Dad to have fresh flowers. It was her way of showing she hadn't forgotten. And perhaps something more: He saw it in the way she moved, her fingers sliding down the flower stems as she propped them against his father's grave— it was the closest she would ever get to touching him again.

Unlike downtown, Carwin University was mostly deserted when they arrived. Mason liked it here too. The buildings were a mishmash of old and new, from modern-day glass towers to century-old Neo-Gothic halls. Although he didn't like the ones that looked like concrete bunkers— brutalism was just too drab, even for Mason. Thankfully, there were trees everywhere, dotting and surrounding most of campus. It meant you couldn't see the downtown skyscrapers from Carwin, but it was peaceful— for now.

They pulled into the driveway of Mason's new home. The house sat on the edge of campus, in a cul-de-sac surrounded by other, much nicer properties. His was the neighborhood's black sheep, the one whose front yard had grown into an unruly jungle. He told himself that he would fix the place up, but he knew deep down that was probably a lie.

Mason stepped out of the car and into the rain.

"Your jacket is in the trunk," his mother said, turning off the ignition.

He sprinted to the front door — at least the porch was dry — then fished out a silver-colored key from his pocket. He struggled with the lock — it was old, like everything else in this house — until finally it clicked. "Stupid thing."

The floorboards creaked as he stepped inside. It had been a year since his last visit, but everything still looked the same, as it had for decades (his father always had better things to do). The clocks, however, were an hour behind— the only sign that anything had changed.

Mason dropped his keys into a small ceramic dish in the foyer then hurried back to the car. His mother popped the trunk open. He grabbed his jacket, a black leather one, and slipped it on before unloading two duffle bags full of clothes. He carried them to the house, one in each hand, and then came back for more.

For the most part, Mason had packed light— with a couple exceptions. Resting in the open box under his arm was a faded wolf figurine, its lifeless plastic eyes fixed on him. It was a gift from his mom, bought nine years ago on a road trip up north. As a child, Mason had been fascinated by wolves. She'd insisted he keep it, forgetting, as she sometimes did, that he was no longer eleven years old.

Once everything had been moved into the house, Mason said a sort-of goodbye — "I guess I'll see you later" — but that wasn't going to cut it.

Mom stepped out of the car and hugged him, leaning her head on his chest. "I'm going to miss you," she said.

"I'm still close by," he replied.

She sniffled. "No, dear, it's not the same. I've got no one to share the house with now." She wiped her face with a tissue.

Mason didn't know what else to say. He considered suggesting she buy a pet but said nothing instead, waiting for her to finish crying, wondering if he should be sad too. He didn't see the big deal.

"You take care of yourself," she said after a minute. "I love you."

"Love you too," he replied.

She kissed his cheek before getting back in the car, and then she was gone.

Mason returned to the house, drenched. His dark hair was a mop, rogue strands patterning his forehead, water dripping down his face. He combed them back with his fingertips then closed the front door and surveyed his surroundings, wondering where to begin.

Because he didn't have much to unpack, the process was relatively painless. The master bedroom upstairs, which had a big window overlooking the backyard, became his new room. It already had a bed and a desk, buried under binders, pens, and loose-leaf paper. His father's notes. Mason piled them and put them aside. Then he hung his clothes, arranged his books, and found a nice spot on the desk for his wolf. The room was his. It looked pretty much the same.

By dinnertime, the boxes and bags he'd brought with him were empty. He tossed them into the recycling bin in the garage then meandered around the kitchen aimlessly, wondering what to do now, as if living alone brought new expectations. Eventually, he fetched an apple out of the fridge. A McIntosh. Mason preferred the green ones, but he munched it all the same, staring out his living-room window at the setting sun— a faint, orange blur buried behind sheets of rain. The downpour still hadn't let up.

He made his way outside to watch the evening sky from under the cover of his porch. Heavy clouds formed a dark canopy overhead, stretching across the sky like an endless grey quilt. Or almost endless. That hint of orange still hung to the horizon, just barely, losing its grip by the minute. Mason sank into a white wicker chair and reached into his jacket pocket for his cigarettes.

Flick.

He closed his eyes, smoke seeping out his nostrils, and listened to the rain drumming on the roof.

Mason had picked up his smoking habit a few months ago as a way of self-medicating. After his dad's death, he'd been offered antidepressants but ultimately decided against them. He wanted his emotions to be authentic, whatever the hell that meant. So he started buying cigarettes instead, and he'd yet to stop— but he would, he told himself, before they killed him. In the meantime, they were one of the few things that helped him relax.

Unfortunately, his most recent meditation would be short-lived. He was halfway through his cigarette when a voice yelled, "Lovely weather!"

Mason opened his eyes.

A short man in a yellow raincoat was walking up the driveway, his suitcase bumping along the pavement behind him. When he got to the porch, he lugged his baggage up each step with both hands and then finally — in the most annoying way possible — stomped his boots on the floorboards, one after the other.

Mason took another drag off his cigarette.

"Does your mother know you smoke?" the man asked, standing still now, panting, every corner of his raincoat dripping.

She didn't, his mom.

"Who are you?" Mason ignored the question.

The small man removed his hood to reveal a bald head and a familiar face. His name was Lester Wright. He was an old friend of Mason's father.

"Lester? What are you doing here?" asked Mason.

"Moving in," said Lester matter-of-factly, followed by a toothy grin.

"What do you mean you're moving in?" Mason cocked an eyebrow.

"I'm going to live here," replied Lester, glancing toward the house appraisingly, "with you. If you don't mind,"

Mason was pretty sure he did mind but was lost for words. Lester had this effect on people. Nine months ago at his father's funeral, Lester had asked Mason if he believed in an afterlife. Mason had responded, in somewhat uncertain terms, that he did not. Lester had then stared at him for a few seconds too long, rubbing his stubble, adding just one word before walking away: "Interesting." They hadn't spoken since. Until now, of course.

"I should explain myself," said Lester. "I'm here on behalf of your dad."

"You're here on behalf of my dead dad?" replied Mason.

"That is correct."

"So, what, you've been talking to his ghost?"

"Well." Lester scratched his head awkwardly. "You might say that."

Mason was baffled. "And?"

"And what?"

"And what did my dead dad say?" Mason finished his cigarette and flicked it off the porch, thinking he should probably pick up an ashtray at some point.

"Right," said Lester, stalling. "It's very complicated."

"I'm sure it is," replied Mason. "Anyway, Lester, it's, you know, nice to see you again and all that, but I don't think—"

"How about this," Lester interjected. "Let me stay here for a week. Just one week. If you still want me gone next Sunday, then so be it. Sayonara, little old Lester. I shall be on my merry way, no complaints. Promise ya. Scout's honor."

Mason seriously doubted Lester had ever been a Boy Scout.

"Kid, it took me twenty hours to get here," said Lester. "Twenty hours on one of those shitty, cramped buses they have." He sighed, wiping raindrops from his face. "I'm not a young man like you, sonny. Look at me." He looked at Mason. "Look how old and feeble I am."

"Jesus Christ." Mason didn't like losing negotiations and yet— "okay, fuck, whatever. You can stay but just for one week," he said. "I mean it, man. After that, you're on your own. Are we clear?"

"Crystal." Lester gave a thumbs-up. "I have just one more request."

Mason shook his head, looking defeated. "What?"

"A cigarette."

Mason passed him his pack. "Does *your* mother know *you* smoke?" he asked.

"Yes," said Lester, sliding a cigarette between his lips. "She does. Lighter?"

"Here." Mason lit it for him before wandering back inside the house, confused and annoyed.

At any rate, he figured he should make dinner or perhaps order some. Mason didn't have much in stock, after all, or an internet connection yet. He found an old phone book buried in a cupboard beside the stove.

Lester stepped inside after his cigarette. "I'm going to bed," he proclaimed. "I tell ya, I don't know how anyone falls asleep on those buses. I might as well be a zombie."

A rather talkative zombie, thought Mason. "Anywhere but the master bedroom," he said, rifling through pages. "That's mine."

"Naturally," replied Lester. "Enjoy your evening, boy."

"Good night, or evening— whatever."

As Lester headed upstairs, Mason stared out the window. That orange on the horizon had faded to black now, gone like the last ember on a cold night.

A door upstairs slammed shut. Mason shook his head. Just what the hell was Lester Wright doing here?

Chapter 3

MASON WAS NIBBLING on his fifth slice of cheese pizza. He could have kept going but figured he should save some for breakfast. The TV was on, if only because it seemed better than staring at the wall. It was some hokey nineties romcom he couldn't name. In the kitchen behind him, a sticky note pasted on the fridge read, CALL CABLE COMPANY TOMORROW.

"Don't ever let me go, James."

"I won't, Sally. Not ever. As God is my witness, from now on I'll be the man you deserve."

Mason ended up staring at the wall anyway. Specifically, at *The Death of Socrates*, his father's print of the famous painting. It had been hanging there for as long as Mason could remember. His dad first told him the story when he was young and again as a teenager. Sitting in a dungeon surrounded by his pupils, Socrates, the great philosopher, hangs his hand over a cup of poison— over death itself. His fatal sentence is punishment for doubting the gods and corrupting the youth, the jurors had decreed. For asking too many questions. All around him, his students despair, save his best, Plato, sitting solemnly in his dim grey robes at the foot of the bed.

"Wise people are rarely safe," Mason's dad had told him one winter morning, "especially the honest ones." The citizens of Athens had silenced their wisest. If only his father's death could have possessed such poetry.

That was another winter morning Mason would never forget. His father hadn't come home the night before, but that was hardly unusual. He'd often stayed on campus writing into the early morning. When genius strikes, hang on tight, he'd said.

Apparently, he hadn't applied that logic to his steering wheel.

Mason first heard their voices in his dreams, the cops who arrived at 6 a.m. to tell his mother her husband was dead. Then came her cries of disbelief. In his nightmare, her screams were his. He'd been walking down the highway to Terminal City, its skyline looming over the horizon like a distant fantasy that never came closer— no matter how far he traveled. Far enough that he collapsed to the asphalt, collapsed under his own weight. That's when Mason woke up and realized his cries were coming from downstairs. But the dread, that was definitely his.

He'd never felt so afraid.

Outside, the wind was howling. The old house creaked after each heavy gust as rain drummed on the windows like pebbles poured over glass.

Mason stood up and walked into the kitchen, carrying the cardboard pizza box, a large, with both hands. But when he swung the fridge door open, ready to put away the last of his dinner, the light inside went out.

"What the hell?"

It wasn't just the fridge. The whole house had gone dark. James and Sally were no more, their movie love forever preserved by their absence. Mason left his pizza in the fridge, closing the door to keep in whatever cold remained, then found a small black flashlight in a drawer beside the stove. It still worked, but its batteries must have been low; it flickered and shined a faint, warm yellow. He would have gone to bed, but he wasn't tired— never was at the right times.

Mason stepped outside to survey the neighborhood. The power outage had hit the whole campus, at least as far as he could see. Resting his arm on the porch railing, he spotted his cigarettes lying a foot from his fingers, apparently where Lester had left them. He figured he might as well have another.

After his smoke, Mason lumbered back inside and headed to the bathroom to wash the cigarette smell from his hands. But he didn't make it very far. His flashlight had caught something unusual— and his attention. It was a door underneath the stairwell, painted white, same as the walls, and blocked by a bookcase. A hidden door, or perhaps just a forgotten one. He'd never noticed it, not once all these years, and he probably wouldn't have were it not for his flashlight, its yellow beam giving contrast to the doorframe's subtle protrusion.

Maybe it was just an empty closet, but Mason wasn't a fan of maybes. He preferred answers, and with nothing better to do, he was determined to get one. And so, resting his flashlight on the carpet, Mason grabbed one end of the bookcase with both hands and dragged it backward for what felt like three feet— it was hard to tell in the dark. He fetched his flashlight from the floor and stepped forward for a better look. The door had a small glass handle. Mason gave it a twist.

The hidden entrance creaked open. Inside, he found unfinished plywood stairs burrowing downward into a black abyss. He hadn't realized the house had a basement. He stepped through. As cautiously as he could, Mason crept down the staircase a step at a time, one hand clinging to his flickering flashlight, the other tracing the cement wall beside him. He could still hear the wind howling outside. The old house moaned.

Mason made it to the bottom and felt the coldness of the concrete floor through his socks. He stepped lightly, scanning the basement with his flashlight— the only thing between him and total darkness. There were no windows down here, or much of anything, really, save three soggy cardboard boxes piled against the wall.

"Smaller than I thought you'd be," he muttered. The basement was unexpectedly tiny, hardly bigger than his kitchen.

Mason ruffled through the boxes, but like the room itself, they were disappointingly empty. He was about to leave, but then, once more, his flashlight caught something on the wall. They were letters this time, or what looked to be letters, carved into the concrete, though he couldn't read them. He'd never seen symbols like these, not even in books. They were simple and rugged, jagged like they'd been spelled out with snapped toothpicks. Mason ran his fingers across each letter and thought he felt two words. Two words that could have meant anything in the world.

His flashlight flickered once more and then died.

"Shit."

Mason couldn't see anything. He smacked his flashlight a few times, but the damn thing was deader than Dad. He took that as his cue to leave, though he couldn't see the exit. He turned on his heel and retraced his steps, until finally he spotted a soft sliver of navy blue above him— the doorway out of here.

Mason stepped toward where he thought the stairs would be, his arms outstretched before him to ward off danger. He nearly tripped on the bottom step, catching the handrail just in time. "Son of a bitch." He took a deep breath then continued upward.

Mason made it out, alive, shutting the basement door behind him. It was still dark up here, but at least he could sort of see — if only enough to keep himself from running into things. He pushed the bookshelf back into place then ambled down the shadowy hallway to his kitchen, hoping to find spare batteries.

Instead, he found the dark silhouette of another man, standing in the middle of the room, staring at him. Then came a loud smash. Mason stumbled backward into the wall, clinging onto his flashlight like a weapon.

"Jesus Christ, son!" It was a voice he recognized. "Don't scare me like that!"

"Lester," said Mason, exhaling relief.

"You almost gave me a heart attack. I'm an old man, you know."

"I thought you were sleeping," replied Mason. "What are you doing down here?"

"Pouring myself a glass of water," answered Lester, gazing down at the shattered remains of his endeavour. "I guess I'll have to pour another."

"Right," said Mason, regaining some composure. "Just watch your step. Clean the glass in the morning. It's too dark right now."

"Yes, sir, housemaster, sir."

Mason ignored that. "I'm going to bed," he said. "Good night."

"Sleep tight," replied Lester, fetching himself another glass from the cupboard.

After brushing his teeth in the dark, Mason felt his way to his bedroom. He locked the door behind him, undressed, leaving his clothes in a rumpled heap on the floor, then threw himself onto his new king-sized bed, which was actually quite old and squeaked.

Mason landed on a book. Immediately, he knew which book it was: his father's posthumous gift. He rolled over, grabbed it from underneath his body, and tossed it off the bed.

Thump.

Mason closed his eyes and did his best to fall asleep.

◆❖◆

Sleep wasn't having him. Two hours had passed and Mason was still awake, wondering about the book on the floor. Curiosity could be a cruel bastard. He sighed, slid out of bed, walked over to his desk, and then shuffled through its drawers. He was pretty sure he saw a candle in one of these— ah, there it was. He placed the candle on his desk, beside his wolf, and found his lighter in the pocket of his crumpled jeans.

Mason checked the time on his cell phone. It said 1:04 a.m. At this point, he'd be lucky if he got five hours of sleep, but he knew the drill— it involved lots of coffee.

Mason lit the candle, grabbed his book off the floor, and then sat down and stared at its silver combination lock, flickering orange from the flame. He was completely clueless. There were four digits, ten thousand possibilities. He started with the year. It stayed shut. He flipped through some of his father's notes, scanning for four digit numbers. Nothing.

It would only take a few hours to go through every possibility. Mason considered it, for another time. First, he would try a few more years. He began with Dad's birth year and the year he married Mom. Then he tried the year after that, and the lock clicked open. It was the year Mason had been born. He lifted the cover, a little hesitantly, his old friend dread marching down his spine.

Mason worried about what he would find inside, but he wasn't sure why. The worst had already happened. Dad was dead. What did his secrets matter now?

The pages inside were yellow and looked old. They smelled old too. The first one was blank, but on the second, written in ink, were three words: *The Necromancer's Grimoire*.

Mason was immediately baffled. It didn't sound like anything his father studied— at least, not anything he was aware of. He turned to the next page, a table of contents. The book had eighty-six chapters in all. He read a few of their titles: *Chapter VII: Incantations*, *Chapter XXV: The Spirit Realm*, *Chapter LXVI: Summoning*. Mason began flipping through the book's many pages. It was biblical in size, but size was about all it shared in common with the Bible.

Somewhere in chapter eleven he found a picture of a deformed human being. The caption said it was a reanimated corpse. He shook his head.

"What the fuck am I looking at?"

On the bottom of the same page were two lines written in a language Mason couldn't understand. But come to think of it, the alphabet looked familiar, like that writing he'd found on the basement wall. That couldn't be a coincidence. He continued scanning the book, finding more lines of the same strange language every few pages. The inscription was always dark, jagged, indented— almost carved into the page. He didn't know what to make of it, or anything in this book for that matter.

Meanwhile, it was only getting later. Mason had to accept that he wouldn't find the answers he was looking for tonight. Hesitantly, he closed the book, figuring he ought to be awake for his first day of university.

He slipped back into bed and stared at the ceiling. Opening the book had only added to his confusion. But not for long, he told himself. He'd figure out what this book meant— and what it meant to Dad. When Mason put his mind to something, he seldom failed to find the answer, even when it wasn't the one he was hoping for. That was something else he and his father had in common.

As tiredness overtook him, Mason closed his eyes. His brain was an impatient animal, always nudging him with its nose, raring to go, when all he wanted to do was sleep. But even the hungriest beasts tire out after a time. Slowly, Mason's clear thoughts turned to mud, until finally he fell from reality and into the chaotic world of dreams.

Chapter 4

WITH THE BOOK still fresh on his mind, Mason went to his first class of the day tired and about five minutes late. Perhaps he had smacked the snooze button too liberally, or maybe he should have just gone to bed earlier. His hair was still wet from the shower when he arrived.

Thankfully, that class ended early. Mason hunted down the campus café, Scholarly Addictions, and shuffled into a long, snaking line of uncomfortably sober students. It seemed he wasn't the only one recovering from summer hours. He bought the largest, a twenty ounce, and headed to his next class, philosophy, realizing, shit, he was going to be late again.

"Where the fuck?" Mason's watch struck 11:03 a.m. He was having trouble finding the right building: Sherwood Hall. He'd written directions on a folded piece of paper, but they were failing him. Finally, he asked a nearby student, who, by the looks of her, was late too. She told him the building was on University Avenue, three blocks that way. He jogged, slipping along the way. The rain had stopped, but the ground was still wet, the sky still overcast.

11:07 a.m.: Mason found his lecture hall and pushed open one of its heavy wooden doors with his right hand, spilling coffee on his left.

"You're late," said the professor, a good-looking woman in her thirties. She eyed him over the rim of her red-framed glasses. For a teacher — a notoriously dishevelled lot, as Mason had learned from his father's friends — she was uncharacteristically fashion forward.

"I'm sorry," said Mason. "Got lost."

"You're forgiven," she replied. "Take a seat."

Mason sat down near the front of the class, but not for the better view; rather, it was the most isolated seat he could find. He didn't like sitting close to people. Most people, anyway.

The professor handed him a syllabus. It was printed on orange paper. Mason scanned the reading list then his professor's name, Dr. Alicia Rutherford.

"All right," she continued. "Now I want you to break into groups of, hmm." She began counting the number of students with her index finger; there were about thirty. "Let's say five. Break into groups of five."

Damn it — Mason hated group activities. And there he was, all by himself on his own little island at the edge of class. Hesitantly, he stood up and began roaming the room, shoulders slouched, failing to take further initiative, until eventually — inevitably — he was the only person left standing. Alicia met his gaze and pointed to the one group still short a person. He wandered over.

"Hi." Mason stole a seat and shifted into the circle.

There were two other guys, both about his age, an older woman, and a beautiful one. They all shook hands, Mason forgetting each of their names in turn— except the one.

"Asha," she said. She looked Indian, roughly his age. Her eyes were big and brown, but her smile was bigger still. She kept her hair unstraightened, voluminous black waves flowing over her shoulders and down her back. Mason liked that. Hell, there wasn't much not to like from where he was sitting.

"Looks like we're good to go." Alicia clapped her hands to get their attention. "Okay," she said, "now imagine this. There's a train barreling past you. Suddenly, you notice five people are tied to the tracks ahead— presumably by an evil man with a twirly moustache."

They laughed. She'd obviously told that one before.

"You're next to a lever," she continued, "which can redirect the train to a different set of tracks— away from the five people. But there's a problem. Another man is tied to the divergent track, only he's all by himself. With no time to stop the train, you're left with just two options: do nothing, be a passive observer, and watch five people die or pull the lever to save them— but you'll have killed the other man in the process.

"So, what do you do?"

Alicia looked at her watch. "Take a few minutes to discuss the question with your group."

After ten or so seconds of contagious silence, one of Mason's group members — Jim or John, something with J — finally spoke up. "I don't think it should be up to us to decide who lives and who dies," he said. "You know, like, who are we to play God?"

"Okay. But then five people are going to die," replied Mason, a little coldly. "If not you, then who else is going to save them? Who else is going to play God?"

"I don't know— God?"

"You really think God is going to stop that train?" asked Mason. "When's the last time God stopped a train?"

"Maybe he stops trains every day, and we just don't know."

Mason tried not to roll his eyes. "You want to bet five lives on that?"

"I see what you're saying, Jason, but I think I agree with Mason," said Asha, more politely than Mason had ever said anything. "Even if it shouldn't be up to me, if I had the chance to save five lives— well, four if we minus the other guy. Anyway, with power comes responsibility— isn't that what Uncle Ben said?"

Mason chuckled.

"So, why's it okay to let one person die?" asked Jason.

"It's not," said Asha, "but sometimes there isn't an okay. Sometimes you need to pick the lesser evil, do what's best for the most people."

"Very utilitarian," added Mason.

"I try not to label myself." She smiled.

"Yeah." Mason leaned back in his chair. "I know what you mean."

The others were already thumbing their phones.

"I take it you've all made up your minds." Alicia faced the classroom like a captain on the bow of her boat, back upright, eyes surveying the sea of cellular devices. "So, what do you guys think? Show of hands: who would kill one person to save five?"

About half the students in the room put up their hands, Mason and Asha included.

"And who would do nothing?"

This time, only a handful of students volunteered their arms. There were a few abstentions.

"Interesting," said Alicia, and then she asked why.

No one in Mason's group weighed in, at least not willingly. Once the discussion had settled down, he figured he'd gotten off scot-free. But that hope dashed when he saw her staring at him.

"What about you?" She nodded toward Mason. "Mr. Latey McLaterson."

Son of a bitch.

"Umm." Mason took a second to gather his thoughts. "I would save the five people. It just, I don't know, it seems like the adult thing to do, taking responsibility of the situation. No one else is going to step in and save the day. No one else is going to rescue those five people. It's just them and me, right?" He shrugged, staring somewhat intensely at the wall. "That's the reality. I can't pretend I don't have a choice when the lever's right in front of me. Doing nothing is doing something. The rest is math, I guess."

And that, apparently, was a wrap. Alicia assigned three chapters in the course pack before dismissing them. Mason, meanwhile, skimmed the syllabus a second time as students around him packed their bags manically, as if in a race to see who could leave first.

"Good answer."

Mason looked up. It was Asha. "Not really," he replied, "but thanks."

"Do you ever feel, like... responsible for each and every person that maybe you could help in some small way?" she asked, with a look that suggested that, clearly, she did. "Until it's kind of overwhelming." She was packing her bag on the desk beside him.

"I'm more of a big-picture guy," he said. "Or maybe you're just a better person than I am." Mason scribbled a sloppy spiral on his syllabus, knocking over his empty coffee cup with the butt of his pen. "Crap."

"The problem with me," replied Asha, "is that I am a hard-core, clinically diagnosable guilt-aholic."

"Well, better that than the opposite— a sociopath or whatever."

"Are you a sociopath, Mason?"

"Of course not," he said. "But that's probably what a sociopath would say. And I am a bit... you know."

She shook her head.

"Strange," he said.

"Because you sit by yourself?"

"Something like that." Mason stuffed his binder into his backpack and zipped it shut. They were the only students left.

"Maybe," she said, "but I don't think you're a sociopath. From what I understand, sociopaths are chronic liars. I got a B in psych 100, so I'm pretty sure I know what I'm talking about. You're too honest, Mason."

"It is a problem," he replied.

"Baloney." Asha wasn't having it. "I'm sure your friends appreciate the real you."

Mason shrugged and then replied nonchalantly, "Don't really have a lot of those."

"Friends?" She raised an eyebrow.

"Well, not lately. I just moved here like two days ago, so yeah, new place and all that. You know how it is." He tried not to look as awkward as he suddenly felt. "See, I really am too honest."

"You're not," she said, walking with him into the hallway. "Well, maybe you are— but I like it." They stepped outside into the concrete courtyard. "I gotta head to my last class now." She was twirling a thick lock of her black hair. "If you'd like, my friends and I were going to get together for drinks this Friday. You're welcome to join us."

Mason stalled but already knew his answer— what the hell else was he going to do? "Yeah, sure, why not," he told her. "We have class that day, right?"

"Yeah," replied Asha. "I'll fill you in on the details then." Her smile seemed genuine, like a friend's. "Have a good one, Mason." She waved and went on her way.

In truth, Mason was actually heading in the same direction, but he wasn't about to spoil a good thing. He took the scenic route home, lighting himself a cigarette along the way. Some smokes were better than others, and this was one of them.

Mason arrived home with a half-empty Scholarly Addictions coffee cup in hand— just a twelve ounce this time. He left the cup on the kitchen counter and dropped his backpack onto the nearest chair. It landed with a thud. He cracked his neck with a pop.

"How was school?" Lester asked from across the room. He was bent over the stove, sipping the end of a reddened wooden spoon.

"It was fine," replied Mason, glancing at him curiously.

"Meet any cute boys?"

Mason smiled in spite of himself. "Unfortunately, no. Just a cute girl."

Lester shrugged. "Suit yourself."

Mason dumped his lukewarm coffee and poured himself a glass of tap water. "What exactly are you making?" he asked.

"Dinner," said Lester, "and there's enough for two. Your timing was impeccable."

Mason decided he should help, or at least give off the appearance of helping. He set down some plates and made makeshift napkins out of paper towel. "So, you like to cook?" he asked.

"Nope," replied Lester, switching off the stove element. "That's why I made spaghetti. You should learn, though. I hear pretty girls like men who can cook. I wouldn't know." Peering over his shoulder, he added, "I do like to drink, however. There's a bottle of merlot behind you."

"Ah." Mason grabbed the wine and poured two glasses, stopping just before the rim.

"Nice pour," said Lester. "Guess I'm not the only one who likes to drink."

"Nor are you the only one who likes spaghetti," replied Mason, sitting down to an empty plate.

"You kids nowadays— always so impatient." Lester was taking his time straining the pasta, banging the plastic strainer against the edge of the sink. Finally, he pointed to a pot on the stove and said, "Pasta's here. Sauce is there."

Mason took generous portions and Lester took only a bit less. Finally, they both sat down, eye to eye.

"How's Julie?" asked Lester, spinning his spaghetti like yarn.

"My mom's fine." Mason left it at that. "I was wondering," he said after a mouthful, "where exactly did you come here from?"

Lester downed half his glass of wine in one fell swig. "From up north," he said. "A big house in the middle of nowhere."

"Sounds like where I come from."

Lester smirked. "Not quite. My home, sweet home is a little more... nowheresy. Trust me. It's good, though. I like it. As I've always said, there's nowhere to lose yourself in the middle of nowhere."

"Clever," replied Mason. "Is it lonely? Don't get me wrong, I like my alone time, but that seems a bit much."

"I live with the people I care about," explained Lester. "Only reason I'm down here — only reason I would come down here — is for your dad." He reached for the wine then topped up his glass.

"About that." Mason set down his fork. "I still don't know what the hell you were talking about yesterday. I appreciate this dinner and the wine and everything, but you still owe me a proper explanation. Why are you here, man?"

"Why is anyone anywhere?" Lester extended his arms and gazed up to the heavens.

"Oh, come the fuck on." Mason wasn't impressed.

"That's no way to speak to a man you're trying to get answers from." Lester was already helping himself to seconds— that pudgy figure of his wasn't going to maintain itself. "You should work on your interrogation skills."

They matched hostile eyes then went back to eating. Mason could hear Lester chewing from across the small kitchen table.

Generally speaking, Mason didn't initiate conversations. With most people, he simply didn't care enough. With pretty girls, he cared too much. But with Lester, Mason had an agenda. As of yesterday, he had a lot of new questions, most of them about his father, and he was hoping this oddball of a man would have at least a few answers.

After a couple more minutes of uninterrupted slurping and fork-scraping, Mason muttered, "My dad left me a book," still with food in his mouth. He didn't look up from his plate. "This really old, weird book. I mean, like, really weird. It was sealed shut with one of those combination locks." He twirled together the last of his spaghetti.

For once, Mason could see he had Lester's full attention. The old man's air of nonchalance had been whisked away like a leaf caught in a cool breeze.

"Well, I got it open," continued Mason, "just last night, in fact. You'd never guess what it was called. The book, I mean."

Lester didn't try.

The Necromancer's Grimoire," said Mason. "It was full of these weird drawings and this fucked-up language. I couldn't make any sense of it." He paused to catch Lester's gaze, which had grown increasingly defensive. "Really, really strange stuff. I was thinking, you two were pretty close. Did my dad ever show you anything like that?"

Lester looked tense. His leg was bouncing beneath the table. "Well." He dropped his fork. "To hell with it." He sighed the words. "I guess now's as good a time as any."

"Good time for what?" Mason sounded wary.

"For the truth, of course," he replied. "I was hoping I could ease you into it or something, but I suppose you're not going to believe me either way — at least not at first."

"Okay…"

"Right, then." Lester exhaled every ounce of oxygen in his lungs. "Let's just do this, kid. Your dad: he was a necromancer. I too am a necromancer." He paused, cringing like a man preparing to take a punch. "What's a necromancer, you ask?"

Mason hadn't asked.

"Let me tell you. You see, your dad and I, we can communicate with the dead — more or less. We use something called spirit energy to perform spells of a sort."

"Spells?" Mason had never felt, nor looked, so taken aback. "Are you saying my dad was in a cult? My dad, the atheist professor? What you're describing — it's like Scientology times a thousand."

"No, no, no." Lester slapped the table. "Just let me finish, kiddo, and then I'll prove it to you."

"Yeah, right."

"Like I was saying." Lester sounded exhausted. "Your dad and I were necromancers. Well, I still am a necromancer, and your dad was up until the end. But he exists in the Spirit Realm now, which is where people go when they, you know." He made a croaking noise.

"The Spirit Realm, eh." Mason nodded mockingly. It was too stupid for an actual rebuttal.

"Yes, the Spirit Realm," Lester said soberly. "A few months ago, I summoned your dad's spirit. He asked me for a favour. He wanted me to — shit, I don't even know — teach you or something. I'm less than thrilled about the whole situation, I assure you."

"You're going to teach me?"

"Well, your pa certainly ain't in any condition to do it himself, now is he?"

"To be a necromancer?" Mason clarified, leaning forward on his elbows like an arrogant debater.

Lester looked a little peeved now. "This was his life's work, kid," he said. "Despite his impressive career and all those books he wrote, this was what kept him up at night. He thought you'd be passionate about it too. Said you would discover great things, said you had the right mind for it, that you were even smarter than he was."

"Personally," added Lester. "I don't see it."

Mason rolled his eyes as far as they could roll.

"Yeah, yeah," said Lester. "I know you don't believe a damn thing I just said. Go ahead and chuckle, kid, but you won't be laughing in a minute."

Mason hadn't actually laughed until he said that.

That's when Lester held up his wine glass, still half-full of merlot, examining it in detail like a piece of art. He started mumbling something to himself.

Mason cupped his ear. "I can't hear a damn thing you're saying."

A second later, he realized he didn't need to. If a picture was worth a thousand words, what came next deserved a goddamn encyclopedia. The wine in Lester's glass was suddenly glowing and getting brighter. Lester's plump face shone even redder than usual, and then it was the whole room, Mason included, bathed in crimson— like a darkroom without the dark.

And then it was over, just like that, at the snap of Lester's stubby fingers.

If Mason could have seen the expression on his face.

He could see Lester's, though. The old codger had stopped mumbling. He was staring straight at Mason, smirking pompously. This was the moment he'd been waiting for. He swirled and sipped his cheap wine like a connoisseur, savoring every drop. "I suppose," he said, "I should have just started with that."

Chapter 5

DOES NECROMANCY CORRUPT? *That is what the inquisitors would have us believe. Certainly, there are bad necromancers. There are psychopaths among us and those who think necromancy makes them something of a superhuman. Indeed, power attracts and exasperates the worst of people, but that is a fact of humanity. Necromancy is simply a tool, and tools can be used for many things.*
  —Samuel Benedict, *The New Necromancer*

Joan Worthington was jet-lagged. She was always jet-lagged for these meetings. She couldn't remember the last time her fellow guardians had visited her in London. It was a good sign, she knew. It meant things were better in Europe, less urgent than in North America, the heart of the inquisition.

Still, she was tired. It was late in Maine, but not nearly as late as it would have been back home. It didn't matter. This was the time Rowland had set, and they had little in the way of negotiating power.

"This the place?" Her cab slowed to a roll, a lone black driveway snaking northward beyond the driver side window.

Joan knew the sight well— her home away from home. "Yes," she said. "Right here is fine."

The bill was thirty-two dollars. She gave him two twenties. "Keep the change."

"Thanks, ma'am," the driver said. "You have yourself a good night."

"That remains to be seen." Joan stepped out of the car and watched him accelerate off into the night, his brake lights vanishing around the bend. She headed up the driveway, heels clicking on the pavement.

A gust of wind threw loose strands of grey hair over her eyes; she swept them back with her fingers, hoping she still looked as she had an hour ago. It was always windy here, a small price to pay for living on the ocean, she supposed. Whenever she stayed with Samuel, she would relax along the cliffs, sometimes just listening to the waves. Joan could already hear them crashing in the distance. She didn't know anyone in London who could afford a place like this.

But London was far away now, and her long trek over. Joan stepped onto the wooden veranda, up to his front door — she breathed — and then knocked three times.

The house was an old, red Victorian. It looked like it belonged in a calendar. Instead, it belonged to Samuel Benedict, with whom she had an interesting relationship. They were close friends, maybe even best friends, they had sex — which she was looking forward to — and, of course, they lived an ocean apart. It had to stay this way. Samuel was North America's guardian, in charge of defending necromancers and their secret this side of the Atlantic, and she was Europe's.

Joan could hear him coming down the stairs now, recognizing the sound of his heavy footsteps. He was a big man, much bigger than she was.

Samuel opened the door, smiling, but she could tell he was preoccupied with thought. He was an intensely smart man, though he was just as single-minded, the darker side of the same coin. Still, she loved the whole package. He was who he was, a man who loved her equally and as an equal.

Samuel craned his neck down to kiss her forehead. "I missed you," he said. It had been four months, longer than usual.

"I missed you too." She ran her hand down his stubble. "Good thing we have a whole month together." It was her reward for putting in extra hours this summer. She would stay with him until her fiftieth birthday next month.

Joan stepped inside, Samuel's hand brushing the small of her back.

"Everyone is waiting in the living room," he said.

"Rowland?" she asked.

"Everyone but him," he clarified. "We're still waiting."

"That figures."

They made their way through the foyer into the living room. The other guardians were already sitting down. There were five of them in total, Joan and Samuel included.

Sitting cross-legged on the brown leather loveseat across from her was Camila Costa, a Brazilian woman from São Paulo. Camila always wore bright heels, and Joan had never seen her so much as slouch. She made beauty seem like a job. Joan wished she knew where Camila got the energy.

"Joan!" Camila stood up for a hug. Some people just weren't very good huggers, and Joan was one of them. Camila, on the other hand, was a fantastic hugger. She embraced Joan with more warmth than all of Britain.

"How was your flight?" asked the man beside them, Hiroshi Saito. Hiroshi was the best necromancer among them, but he would never admit to that. Boasting was beneath a man like Hiroshi. He was a wanderer, as much as anyone could be these days, though he had a home in Tokyo. "To be near the airport," he'd once said. When it came to flying, Hiroshi was full of opinions.

"My flight was delayed," replied Joan. "I apologize. I meant to be here hours ago."

"Punctuality and planes go together like oil and water, my dear Joan." Hiroshi took a slow sip from his tumbler of scotch.

Lastly, there was Abah Okoro, the Nigerian. He nodded in her direction. It was as much as Joan would get from Abah. She'd never met anyone so stoic. She used to think it was all a facade, but not anymore. Abah had iron coursing through his veins. He was rock, hardened all the way through. She didn't know much else about him, but she knew that.

Joan and Samuel took a seat together on the long sofa by the fireplace. The flames had retreated to the embers below, but Joan savored the smoky smell. She wanted to sit closer to Samuel, but that could wait. This was work. Her vacation hadn't started yet, she reminded herself.

Camila sighed dramatically. "Where is this stupid guy already?"

"He is not a… stupid guy." Abah didn't look impressed. Then again, he never did.

"Stupid, no," added Joan, "but he is a lot of things. After twenty years, I had gotten my hopes up, thought maybe he was gone for good this time. I should have known better."

She could tell from the way Samuel stiffened his neck, staring intensely at nothing in particular, that he was about to disagree with her.

"I don't know," he said, right on cue. "Times have changed. The inquisitors are getting better at tracking us— at killing us. They never used to have the internet. Just last week, they got an acquaintance of mine, Simon Paisley. Burned him alive." Samuel sighed, shaking his head. "Man never hurt a fly. So yeah, I don't know. Maybe Rowland will level the playing field."

"He's an awfully blunt instrument," replied Joan. "Too blunt. He doesn't just kill inquisitors."

"I know, I know." Samuel sounded apologetic. "But what if he saves more people than he kills? If we're being honest, no one has taken out as many inquisitors as Rowland. Not even close."

"That's not how we do things, Samuel." She was using his first name— her tell that she was annoyed with him.

"Perhaps. Then again, it's not up to us anyway," he said. "Rowland's going to do what he's going to do. I'm just pointing out that there's a silver lining."

The others stayed silent, but Joan could see in their eyes that they agreed with Samuel, which annoyed her further. They were wrong, but it was hard to blame them: they'd all lost friends to the inquisitors, and she knew how that felt.

Someone knocked on the front door— a slow, heavy knock. It was him. It had to be. Joan could feel his energy from here, his radiation. Rowland was the atomic bomb of necromancers.

Samuel stood up, as silent as a prayer, and headed to the door. They heard it creak open a moment later. They heard it shut. No words were exchanged. Samuel came back first and nodded. At long last, Rowland stepped into the living room.

He was a hard man to look at. He was tall and skinny, more starved-looking than trim, and paler than most corpses. His hair was a wintery white and his eyes a poisonous red. His sclera had turned pink, his pupils maroon— the aftermath of too much necromancy. He looked like the product of his own experiments.

Then again, appearances were relative. Perhaps he didn't look so bad for a man his age, thought Joan. Rowland rarely revealed anything about himself, but she knew he was over three-hundred years old, kept alive by his own spells. It was older than she'd ever wanted to live, that's for sure.

Samuel returned to the cushion beside her, but Rowland stayed standing, still wearing his black overcoat. He wasn't planning on getting comfortable.

"I will be brief," he said. His voice was raspier than an old smoker's. "Then I will go." Even after twenty years of self-imposed isolation, it seemed he wasn't feeling particularly social.

"I have returned with a plan," he continued, lingering between sentences.

"A plan for what?" It was Joan. She was already growing tired of this theatrical bullshit. The other guardians gave her sharp looks. But not Rowland. He was too conceited to care. She was simply some yammering kid as far as he was concerned.

"Telling you my plan," he said, "is not part of the plan."

Of course. Children needn't understand the adult in the room— only listen and obey.

Arrogant bastard.

"Here is what you need to know." Rowland stepped up to Joan, not exactly threateningly but without concern for her comfort. He was even uglier up close. She could see the thick veins texturing his temples and gnarled hands. His skin was thin and patchy, like a pale balloon stretched over a skeleton, ready to pop— if only it weren't held together by forces greater than flesh.

"First, know that I have returned, as you can all see for yourselves, and that I am here to stay."

Joan flinched at the news.

"Second," he said, "let it be known that I will end the inquisition, once and for all."

"How so?" asked Camila, arms crossed. "You're going to kill all the inquisitor men?"

"Correct."

"When?"

"Soon."

"I thought you said you weren't going to tell us your plan." It was Joan again.

"That is only a small part of my plan," replied Rowland. "The only part you need to know, for now."

"I beg to differ," she said.

"Begging is for dogs."

"It's an expression." *So go woof yourself, asshole.*

"If that is all, I am done here." Rowland eyed each of them in turn.

"Where were you all this time?" asked Joan.

"Next question."

She sighed. "Are you going to tell us anything you haven't already?"

"No." At least he was honest.

"Then I guess we're done."

It appeared Rowland and Joan finally agreed on something. "Good," was all he said, turning toward the exit. No one offered a goodbye. Wordlessly, they watched him disappear into the hallway. They heard the front door swing open. For a few seconds, sound seeped in from the windy night, and then he was gone. It was a little anticlimactic.

Hiroshi poured himself another scotch.

"An end to the inquisition," said Samuel, setting his hand on Joan's shoulder. "That would be one hell of a silver lining."

She shrugged out from underneath his fingers. No, he was still wrong. This would end badly. It always did with Rowland.

"Pass the whisky, Hiroshi." Samuel looked a little too comfortable.

Joan got thinking she might not sleep with him tonight after all.

Chapter 6

MASON WASN'T SURE why he kept antagonizing Lester. Sure, he was weirder than an elephant's dick, but he didn't hold that against him. Mason had never fancied himself particularly normal either. And yet he was being a jerk, but then so was Lester.

It was Friday evening and enough time had gone by for the truth to sink in. Mason now accepted the fact that the man living with him was a necromancer (though he remained a little fuzzy on what being a necromancer entailed) and that the same could have been said of his father. That pill was a bit harder to swallow. Still, something about Lester continued to piss Mason off. Or maybe it had nothing to do with him. Maybe he was just pissed off.

Lester seemed pissed off too. He hadn't wanted to come down here, nor had he ever wanted to teach anyone anything. It was a favour. And yet, from the way Mason treated him, you wouldn't know it. He'd said as much last night, before Mason reminded him that he was an uninvited guest. Neither one of them was wrong, strictly speaking.

But sometimes, when their guards were down, they acted almost like friends.

"Going on a date?" asked Lester, emphasizing the word *date*.

"It's not a date," clarified Mason, tying his shoes.

"Well, not with that attitude." Lester was sitting in the kitchen, eating rice from a bowl and reading obituaries in *The Terminal City Chronicle*. He looked up. "*Date* is a rather superfluous word, anyway. I wouldn't dwell on it."

"You brought it up," said Mason.

"I suppose I did." Lester returned his gaze to the paper. "Any progress with the illumination spell?"

The illumination spell was, according to Lester, one of necromancy's simplest. The goal was to manipulate energy from the Spirit Realm into light in the Living Realm. Lester had shown the spell to Mason many times now. On each occasion, after only a few seconds of chanting, an orb of red light would manifest over Lester's palm.

"Remember, it's not just about the chant," Lester reminded him again. "The chant only helps you focus your power on the right spell. It's like a filter. In theory, not even necessary. What matters is that you *feel* the spell."

"Well, I don't feel shit." Mason shrugged into his leather coat. "I can't seem to pronounce the words right either." So far, his venture into the world of necromancy had been fruitless and frustrating. "Maybe I'm just not a necromancer," he added. "Not everything runs in the family."

"Maybe not," replied Lester, "but you wouldn't know it yet. It's only been a few days. And need I remind you, my young apprentice, that necromantic ability has nothing to do with blood?" He placed a finger on his temple. "It's all about your mind."

"Ah. Gotcha." Mason had one foot out the door. "So, what you're saying is that I'm just too stupid."

Lester sighed. "For fuck's sake, kid, it took me three whole months to get my first spell working."

Mason considered this. "I did say a week," he said. "The week's almost up. I hope you didn't think you'd be staying here for, what, three months? Yeah, I wouldn't count on that." Mason wasn't sure he meant what he said, but Lester was pissing him off again, though he wasn't entirely sure why.

Lester put on a show too, burrowing his face between both hands. "The prospect isn't appealing to either of us, believe me."

At this point, Mason left, locking the door behind him.

Mason showed up to the bar before Asha, who had said to come around nine. It was 8:56 p.m. If some of her friends were already here, he wouldn't have recognized them. He decided to settle down at the bar with only a pint of beer for company, playing around with his phone so passersby would believe he had friends. Not that anyone noticed or cared.

The bar was close to home so getting here had been easy enough. It was a casual place and no stranger to graffiti, nor spilled beer. Basically, a dive bar, which quite honestly he preferred. According to a flyer pinned on the wall beside him, Tuesdays were open mic nights. Mason knew a few chords and a couple songs, but quickly thought better of it.

"Mason." It was Asha, twenty minutes late. "Hey. Hope you haven't been waiting long."

"No, no. Just got here," he replied, holding up the nearly-full pint he'd been nursing as proof.

"Cool. We're over here." She gestured him to follow.

She led him to a long, people-packed table out on the patio. He didn't mean to check her out from behind, but it somehow seemed impossible not to. He told himself that, since he respected her, it was okay. Asha was on the tall side, maybe an inch or two shorter than he was. Mason was an average-sized dude, who, like all average-sized dudes, would rather have been six feet tall. Reality being what it was, he made sure not to slouch.

Mason relaxed when they took their seats across from one another at the end of the table. She began introducing him to her many friends, all of whom seemed like normal enough people. As usual, Mason wasted no time forgetting their names.

"Craig," the guy to his right reminded him a minute later. "Craig Patterson."

"Mason. Mason Cross." The two men exchanged a sloppy handshake.

"Shit, man." Craig slapped the table, beer splashing his hand.

Mason looked confused and then toward Asha, who looked confused too.

"Your name," said Craig, "is so fucking cool. Mason fucking Cross? I wish I had a name like that. You should be like a fucking, I don't know, superhero or some shit."

Briefly, Mason wondered if being a necromancer would be anything like being a super hero. Then he thought of Lester. "The Super Hero Academy rejected my application," he replied. "So here I am."

Asha was the first to laugh. In his mind, Mason did one of those victorious fist-pumps. Craig, meanwhile, started talking to some other guy.

Good.

In an attempt to loosen up, Mason gave a little more love to his pint of beer. He craved a cigarette — beer had that effect — but worried Asha would disapprove. It wasn't worth the risk.

"Do you live on campus?" he asked her.

Asha nodded. "Got one of those studio apartments," she said. "It's super small. My mom and dad live like an hour away, but I couldn't, you know, stand living with them. As much as I love them, my parents can be a bit overbearing." She grinned and added, "I told them I couldn't study on the bus, said I'd have more time to buckle down if I lived here."

"Beerology is one of my favorite subjects," said Mason. They clinked glasses.

"Cheers to that." Asha downed a mouthful.

Man, she was cool. "What do you take here?" he asked. "What's your major?"

"Classical studies."

"Really?" He sounded surprised.

"Yeah, I know," she replied. "Don't tell my parents."

"Well, I was going to call them," he said, "but if you insist."

"What about you, smarty-pants? What are you studying?"

"That's a very good question." Mason looked up to the night sky for an answer. "Honestly, I have no idea. Whatever I end up hating the least, I suppose."

"Sounds practical," she said.

Mason sipped his beer slowly, tilting his glass just so as he racked his brain for a witty reply, but he came up short. Instead, he put the crosshairs on her: "What about you? What are your big life plans once you get out of here?"

"Worst question ever," replied Asha. "I guess I kind of want to move someplace I haven't been. You know, just for the hell of it."

"Sounds nice," he said.

"Are you also itching to explore?" she asked.

He set down his drink. "Just itching to start."

This time, it was Asha looking at the stars. "For me, it's not about one place. Terminal is nice, but I want to see the world."

"And save it along the way, right? Ms. Guilt-aholic."

She returned her wandering gaze to Earth and then toward Mason. "You got me," she said, her smile splitting the night like a beautiful scar. "I'm such a cliché, I know."

"Yeah," he replied, "you are. But so am I. So is Craig here." Craig didn't hear him. "There are, what, seven billion of us on this planet? Statistically speaking, it's damn near impossible not to be cliché."

Asha's grin grew just a bit. "Well, at least we're self-aware. That's gotta count for something."

Briefly, Mason contemplated whether self-awareness could be considered cliché, but his wit waned the second a stranger sat down next to Asha. He was a tall man, about their age, and handsome— in that objective sort of way. He had short blonde hair and olive skin, almost the same tone; the opposite of Mason, whose dark hair stuck out like black bark in a snowy field.

The handsome man slung one arm around Asha and kissed her on the cheek. She was more of a passive participant. She didn't say anything, but if expressions could talk, hers would have said, *please, not in public, thanks.*

"Hey, babe." He seemed oblivious to Mason's existence.

Asha's smile looked forced. Pointing with all five fingers, she introduced them. "Josh, Mason. Mason, Josh."

The two men shook hands — Josh had a firm grip — if only because it seemed like the proper thing to do. Obviously, Josh could go fuck himself. He didn't care much for Mason either, or at least that was the impression he gave. He skipped any semblance of small talk and went back to chatting up his girlfriend— some crap about his construction job. Mason figured he must be smarter than Josh.

And yet he imagined he looked pretty pathetic just then, Mason did, staring down at his shoes, sipping away the last of his beer, thinking about stuff. So, Asha had a boyfriend. He quickly came to terms with this fact— a fact that made him uncomfortably sober. Needless to say, he was no longer enjoying himself. Sitting beside him, Craig was anything but sober, laughing, slapping the table, generally having a fantastic time. Mason resented him for it.

He checked his watch. It was 10:16 p.m. The night was young, but already he wanted to leave. He was the only stranger at the table. If there had been other outsiders, lost like he was, Mason could have found common ground. But it was a table for friends, and he was just some dude with a cool name.

Mason got to the bottom of his beer then made up an excuse. "I think I'm going to head home," he told Asha. "I'm really tired. Didn't get much sleep last night."

"Aww. Are you sure you don't want to stick around a bit longer?" She looked disappointed. "Come on. Next beer's on me."

"It's okay." Mason was already sliding on his jacket. "But thanks for inviting me out. First week, you know. Not used to the early mornings. Guess I haven't really adjusted yet." He pretended to yawn. It was too much. He was terrible at this.

"Okay, Mason." If expressions could talk, this one said, *that's bullshit, but I get it*. "Have a good night."

"You too." He waved. "I'll see you Monday."

"Yeah. See ya Monday."

On his way out, Mason bought a shot of tequila. He hated tequila, but he felt like he deserved tequila. He'd smoke that cigarette he was craving too. Then he'd smoke another. He'd smoke as many cigarettes as he damn well pleased.

The walk home didn't take long, but Mason powered through four cigarettes, just enough to make him feel even worse.

"You're home early," said Lester from the living room. He was watching some nature show.

"Yeah," replied Mason, kicking off his shoes. Without saying another word, he went upstairs to his room and slammed the door.

He sighed. *Now what?*

Despite what he'd told Asha, Mason wasn't particularly tired. Just a little sucker-punched and now suddenly bored. He considered studying or starting a new book, but he was too on edge to settle down. Instead, he began practicing the illumination spell again, as infuriating as it was. He figured he couldn't possibly get any more frustrated, after all.

Sitting on the corner of his bed, Mason began reciting the chant. He had it memorized now, but the words still sounded and felt like gibberish.

He tried and tried again, until he proved himself wrong: it turned out his frustration knew no bounds. And then, when he was least expecting it, Mason felt something. It only lasted a second. It struck him like an idea making sense, an argument coming together. In his mind, he chased the feeling. His lips moved as methodically as they did mindlessly. After so many failed attempts, the chant had become second nature. He was lost in his head, doing everything he could to find that—

And there it was, like snapping together the first two pieces of an enormous puzzle. Right before his eyes, a faint orb of red light faded into existence, illuminating the palm of his hand.

It lasted for a second or two, disappearing when he paid it too much attention.

Mason wasted no time starting from scratch. His second attempt proved even more successful: it took him under a minute and the orb glowed brighter than before. It stuck around longer too.

Mason repeated the spell three more times, always with improvement. Finally, he decided he should show Lester and headed downstairs.

Lester was still watching TV, some late-night show now, shaking his head at the screen. "Can't say I recognize any of these so-called movie stars," he said as Mason entered the room.

"That's because you live under a rock."

"Maybe so." He didn't seem offended. "In my day, it was all Charlie Chaplin and James Dean."

"You're not a hundred," replied Mason. "Those guys aren't even from the same era."

"Indeed," said Lester. "I was testing you. What's up, boy?"

"Right. Just look over here for a second."

Lester was hardly married to the screen.

Wasting no time, Mason bathed the room in bright red light. The spell lasted until he decided to end it.

Lester looked impressed — hell, his jaw dropped a little — and Mason looked proud. He wasn't feeling frustrated anymore, not one bit. It was a rare sensation, indeed.

"Jesus H. Christ," said Lester, wide-eyed. "Maybe your father was right about you. I mean, you're a brat and all, but holy hell. I've never seen a necromancer learn their first spell so fast, or that well."

"So, I'm a necromancer now?" asked Mason. He tried to sound tongue-in-cheek, but the truth was he wanted to be one. He wanted Lester's goddamn validation.

"I guess so," said Lester. "Not really a fan of labels, though."

"Right. They're superfluous. Like the word *date*. Got it. Any other pearls of wisdom, master?"

"You really are a brat."

They were both smiling, more so like friends than ever before.

Lester pushed himself off the couch. "Come on." He cleared his throat. "I have something to show you."

"What is it?" asked Mason.

"You'll see. It's in the basement. Or should I say it is the basement."

CHAPTER 7

AT SOME POINT, every necromancer is bound to wonder when and where necromancy began. While no one can say for sure, there are tales and theories— though little is proven.

In one of the more popular stories, a woman dies, comes back to life, and discovers necromantic powers. Isidora, an Athenian slave in Ancient Greece, is impregnated at fourteen. Her young body does not handle the birth well, and while her son lives, Isidora dies.

She awakens in the Spirit Realm, unready for death, unable to handle the thought of her child sharing her fate as a slave. Isidora pleads with the spirits to give her another chance at life— a wish that is ultimately granted.

Fearful of slave traders and distrustful of humanity, Isidora begins her new life in the mountains, but a piece of death lingers with her: Deathspeak. With it, Isidora discovers how to channel, and eventually control, energy from the Spirit Realm.

Newly powerful, she returns to her former master, killing him and retrieving her son. The two flee back to the mountains, where she teaches him what she has discovered, until he too can perform spells. Thus begins the tradition, the passing down of necromantic knowledge.

That, of course, is just one version of the story.

Others say necromancy always was, a faint noise in the background just waiting to be discovered. Until, like fire, we learned to harness its power. The theory goes that Deathspeak was learned not from revelation but over thousands of years of trial and error. That like every other language, it too evolved, only in history's shadows.

And that is precisely where necromancy has always existed — somewhere unseen — and why we may never know where this strange, wonderful, terrifying force came from. Was spirit energy a gift from the

Spirit Realm, or was it a resource we humans discovered, dug up, and began burning like oil from the ground? Was it given, or was it taken?
—Samuel Benedict, *The New Necromancer*

Mason and Lester were standing in the former's seemingly small basement. The room was lit this time, though rather poorly, by an old light bulb hanging from the ceiling, swaying and flickering.

"Okay," said Mason. "Now what?"

"I'll show you what." Lester walked over to the far wall.

With his back to Mason, Lester pressed his palm against the concrete. He was touching those carved letters Mason had found the first night he moved in.

Mason now knew they were written in Deathspeak. "What do they say?" he asked.

"It's the chant that gets us through this door," explained Lester.

"What door?"

"Hold your horses." Lester began mumbling a spell, until a faint flash of red framed his silhouette. More startling, however, was the sudden appearance of a door.

"Ah," said Mason. "That door. Neat trick. I didn't know we could conjure up, you know, doors."

"The door was always here," replied Lester, "just hidden. Come." He swung it open with one hand and beckoned Mason with the other. Behind him, the newly revealed room emitted a familiar shade of red.

"I feel like I'm about to walk through the gates of hell," said Mason.

"Yes, yes, come now. The Dark Lord awaits."

Mason obeyed.

The room was a lot bigger than its facade suggested and as weird as it was red, though that was to be expected. Something that looked almost but not quite like a black chandelier hung in its center, only instead of light bulbs or candles, its wiry arms supported hovering orbs of light.

"Hey, I can make those," said Mason. "But mine don't last. How do you make them stick around like that?"

"It's complicated," replied Lester, standing idly by as Mason took in the room.

The place was messy and full of old books, like a library that was actually used. It had been his dad's real den, Mason realized, unlike the fake one he'd grown so fond of as a kid. "Second question, then," he said. "Why not just use regular lights? Those orbs are neat, I'll grant you, but it's pretty freaking dim in here."

"Indeed," said Lester. "The light uses necromantic energy because— how should I put this." He scratched his chin. "Because it's good ambience for doing necromancy."

Mason looked a little humored.

"It's like when you want to write," continued Lester. "You don't want to be somewhere noisy and intrusive. You want to be somewhere quiet, maybe with music you like. Your old man, for example, when he was writing, I remember he'd always put on jazz and lock the door."

"I'm well aware," said Mason. He got the analogy too. "So, what the hell is this place?"

"It was our library. It was our lab. It was all things necromancy." Lester sounded nostalgic. "We studied here, practiced spells, sometimes even discovered new ones. This was our safe haven. I guess it's yours now, kid."

"Why do we need a safe haven?" asked Mason. "Who aren't we safe from?"

"Ah, yes." Lester prepared his next words carefully. "Perhaps it's time you learned about inquisitors. There's another group out there that knows about us, and they're not our biggest fans. Inquisitors, those bastards, their job is to— well, there's no nice way to put this. They hunt us down and kill us, or at least they try. They do sometimes succeed. The inquisitors are religious fanatics. They think we're corrupted, irredeemable. They think we deserve to die."

"We don't, do we?" Mason smiled.

"You tell me. Do you feel corrupted?"

"I don't know, sensei. Maybe I'm so far gone, I just can't tell anymore."

"Well, try not to kill me in my sleep," said Lester. "Anyway, there are bad necromancers too, Mason. Not that it justifies what the inquisitors do, but they're out there. Power attracts the worst of us human folk."

On that note, Mason explored the room some more. The shelves and tables were dusty and battered, the books likewise. And Jesus, there were so many. Stacks of books veiled the floor where shelving had run out.

"I never imagined so much had been written about necromancy," said Mason.

"Gotta maintain the knowledge somehow," replied Lester. "This is just a small sampling. There's an academy of a sort — I don't know if I'd call it that. It's a place where necromancers get together and study, a hidden oasis in the frozen wastelands. I went once. I dare say their library puts ours to shame. When you've got secrets to hide, you gotta go old school. Can't exactly put this shit up on — what do you kids call it — Wikipedia."

"I suppose not." Mason was kneeling over one of the stacks, flipping through books at random.

"There are more spells than any necromancer could ever remember," Lester continued. "Think of necromancy like you would a paint brush. Painting won't cure cancer, but there's no limit on how many things you can paint. In layman's terms, we're painters of spirit energy. Necromancy can't do everything, but there are an infinite number of things it can do."

"You sure like your artist analogies," said Mason. "Speaking of cancer, can necromancy cure disease?"

"Depends on the disease," replied Lester. "As for cancer, it can help. Cancer's a persistent son of a bitch, so it takes upkeep. With humans, everything does."

Mason stopped in front of a small, oval mirror hanging crookedly on the wall. It should have been unassuming, but there was something about his reflection that seemed off. For the life of him, he couldn't figure out what.

"What's with this mirror?" he asked.

"You tell me." Lester obviously knew, but the old bastard enjoyed playing games.

"Everything looks in place," replied Mason. He checked his cheeks, his nose, his lips, his eyes and ears — they were all his. "You know when you see yourself on video from a strange angle, and it's obviously you, but you feel like you're watching someone else? That's what this is like."

"An apt description." Lester nodded approvingly. "That face you're seeing isn't real. At least, not in this world."

"Then what's it doing here, staring back at me?" Mason rotated his face, analyzing each angle.

"That mirror reflects perception," explained Lester. "You're seeing your face as you perceive it. That's why nothing looks out of place. It just seems a bit off."

"Yeah," replied Mason, still looking for a detail to disagree with, but the moles he remembered were all there.

"The trick," said Lester, "is to first observe a part of yourself in the mirror. Let's say your hand. Look closely. Memorize details— moles, bumps, hairs. Then look at your real hand. You'll see a difference. Just make sure you look at it in the mirror first. If you do it the other way around, everything you remember will show up in the mirror. You'll perceive what you just saw. Perception is always changing, my boy. Hell, look at us. I'm almost starting to think you're all right. Almost."

"That's cute," replied Mason. "This time tomorrow, we'll be BFFs."

"What's a BFF?"

"Never mind."

"You know, on good days, I look about fifty in that mirror." Lester seated himself on an old rocking chair in the corner of the room.

"You look closer to seventy in that rocking chair, grandpa." Mason was staring at his forearm in the mirror, counting the blemishes as per Lester's instructions. "How old are you anyway?" he asked.

"Older than you," replied Lester.

Mason shifted his gaze from the mirror to his flesh-and-blood arm. He immediately saw Lester was right. His real arm looked a lot different. It was uglier, for one, more speckled and bumpier than he had remembered. He'd also forgotten about a small white scar he got cooking a few years back (like Lester, Mason was no master chef).

"I thought I knew myself better," said Mason.

"We're more complex than we realize," replied Lester. "Inside and out."

"Is that the point of this mirror?" asked Mason. "To show people how complex they are."

"Sort of." Lester looked to be enjoying his chair, swaying slowly like a boat on calm water. "But it serves another purpose. That mirror shows you what you'd look like in the Spirit Realm. You see, Mason, when the body dies and decays, all that's left is perception. How you remember yourself. How others remember you. That's how spirits exist— like memories trying to remember themselves."

"Do they ever forget?" Mason met Lester's gaze.

"They all do," said Lester, "eventually. It gets harder and harder to tell fact from fiction, your experiences from somebody else's. Our memories are far from perfect. It's reality that keeps us in check, old sport. But reality doesn't exist in the Spirit Realm, not like it does here. The Spirit Realm is formed from perception. Some spirits fare better than others."

"And here I thought I'd live forever," said Mason.

"Everyone dies sooner or later." Lester shrugged. "It just takes a little longer than most folks realize. We all fade away in the Spirit Realm. Even here, in the Living Realm, some of us get off to an early start."

Mason leaned onto a small oak table across from Lester. "I guess it's good my dad didn't go out that way," he said. "He valued his mind above all else, as I'm sure you know. I suppose there are silver linings in every tragedy. Speaking of my dad, is it true what you said when you first got here? Did you talk to him— his spirit, I mean?"

"Yeah, kid. I did."

"What did he say?"

"It's not easy talking to the dead." Lester hesitated. "He still had his wits about him, but a lot gets lost in translation. It's a difficult spell. I remember the big thing was you. He wanted me to show his boy the ropes. He wanted to live on through you."

"I see." That should have bothered Mason, as adamantly independent as he was, but not this time. "Did he say anything else?"

Lester stalled once more. "Nah. Just that."

Mason wasn't sure he believed him, but for once didn't feel like arguing.

Lester changed the subject: "Speaking of living a long time, there are spells for that."

Mason cracked a much-needed smile and said, "That must be why you're still around."

"Hah. Hah." Then a little more seriously, Lester added, "It's not a path I plan on going down, kiddo. I'm probably not smart enough to cast the necessary spells, for one. More than that, I'm just not sure it's healthy. Living too long, that is. There's this necromancer named Rowland— the guy refuses to die. He must be a few hundred years old if he's not dead yet. Haven't heard anything about him in a while. Anyhow, for all the years Rowland gained, that old bastard lost more and more of his humanity. I guess you could say parts of him have faded. He's a smart son of a bitch, but he ain't whole— not anymore."

"Is he one of those bad necromancers you mentioned?" asked Mason.

"Yeah." Lester looked him in the eyes. "The goddamn king of them."

Chapter 8

MILES HUXLEY HADN'T always been an inquisitor. He'd once been a realtor, a pretty damn good one in his opinion. But above all else, he'd been a family man, a husband and a father of two. Both girls, six and four when they died.

In a different life, Miles had had a tender soul. But sometimes people really do change.

It happened ten years ago, and every day since it grew harder for him to remember how things used to be, how he used to feel. Now, he mostly felt hate. Whenever he tried to remember love, he was reminded of loss— of the night that changed everything.

Still, Miles would force himself to remember Jennifer smiling at her last birthday party — she'd just lost her first tooth — until a crisper image of her lifeless, six-year-old body, lying face down in his old backyard, flashed cruelly into memory. When he tried to recall his wedding, it was the same thing: he saw his wife lying on their bed, her dead eyes staring vacantly at the ceiling.

Miles remembered that night as if he had never slept since. It had been a cold November day, autumn leaves skipping down the pavement, caught in a frigid breeze that warned of winter. He'd just come home from work and another big sale. Up until everything went to hell, it had been a pretty good day. He was taking them all out for dinner.

The first thing that seemed off was the quiet. He had two girls— his house was never quiet. Shutting the front door behind him, Miles figured he must be the only one home. He hung his jacket up and walked toward the kitchen, briefcase still in hand— but only for a second.

He dropped it the moment he stepped into the room.

Miles didn't believe it at first. It was his four-year-old, Lisa, lying in a pool of blood.

He fell to his knees and turned her over. His Lisa. Her glossy green eyes gazed through him, as uncertain as his own. Red lines ran from her mouth and nose, transforming into drops that fell from her chin.

Without thinking, without comprehending, Miles lifted her weightless body out of the blood, trembling but clutching her tightly, as if she might fall from him forever— had she not done so already. And still, he didn't really believe it. He could he? How could he believe his baby girl was dead? That sort of thing didn't happen. Not in the suburbs, not to men like him.

Miles would have held her until God knows when, but uncertainty struck him like a second bolt of lightning: where was the rest of his family?

He could barely bring himself to set Lisa down, let alone back on the floor. Instead, he eased her onto the couch, resting her on her back, closing her eyes with his fingertips so that she might sleep. If only the nightmare had ended there.

He found his second girl, Jennifer, lying on the pool cover outside. She must have tried to escape. She'd always been a brave girl, ever since she could walk. And until she couldn't, it would seem. Miles carried Jennifer inside and set her down on the loveseat near her sister. He almost threw up. He felt sick and dizzy, sweating when he should have been crying. But the truth was toxic; his body wanted to reject it, not mourn it.

He still had a wife to find, however. In what state— well, he didn't want to think about that. Hell, he didn't want to think ahead at all. Not about anything, not ever again. Light-headed, Miles marched upstairs, the only place left to look.

He found Rosetta in the master bedroom, just as he'd expected, just as he'd feared— lying dead and bloodied on their bed. At least she'd had a soft landing.

And there he was: the son of a bitch responsible for all this. The intruder was a short, scruffy man. He walked with a limp but no sense of insecurity. Quite the contrary. He stepped toward Miles, looking distracted, an aura of invincibility about him.

Miles went to grab the man who'd murdered his family, but there was just one problem: he couldn't move. He was stuck in space, a standing paraplegic. The intruder, meanwhile, was mumbling under his breath. Miles couldn't make out what he was saying, but it didn't sound like English. And his eyes, they were... unnaturally red.

He remembered thinking in that moment that he wouldn't mind dying. And only five minutes earlier, he'd been living the American dream. How quickly he'd lost it all, even the dream itself. Suddenly, nothing mattered, save one thing: the man in front of him. Miles would have killed him a million times over if only God had offered him the opportunity. But in that instant, he still couldn't move, and for the life of him — literally — he didn't know why.

The stranger went quiet and walked forward until he was a foot from Miles. "Bad timing," he muttered and sighed, looking past Miles. His breath smelled like sulfur.

"Who the fuck are you?" Miles could speak, if nothing else.

"Jared, obviously." He certainly said it like it was obvious. "Okay, how should I do this?" It wasn't a question for Miles. He spoke as if having a conversation with someone else in the room, as if Miles were interrupting.

"I do apologize." Jared finally made eye contact; the red in them had dimmed. "You see, I don't like people very much. This conversation, even, I find it... uncomfortable. So I will have to kill you. Sorry." He didn't sound it.

Miles was angrier than he'd known possible. "Or how about I kill you, you crazy son of a bitch," he said, still unable to break free from his invisible bonds.

"That's not likely." Jared shook his head, looking away from him again. "Not likely at all." Whatever was holding Miles in place, it held Jared's attention too. "If you want to say something quickly. I don't know. Some quote or whatever it is you people say at times like this. Just be quick about it. I have things to do."

That's when the pigeon hit the window.

It struck with a loud crack. Both of them jumped, Jared spinning sideways. Miles, meanwhile, realized he could move again. He couldn't explain it, but he knew there was no time for questions— this was his chance. He reached into his jacket pocket and felt for his pen, the one that had sealed his last sale. He pulled it out like a knife and lunged toward the intruder.

Jared turned just in time to face him — and the consequences. Miles drove the pen through the side of his neck, twisting it deeper and deeper into his throat, until Jared couldn't breathe or speak. It hadn't hit an artery, but he was as good as dead; without his voice, Jared couldn't chant, couldn't cast spells. He was back to being his old self: a powerless predator. Not to mention the pen in his neck. Of course, Miles didn't know any of this at the time, and he wasn't taking chances. Nor was he offering mercy.

Jared stumbled backward, grabbing the dresser beside him for balance. It didn't stop Miles from knocking him to the floor with a brass candlestick.

"Not likely? Not likely!" Spit flew from Miles's mouth, spattering Jared's bloodied face. "I'll show you what's fucking likely." He wasn't making sense, but Jared probably got the gist when Miles knelt over him and swung the candlestick again, this time bashing his right eye. Jared threw blind punches, hitting Miles once on the nose. After that, Jared never hurt another living soul.

Miles couldn't say how many times he'd swung that candlestick. By the time he stopped, the bones in Jared's face were broken, his teeth shattered, his skin torn, his identity mashed into a gory pulp.

Slowly, Miles's rage simmered, and he remembered his wife.

He ran to her then clasped her palm with one hand, holding her head with the other. That's when it really hit him. He was the only one left. There were five bodies in his house but only one beating heart. Bent on his knees, Miles rested his head on her chest, letting sorrow finally take hold. He sobbed on her stomach for what might have been twenty minutes or two hours.

Miles would later find out the intruder had been a necromancer named Jared Snow. He'd killed hundreds of people, the inquisitors claimed. Families, they said. Children. Jared Snow would kill them all. He was a vagrant who drifted from one home to the next, murdering and pillaging. He was a modern-day Viking.

Miles hated the dead man with every ounce of his being and couldn't shake his desire to kill him again, if only he could. The inquisitors took notice.

It was two days after news stations began airing Miles's story — or a version of it, anyway — when the two men who called themselves inquisitors showed up on his doorstep. They were careful with their words. There was only so much they could tell him, they said, unless he came with them. They told him he had great potential, that he'd killed Jared Snow before they'd been able to. They told him they had a cause worth fighting for.

They mentioned the pigeon too. The dead bird was still lying in his backyard beneath a spider-web of window cracks, its neck broken, its wings spread out like an angel's. That bird was sent by God, the inquisitors said. God had saved Miles, and God had brought them together.

Miles slept on it. The next morning, he told them he'd join.

Miles spent the next year of his life training. He learned the inquisitors' ways and about necromancers. He learned how their power corrupted and turned them into evil men and women. Even the young ones— it was only a matter of time, they told him. And if Miles knew one thing, it was that he wouldn't let another Jared Snow wander this world. He'd pay any price to make sure of that. He would fight the dark. He would be God's hand here on Earth, snuffing out evil until the day he could be with his family again.

Over a decade had passed since Miles transformed into the man better known as Mr. Huxley — or James Harris, if you believed his passport — and he'd yet to change his outlook. But he had grown tired. It showed in his eyes.

Mr. Huxley glanced over at Mr. Underwood. He and his partner were walking down a long corridor at the Terminal City International Airport, minimal luggage in tow. They'd grown comfortable with not speaking when they were together, which was often. The two of them had already connected as much as they were going to connect. They'd shared as much as they were going to share. Mr. Huxley sometimes resented his partner for not being as smart as he was, but after eight years of working together, he loved the big oaf as much as he loved anyone left in his life. Indeed, Mr. Underwood was all he had. Well, besides his cause. He always had that.

Mr. Underwood didn't share his partner's ideological bent, though sometimes he feigned it. He had other reasons for being here, for being an inquisitor. He'd found unconditional acceptance among them. Mr. Underwood had been in and out of jail most of his life, but that all changed the day a couple strangers saw something in him. Despite his bear-like stature, Mr. Underwood was a modest man, and he'd told them straight up: he wasn't good at nothin', 'cept crime. The inquisitors would prove him wrong. Strictly speaking, they didn't operate within the realm of legality either, but they downplayed this technicality. Instead, they talked of God and forgiveness. He'd be a new man, they told him— one with a place and a purpose.

Mr. Underwood was a veteran now, having joined three years after Mr. Huxley, and not once had his devotion ever come into question. Mr. Underwood was a true hand of God: he moved without asking questions.

Mr. Huxley supposed there was more to the big man's life than the simple stories he told, but he'd come to realize that Mr. Underwood was too dim to think outside the simple narrative he had created to explain himself. No matter. It served the cause well enough.

The two inquisitors stepped outside the airport terminal, a still stream of black taxis ahead of them. Before they could hail one, Mr. Huxley's phone rang. His work phone.

"Hello, Ms. Westcott."

"There'll be a slight change of plans, sugar." Ms. Westcott sounded out of breath; she sometimes made calls from the treadmill. "Lester Wright may have to suffer another night or two of his miserable life. A shame, I know, but we've got a lead on someone else in Terminal City, where you just happen to be. Unlike Mr. Wright, we have an address for this one, so let's start there. Who knows— maybe the two are connected."

"Who is he?" asked Mr. Huxley, pacing around his partner.

"She," clarified Ms. Westcott. "What is it with you boys? Always so presumptuous."

"Sorry." Mr. Huxley rolled his eyes. "*She*."

"Her name is Lisa Sharpe," said Ms. Westcott. "She just appeared on our radar. We traced a suspicious blog post to one of her online profiles. Now, be careful what you say to her. She may not be the real deal. But she certainly knows more about necromancy than an innocent girl ought to."

"We'll pay her a visit," replied Mr. Huxley.

"Yes. That is your job, Mr. Huxley. Just remember you're dealing with a lady. A *she*. I know we're not your forte, hun. I'll message you her address." She hung up.

"Bitter old bitch," Mr. Huxley muttered as he snapped his phone shut. A woman walking past them shot him a mean look.

"Should we get a cab?" asked Mr. Underwood.

"Not yet. I'm waiting on an address. There's been a change of plans." Mr. Huxley reached into his jacket pocket. "Besides, we just spent half the day on a plane. I need a bloody smoke."

◆❖◆

Evening was setting in as Mr. Huxley and his partner marched down a long, fluorescent hallway. They had found the apartment— but not before taking a few wrong turns.

"What's the number again?" asked Mr. Underwood.

"Three-fifteen," said Mr. Huxley. "That's about the fifth time you've asked." In truth, it had only been the second, but Mr. Huxley was sleep-deprived, jet-lagged, and in a generally bad mood— even more so than usual.

"Here it is," said Mr. Underwood.

"Yes, I see that." Mr. Huxley knocked.

They waited and then knocked again, but still no one answered. Mr. Underwood shrugged. "I guess she ain't home."

Mr. Huxley tried turning the knob— it was always worth a shot. Lo and behold, the door creaked open. "Well then, let's find some evidence."

The apartment was like a cave, its blinds drawn shut. The two inquisitors tiptoed inside, hands hovering over their guns. Their faint footfalls made the only sounds. Mr. Huxley felt a light switch around the corner and gave it a flick. The living room popped into view. It wasn't pretty, full of mismatched furniture well past its prime. The walls were bare, but the floor was littered with crumpled clothing and faded magazines.

Then they saw the body: an elderly man's, pale and gaunt, no more than a day dead by Mr. Huxley's estimation. The corpse looked comfortable in its reclining chair, its hairless head resting on one shoulder, napping the night away— but Mr. Huxley knew a dead body when he saw one. He stepped forward and examined it more closely. No blood, no marks, nothing. The man's death had no discernible cause. "Old age, I guess," he said. "I wonder how long it'll take for anyone to realize."

Mr. Underwood emerged from the bedroom. "No one else home," he said. "But it sure don't look like a lady lives here, or ever did."

"What a complete waste of time. It was a shitty lead— I thought so from the start." Mr. Huxley sighed. "Well, screw it. Let's go."

But they didn't make it very far. A fourth body revealed itself, this one living— though it could have fooled some people. He was tall and skeletal and, for a second, see-through, a ghost fading back to life in the dead air between the inquisitors and the way out of here. The first thing Mr. Huxley noticed about him was his eyes: they were red in a way eyes shouldn't ever be.

The inquisitors were frozen in place before they even thought to reach for their guns. Just like that, the necromancer had them in his spell. Mr. Huxley hadn't seen it coming, hadn't heard him chant. He'd met a lot of necromancers, never on good terms, but this was a first.

"Do you know who I am?" the stranger asked.

Mr. Huxley had never seen the necromancer before, but there was no mistaking him. He'd heard all about Rowland. "Imagine a demon fucked a corpse and the two had a kid," his colleague, Mr. White, had once said. "That kid would grow up to look like Rowland." Mr. Huxley more or less agreed. What concerned him more than appearances, however, was that other thing he'd heard about Rowland: that if you ever run into him, make peace with God.

Perhaps no one had told this to Mr. Underwood. More likely, he just hadn't listened. "You're gonna get it, you ugly freak." The hulking man growled and grunted, but his body didn't, couldn't, move.

"I am afraid not," said Rowland. "For you see, I am rubber, and you are glue. That which you say bounces off of me and sticks to you. Consequently…"

It was like Rowland had flipped a switch and that was all it took. Mr. Underwood collapsed like an unplugged android, his head hitting the carpet with a soft thud. He was dead even before the blood began dripping from his nose.

"And then there were two." Rowland looked up.

It was the angriest Mr. Huxley had felt in a decade. Probably the most hopeless too. After all, Rowland wasn't Jared Snow. Mr. Huxley tried to convince himself otherwise, but there was no having it. There wouldn't be an opening this time. Rowland was good at many things, chief among them staying alive. No one on Earth had done a better job evading death— or serving it to others, for that matter. No, Rowland wasn't Jared Snow. Rowland was the devil himself— at least some people thought as much.

"Just kill me already," said Mr. Huxley, trembling in his invisible shackles. He peered down at his partner, his only friend. "Just get it over with."

"Interesting," said Rowland. "Most people beg for their lives before conceding them." He took a slow step forward. "Alas, for the time being, your request is denied. I will kill you eventually, however. You have my word. But not until you have passed along a message for me. To your fellow inquisitors. To Victoria Westcott. Especially Victoria Westcott. Tell her to bring her war to Terminal City. Tell her I will be waiting here. Tell her I will kill her this time. And that goes for the rest of you as well.

"Only then, inquisitor, will I kill you." Rowland squeezed Mr. Huxley's shoulder. "Just like I killed your large friend. The next time we meet— I promise."

A red stain had formed beneath Mr. Underwood's head. It was spreading and sinking into the carpet.

"What makes you think I'll tell them anything?" asked Mr. Huxley. He would tell them, of course — he had every reason to — but right now he'd have said the moon was made of cheese just to be difficult.

"You kill countless weak and innocent necromancers," said Rowland, eternally emotionless, "because you think — incorrectly — that they could turn into me. You will tell them, inquisitor, because you believe I am the reason people like you need to exist. Because there is nothing you want more than to see me dead. And because I will kill all of you regardless. In the end, it makes no difference whether I go to you or you come to me."

"Then why do you care if I tell them anything?" Mr. Huxley snarled.

"It is the fastest way," replied Rowland. "Tracking you is tiresome. Writing fake messages on the internet is not my preferred method of acquiring your attention, although I will admit it was effective. Here you are, after all."

"You'll regret this," spat Mr. Huxley, but his threat felt empty. He stopped short of saying he'd see the necromancer dead, as his partner had done. He wagered Rowland was still made of rubber and that he, like Mr. Underwood, was a man of glue.

Rowland inched forward, just close enough to look down on him. "We are done here," he said. "For now." With one hand, he covered Mr. Huxley's face, consuming it like a carnivorous maw.

Mr. Huxley fell unconscious in an instant, his body folding in on itself before hitting the floor— just as his partner's had. And there they were left, two suits sprawled over an old man's garbage and a young man's blood. But only one of them would ever wake up again.

Chapter 9

"**DO YOU HAVE** any siblings?" Asha was staring out the window.

"Nah," replied Mason. "Don't think my father ever really wanted kids. My mom, on the other hand, she was probably hoping for three or four. I suppose I was the compromise." He let out a single chuckle. "What about you?"

"Two sisters." She turned and met his gaze.

"Are you close?" he asked.

"Very," replied Asha. "We're on the phone every day. Same with my parents. We're a bit codependent, I guess." She smiled. "Well, they are. It's more for them than me — at least, that's what I tell myself. What about you? You talk to your parents much?"

He took a moment to consider his answer. It was lunchtime and they were sitting in the cafeteria, a small table between them. Mason tore off a piece of his sandwich and chewed it leisurely like a cow, stalling for time.

"I love my mom very much," he said finally, "but we don't communicate too well. Different wavelengths and all that. We're close in our own way." He took a slow sip from his cup of orange juice. "And my dad, he's, umm. He's dead. When he was alive, I guess he frustrated me sometimes, but other times — other times were good. People tell me we're a lot alike." He shrugged. "Might be true."

"I'm so sorry, Mason." Asha rested her hand on his.

"It's… it's nothing. I mean, it's something, but people all over the world deal with much worse, you know?" Mason didn't do well with sympathy. "He died in a car crash nine months ago, almost ten now. Anyway, it's been almost a year. I'm fine."

Asha decided to change the subject: "Have you picked up your student card yet?"

"Not yet," he said. "I suppose I should. It hasn't really been priority number one. What about you?"

"I picked mine up a few hours ago," she replied, "but it pains me to look at it."

"Bad picture?" Mason was absent-mindedly twisting his straw into a hypnotic circle.

"The worst," she said, "in the history of humankind."

"That's a bold claim." Mason released the straw and watched it expand like a mini Big Bang. "I'll need proof. Let me see. I'll tell you if I've seen worse. Bet I have."

Asha hesitated. "It's really bad." She said it like a warning.

He considered giving her a compliment — *you're too pretty for bad pictures* — but knew he didn't possess the nonchalance to make it fly.

Asha sighed and reached into her purse. "I'm going to regret this." She shuffled through leather, plastic, and tissue until she found her wallet. She flipped it open and slid out her student card. Then she held it out before her, frowning like a disappointed artist, and finally handed it to him.

"It's not so bad," he said without hesitation, though to be totally honest, it was pretty unflattering, which surprised him. He really had thought she was too pretty for bad pictures. But pictures lie, he knew.

Mason lied too— not often, but when it was the right thing to do, or occasionally, when it spared someone's feelings. "Really, it's not that bad," he told her again. "Asha Sarai," he said, reading her name aloud.

"Good job," she replied. "You pronounced it right."

"Lucky guess." Mason handed her back the student card. "My driver's license is ten times worse." It really was.

"Your turn, then." Asha poked the table.

Mason didn't put up a fight, but he did offer a disclaimer. "It's really old," he said. "The picture, I mean. A lot of the information on it too, I think." He unfolded his wallet, took out his license, and dropped it into Asha's eager, open hands.

She looked at it without saying a word, but her smile said enough.

"See," said Mason.

Then Asha furrowed her brow, her smile dropping as if suddenly hitched to a sinking anchor. She looked at the license a second longer before returning her eyes to the real him— not the one in the picture. "Mason," she said with emphasis. "Why didn't you tell me it was your birthday?"

Because I couldn't care less, he thought. He figured she'd probably want a better answer than that, however. Damn. He forgot licences showed birthdays. Meanwhile, the lunch rush was over and the cafeteria had turned quieter than he would have liked, at least at this very moment.

"It just seems sort of weird, telling someone it's your birthday," he said to break the silence. "Like you expect them to give you something." He tossed his hands into the air. "I don't know."

"Well, happy fucking birthday." She handed him back his license. "Do you have any plans?"

"Not really. I think my mom might visit this weekend."

"No party?" she asked.

Mason stared at her like she'd told a joke. "Who would I invite?" He figured Lester would probably come— he did now apparently live with him, after all.

"How about me?" Asha leaned forward. "We're friends, right?"

He nodded. "Yeah." *At least until I profess my undying love for you and fuck everything up.* "We're friends."

"Good." She nodded. "Then let's have a party. How do you feel about cake?"

"It's good. Tastes nice." He shrugged. "I like it about as much as the next guy."

"Then cake it is." She slapped the table. "We're going to make a cake, Mason." She wasn't asking, she was telling. "And put twenty-one candles on it."

If anyone else had insisted Mason bake a cake, he probably would have resisted. But this was Asha. He wouldn't pass up a chance to spend time with her— well, so long as her boyfriend wasn't involved.

"Okay," he said after a moment of feigned hesitation, "but I don't have any of the ingredients or anything."

"We'll buy them," she replied.

"When?"

"No time like the present." Asha stood up. "Your birthday is half over. We still have to bake this thing and make it look pretty. Let's get to it." She kicked his boot and nodded toward the exit. If Mason hadn't known better, he might have thought she was flirting with him, just a little.

On the way out, they spotted their philosophy professor, Alicia, walking down the hallway with a stack of papers under her arm. Mason wondered if their essays were bunched in there. They'd only been in class four weeks now, but already Alicia had her students writing papers. She noticed them and waved. They waved back. Mason was quite fond of her. He figured Asha was too.

The first leg of their mission was pretty painless. This was because the campus had its own grocery store. Mason had grown to appreciate the convenience, if not the selection. It was a small place, but it did have most of the essentials, plus a wide array of Chinese imports he was too intimidated by to purchase.

It also had cake mix.

"Angel's food or devil's?" Asha had a box in each hand.

"I am an atheist," said Mason, "so we better go with devil's." Not to mention a necromancer.

"Good, because the only frosting they have is chocolate." Asha shelved the angel's food cake mix and fetched the last can of frosting.

Meanwhile, Mason grabbed a pack of one-hundred candles from the next aisle over. He doubted he'd ever use the seventy-nine spares, but it was all they had. Might be useful if the power went out again.

When it came time to pay, they both pulled out their wallets. Asha insisted that it was his birthday, and Mason just insisted. In the end, they split the bill, a compromise neither one of them found satisfactory.

On the way to Mason's (it was closest), Asha asked him a question: "So, you're an atheist, are you?"

"I guess I am," he replied. "I don't buy into the whole God thing, so yeah. Why do you ask? Does that surprise you?"

She didn't look surprised. "No," she said. "Not at all. You philosophy types usually are."

"Suppose so," he said. "What about you? What do you believe, or not believe?"

"I believe there's something out there," she replied. "Call it God if you want. My parents are Hindu. They probably think I am too. In my own way, I guess I am. I like to imagine different religions as separate rivers all flowing into the same lake. Does that make sense?"

Mason nodded. "It makes sense. I'm still an atheist, but it makes sense."

It started to rain. Asha looked up toward the sky, unimpressed, holding one hand over her hair. Mason reached into his backpack and pulled out an umbrella. He popped it open; Asha moved closer to get underneath. Mason began hoping it would pour.

"Is it hard being an atheist?" she asked. "Is it hard not believing in anything?"

"I believe in things," he said. "Just not God. We live. We die. We fade away." The fading part was more literal than he would have imagined a few weeks ago. In truth, learning about the Spirit Realm had only reinforced his atheism. He now knew just how uncaring the universe really was, and that no one could ever be immortal. He knew that time ended everyone.

"That sounds depressing," said Asha, twirling a lock of her dark hair. She bit her bottom lip then added, "So, you think life is just random and meaningless?"

They turned the corner, Mason's house popping into view.

"Random, sure," he said. "But meaningless? No. We don't need God for that. Hell, I think our lives are more meaningful without God."

"How so?" she asked.

Mason hesitated. "It means our experiences are earned, not just given to us," he said. "If God is up there plotting our lives, then we're basically carts on a rollercoaster. This moment, us walking together in the rain— all part of God's plan.

"Or," he continued, "maybe there is no track. Maybe we're the drivers. Maybe you're here because you want to be. Because I want to be. Because we got to know each other. Because you thought I should have cake, and now we're having this conversation under my piece-of-shit umbrella." Its metal spine had been disfigured in a windstorm.

"The way I see it, we made this moment," said Mason. "It's ours."

They stepped onto the veranda, Asha's heeled boots clicking on the wood. Mason collapsed his piece-of-shit umbrella and walked to the front door, leaving a trail of raindrops behind him. He turned the lock and stepped through.

Asha followed him inside. "You've got a way with words, Mason."

He led her to the kitchen and tossed their grocery bag of ingredients onto the counter. "You can put your jacket wherever," he said.

She wrapped it around the back of a wooden table chair and left her purse on the seat. "Nice place." She peered around the room. "It's big."

"Yeah," he said. "Maybe too big."

"I thought you said you lived alone. How do you have a huge house like this?" she asked. "Are you, like, super rich or something?"

"I wish," he replied. "It's family-owned. Well, it's mine now, but it belonged to my dad. He used to teach at Carwin." Mason spotted sympathy in her eyes at the mention of his father. "Right. So, how about this cake?"

Asha pulled the box of cake mix out of the bag and scanned it for instructions. "Do you have a cake pan?" she asked.

"I… umm. Hmm. Let's find out." Mason sifted through cupboards then checked under the stove. "Will this square thing work?" He held the pan over his head, his body bent over the stove drawer, his eyes scanning hers for approval.

She nodded. "Just got the one?"

"Looks like it." He handed it to her.

"Let me guess: you don't know the first thing about cooking." Asha poked him. She was more comfortable with touching than Mason was used to, not that he minded.

"Clueless as the day is long. I'm not really a hands-on type of guy," he said. "But I can follow instructions. Well, I can try."

"We need eggs."

He checked the fridge. "I have egg-zactly seven."

She tried not to smile at that one but failed. "You're so fucking lame."

"Jeez, it was just a yoke."

Asha snatched the eggs from him. "Mixing bowl?"

Mason grabbed a metal one and handed it to her. She cracked the eggs into the bowl, flawlessly, handing him the discarded shells one at a time. After that, she added a bit of water, a bit of olive oil, and, last but not least, the cake mix. As she stirred them together, Mason asked if there was anything he could do. Asha reminded him that it was his birthday, but the oven needed to be preheated to 350 degrees if he didn't mind. For a few seconds, Mason made himself useful.

Once Asha slid the uncooked cake into the oven, there wasn't a whole lot left to do, not for a while anyway. Mason busted out some wine, a chardonnay.

About halfway through the second glass, Asha made a confession. "I don't know what to do, Mason," she said.

"What do you mean?" he asked.

She sighed. "It's Josh. You know how you can really like someone, but, I don't know— you hit a wall with people. Most people. This point where you've said all you have to say to them, and everything from then on feels like… filler."

Mason could definitely relate. "Sounds like most of my relationships."

"He's great, though," she said. "Josh. He really is. People love him. At the start, it was a lot of fun. I mean, it still is sometimes. It's just… it's all the in-betweens. And I don't know if it's specifically our problem, if maybe we're too different from each other, or if it's simply something every couple goes through— this lull. I don't know. I really wish I knew, Mason."

The rim of her wine glass teetered on her lower lip. "Sorry. Sometimes I open up too much with people— like, way too much. It's a bit of a problem with me."

"Well, I probably don't open up enough," said Mason, "or so I've been told. Point being, I'm in no position to judge."

"Thanks for listening." Asha looked longingly toward her wine, swishing it around like a gentle tornado. "You're a good guy."

"I'm okay." Mason cleared his throat then stood up to check the oven. He turned to her. "I think it's ready."

Asha leaned down beside him and peered inside. "Yeah, looks pretty good. Let's pull it out."

With the cake finally cooked, it was time for frosting. Mason and Asha smothered it uncompromisingly. It was his birthday, after all.

"I think I have sprinkles," said Mason. He did. "Shit. Is that too many?" It was.

Asha laughed. "Your cake, birthday boy." She tore open the plastic bag of candles and began placing them around the cake in a circle, which turned into a spiral as she ran out of room. Mason really was getting old. He helped her finish, shoving in the last one like a spear through flesh.

"Twenty-one. I don't feel it," he said, staring down.

"Don't look it either," added Asha.

"Hey, I got stubble." Mason stroked his chin. "Well, kind of."

Asha nudged his shoulder with hers. "It was supposed to be a compliment," she said. "Got a lighter?"

He pulled one out from his pocket and started lighting.

Asha plucked a lit candle out of the cake and helped light the rest. "You really shouldn't smoke, Mason. Don't think I haven't noticed." She leaned toward him until they were touching. "I'm very perceptive, you know."

Mason wasn't quite sure how to interpret that, but he could feel himself blushing all the same. He turned his head away from hers, hoping her senses were less keen than she claimed. They weren't drunk, but they weren't entirely sober either.

"Make a wish," she said.

"All right." Mason was sweating under his T-shirt, but it wasn't from the fire. He made his wish and then blew out every candle in one good gust. She clapped for him as he took a deep breath, knocking back oxygen like a cold beer.

"What did you wish for?" she asked.

"I can't tell you," he replied.

"Why not?"

"Because then it won't come true."

"Oh?" Asha looked incredulous. "You're telling me you believe in magical wishes, Mr. Atheist? I don't buy it."

Mason laughed. "Clever girl. Still, some things are best kept secret."

Her face was inches from his. He could feel her warmth. The wine bottle was sitting across the kitchen table, empty.

"Do you have a lot of secrets, Mason?" Something in the tone of her voice washed over his skin like a warm bath.

"A few," he said.

"You're just so dark, aren't you?" She poked his chest teasingly. "Dark and brooding. With your black hair and your pale skin. Like one of those emo vampires all the teenage girls are into these days."

He coughed up the last of his chardonnay, a grin stretched across his face. "Well, that is what I'm going for."

"Tell me one of your dark secrets, emo vampire," she said.

Mason considered this. The necromancy stuff was entirely out of the question, of course, and hardly appropriate. He pondered some more. "Like most vampires," he said, "I suppose I can get a little lonely."

She laughed — then stopped herself.

"Yeah, maybe that's obvious," he continued. "But I'm not lonely in the way people think I am."

"How's that?" Asha wasn't just being polite; he could tell he had her full attention, that she cared.

"Well, I can't be out in the daylight, for one."

"I think the joke's dead, Mason."

He sighed dramatically. "Just like me."

She shook her head.

"Anyway, as I was saying, it's a different kind of lonely," said Mason. "It wouldn't matter if I had a bunch of friends. You know how people get a boost of energy when they're around others? At parties, concerts, whatever. I've never felt that. Like, probably ever. I get invited out to things, sometimes, and everyone seems to have fun, everyone seems to connect, but I never do. It's kind of like being a picky eater. People tell me lobster is delicious, and I can tell they love it, but for the life of me... all I see is this disgusting sea scorpion."

"So, you're introverted," said Asha.

"Super introverted," replied Mason. "I took that Myers-Briggs personality test online and got literally one-hundred per cent on the introvert part."

"Do you feel lonely right now?" she asked.

"Like, this very second?"

"Yes, Mason. This very second."

He could have just said no. It was the truth, after all. Instead, he got reckless, like everybody else always did, but not him, never him— except at this very second. "I've got another secret for you," he said.

"Two dark secrets?" Asha slapped her cheeks like that kid from *Home Alone*. "I don't know if I can handle two."

Maybe it was the booze. "Too bad. Because I think you... Asha... you are... ridiculously beautiful." Maybe it was her. "Like, in every conceivable way."

In any event, Mason immediately regretted it. His confidence flew from him as quickly as it had found him, and he turned even redder. "I'm sorry." He took a step back. "I didn't mean that. I mean I meant it, but I didn't mean to mean it. No, that's not what I mean either. Ah, fuck my life."

But Asha didn't look displeased. She looked serious, the good kind of serious, and she wasn't going to let him walk away. She grabbed the neck of his T-shirt and pulled him forward until he fell into her. She kissed him, or he kissed her — it didn't matter. Mason felt doubly drunk. He pulled her pelvis toward his, but then she pushed back. She stopped kissing him — it was definitely her this time. Now the expression on her face was the bad kind of serious.

"I'm sorry." Asha yanked her hands from his chest as if he were suddenly contagious. "I can't do this. I know what I said, but I still have a boyfriend." She stood up straight, sounding clinical. "This is wrong." It was a matter of fact. She turned around and started for her coat.

"I'm sorry." Mason didn't know what else to say.

"It's not your fault, Mason. It's mine." The jacket was on now. "Anyway, I should go."

"You sure you don't want some cake first?" he asked. "You're welcome to cake around here a bit longer." She didn't find that one funny, and neither did he. "Shit, I'm sorry."

Asha grabbed her purse then went for her boots. "No, I'm sorry. I'm sorry I ruined your birthday with my unresolved bullshit." She was fighting with her footwear now.

It was a lot of sorrys. They were both being very Canadian.

"You didn't ruin anything," he told her. "You made my birthday way better. Trust me." Admittedly, the bar hadn't been set too high.

Asha stood up, boots on, coat buttoned, purse snug around her shoulder. "You're sweet, Mason," she said. "Happy birthday." She left out the front door.

"Good night." Mason wasn't sure she heard him. He stumbled back into the kitchen then looked at his cake. "Fuck it." He cut himself a hefty piece.

As he set down the knife, the front door swung back open. For a fleeting moment, he thought it was Asha, thought she had changed her mind. Boy, was he disappointed.

"Happy birthday, kiddo." Lester sniffled. "Mmm, cake. Cut me a slice, will ya — a big one."

"Whatever." Mason did as he was told, too annoyed with life to be annoyed with Lester, then grabbed a couple plates from a high-up cupboard. He slid them onto the kitchen table. "How'd you know it was my birthday?" he asked.

"Great question!" Lester said it like some horribly chipper professor. "I uncovered the moment of your birth by casting a mind-bogglingly complex necromantic spell that reveals... birthdays. Also, your dad may have mentioned it once or twice."

Lester sat down first. Good cake, they agreed. Mason credited Asha and blamed himself for the sprinkles.

"No such thing as too many sprinkles," said Lester, still chewing. "Speaking of sprinkles, I have something for you. Actually, it has nothing to do with sprinkles."

Mason swallowed before speaking. "What is it?"

"A birthday gift."

"Really?"

"Don't sound so disappointed."

"I didn't mean—"

"Hold that thought." Lester reached into his blazer and pulled out the gift in question. It was even wrapped. Not well, but still. Mason was impressed. Lester slid his present down the table toward Mason. "Happy birthday, little necromancer."

"I'm like four inches taller than you." Mason ripped off Lester's crude wrapping paper, which was covered in snowmen and candy canes. "A book." He held it up. The book was small, black, and leather-bound— though not nearly as old as *The Necromancer's Grimoire*.

"Not just any," chimed in Lester. "Your father's. He used that notebook for all his favorite spells, including a few he worked out himself. They're mostly complex spells. I doubt you'll be able to perform any of them, but hey, something to strive for, right?"

Mason flipped through the pages, his dad's penmanship and prose illuminating every line, every margin. He imagined more work had been put into this small book than all his father's other works combined. "Thank you." Mason meant it.

Lester nodded. "You're welcome. Just remember that's complicated necromancy in there. Some of it's very dangerous, so be careful. Don't, you know, shoot your eye out."

Mason flipped a page, his gaze glued away from the conversation. "Yeah, yeah. I'll be careful."

Chapter 10

THEY FINISHED WITH a hug. Mason hadn't grown used to hugs, never had to, but now, every time he said good bye to his mother, they seemed obligatory.

"Love you," she told him. "Glad everything is going well. If Lester is making you uncomfortable, you can ask him to leave, you know. This is your home, Mason." She shivered. It was an unusually chilly day in early October. "Don't feel that you have to let him stay. He's a bit of an oddball, that one. Your dad liked him well enough, I suppose, but that doesn't mean you have to."

"Mom, it's fine." Mason stopped her. "Really. I know it's my house. And my decision."

"I know, dear. I'm just trying to look out for you."

Mason knew she meant well but didn't like being looked out for. Still, he said, "Thanks. I'll be all right."

She nodded, hugged him, and then stepped into her car. "I love you," she said a second time, looking for confirmation that he loved her too. Mason said he did, and he did. She started her engine and then backed up slowly before idling at the tip of his driveway to wave goodbye. He waved back, and then, finally, she drove off.

Mason went back inside the house. No one else was home, which is to say he didn't know where Lester was— the little man could be quite elusive. Of course, Mason enjoyed his alone time, though he didn't know what to do with himself now. It was Saturday afternoon, and with no imminent deadlines, he knew he wouldn't be able to muster the willpower to study. He wasn't even going to try.

Then he remembered Lester's birthday gift, his father's notebook. His mother had bought him some books too (and a gift card), but Mason was feeling that necromantic itch — something he felt increasingly often.

He fetched the notebook from his bedroom and began flipping through pages, pacing up and down the hallway. He was looking for something he could try. Something interesting yet doable. But just as Lester had forewarned, many of the spells seemed incredibly complex, some with chants that filled the length of a page. Mason crossed those ones off his mental list, perusing page after page for the shortest spells he could find.

There were a few shorter ones, as it turned out, and a couple that caught his eye. There was one spell that used spirit energy to help heal superficial wounds, but he had no injuries (nor the desire to give himself any). There was another for making static orbs of light, like the ones in the basement lab, but he'd already seen those. Finally, there was the spell that interested him most — it said he could reanimate corpses.

At first, Mason figured it wouldn't be feasible, practically or ethically. He didn't have a corpse lying around and certainly didn't plan on digging one up. But then he read on: it didn't have to be a human corpse. Even an insect's would do. He had no qualms about killing bugs. He did it all the time.

And so the hunt began. Mason looked for insects in every room of the house, with no luck. He thought he'd find one or two in the basement lab if nowhere else, but he came back upstairs disappointed. *Bastards only show up when you don't want them to.*

Mason slid on his jacket and a pair of boots before heading out the front door, locking it behind him. He tucked the notebook into his inner coat pocket — it was just small enough — determined to find a bug. He wouldn't mind going for a walk either. Mason liked walks.

Of course, practicing necromancy required a degree of privacy. In fact, Lester had said not to even consider casting spells outside the house, but he wasn't the boss of him. Mason would settle for the woods, he decided. If he went deep enough, no one would be around, and there should be lots of bugs.

There was a small evergreen forest fifteen minutes from his house, bordering Carwin's campus from the ocean. He followed a thin, well-worn dirt path, winding deeper into the woods, never once spotting another living soul. The day was cool and overcast, not exactly inviting, unless you were a loner necromancer.

Mason deviated from the trail and made his way to the ocean. He sat down on a large wet rock, maybe five feet from the water; fewer when heavy waves crashed against the rocky shore, spraying his boots. It was windy down here — he zipped up his jacket to its collar — but Mason savored the scenery, shivering peacefully. "I wonder if this'll be good ambience for doing necromancy," he said under his breath. It was either a joke or a good question.

Mason let the waves massage his mind a few minutes longer before returning his attention to the task at hand: finding a bug. He stood up and started hunting. "Here, buggy, buggy, buggy."

Mason went back into the woods and knelt down on one knee, surveying the forest floor. He snatched a small twig off the ground and held it like a wand. For a while, he sifted through the dirt with his new weapon, poking holes and drawing smiley faces. Then he saw his first bug: a beetle, a big one. He stabbed at it with his stick, missing by an inch. The bug scurried away, but he kept stabbing, until finally— "Got you!"

Mason had cracked the insect's shell in half. It was stuck on the end of his stick, split open, oozing. He went back to the rock and wiped off the corpse, smearing it along the stone like a condiment, mangling it further.

Mason threw his makeshift spear into the ocean and pulled out his dad's notebook. He thumbed through a flurry of pages until he found the reanimation spell again. He read it carefully a few more times and then began the chant, holding his free palm over the beaten beetle. At first, he felt nothing, tripping over each word, unable to focus, unable to find that familiar feeling. It wasn't until he'd read it through at least a dozen times that he felt any sort of spark. Still, nothing happened to the beetle. He tried a few more times, and then, finally, he saw its leg twitching, just barely. He kept his attention locked and steady, until his chant became background noise, like the waves crashing at his feet, but the beetle had reached its limit. He'd disfigured it too badly, he realized, feeling stupid for not seeing that sooner. But the spell was working — he was pulling it off — and that was enough to get him excited. Mason headed back into the woods.

No beetles this time, but he did find a worm. He picked it up between his index finger and thumb then dropped it down next to the beetle— his new sacrificial stone, apparently. He was a bit disgusted with himself, but he was far more curious.

"How the hell should I kill you? I can't squish you." Mason picked up a small, sharp stone, took a deep breath, and then sliced off part of the worm. It kept squirming, discarding its severed tail. "Oh right. Worms do that. Weird sons of bitches."

Then he heard footsteps.

Mason peered down the rocky shoreline and saw a tall-looking man in the distance, walking toward him. Mason quickly tucked away his notebook and returned his attention to the ocean's hypnotic waves. *You win this round, worm.*

But the stranger was slowing his pace. He stopped between Mason and the water, staring at him unabashedly. "You do not look very much like your father, Mason Cross," he said, a little too nonchalantly.

"Do I know you?" asked Mason.

"No," the stranger replied. "Nor I you." He was a weird-looking man, that's for sure. Pale, and going by his eyes, Mason might have thought he was stoned if not for his severely sober demeanor.

"Who are you?" Mason wished he still had his stick.

"I am a necromancer." There was no hesitation.

"You knew my father?"

"Yes. I know most necromancers. He was… one of the few interesting ones." The tall stranger looked down toward the rock Mason was sitting on. "What were you attempting?" He must have seen the disfigured insects.

Mason didn't know if he should answer honestly. "What do you mean?" He stalled.

"I know you are a necromancer, Mason Cross." It wasn't a threat, but it wasn't exactly a peace offering either. "That is how I found you. When you disturb the Spirit Realm, as all necromancy does, it leaves a trace. Invisible to most people, most necromancers as well, but not to me. There is no point in lying, necromancer."

Mason couldn't come up with a convincing counter-argument — convincing enough for this man, anyhow — but maybe it didn't matter. Still, he wasn't sure he was safe. The stranger's gaze gave away nothing.

"I was trying to reanimate these bugs," Mason finally admitted.

The stranger didn't immediately reply. Instead, he walked into the forest and then went down on one knee and reached into the decaying stump of a fallen fir. He pulled out something small and black. As he approached, Mason saw it was a beetle — this one still alive. The stranger set it down on the rock with the other bugs. It tried to scurry away but then stopped dead in its tracks. Literally.

Mason saw red flash from the stranger's eyes, but he'd heard no chant. He remembered something Lester once said: chanting only helps focus spells and isn't actually necessary — in theory, anyway. He'd never seen Lester pull one off like that. Mason suspected this necromancer was pretty powerful.

"If you aim to use the body, it is best to keep it intact," said the stranger. "Necromancers need not use sticks and stones. Simply tear out its spirit. Now, try your reanimation spell again."

Mason found it difficult to regain his focus, and his first few attempts were fruitless. The stranger's stone-cold stare was a relentless distraction. But after a while and enough failure, he found that feeling — that sense of control — and watched his beetle crawl, slowly in aimless directions.

"Now guide it," said the stranger. "Give it motivation. Give it a goal. Bend it to your will."

Mason tried to do what he said, but stress once again got the better of him. His concentration broke, and with it his spell.

"Try again." The stranger looked as if he'd expected that to happen.

Mason wasn't sure he wanted to, but he gave it a shot anyway. This time, he managed to make the beetle move in one direction — away from him — before losing control for a second time.

"Better," said the stranger, though it hardly sounded like approval. "There is no point in creation without control. Without it, your creation could just as well turn against you."

Mason nodded. It's not like he knew better.

"How long have you been a necromancer, Mason Cross?"

"About a month, I guess."

If the stranger was impressed, he didn't show it. "So, Lester Wright taught you. Not your father."

It was a statement of fact, not a question, but Mason still nodded.

"Have you noticed anyone suspicious lately? Anyone who might be following you?"

"Besides you?" asked Mason.

"Yes. Besides me."

"Then no."

"I see," he said. "Have you learned the invisibility spell yet?"

Mason shook his head. "Don't think so."

"If you mean no, then say no."

"No."

"Learn it." The stranger looked down the length of the beach. "Find the spell in your father's library. Invisibility will save your life one day. An invisible man always gets the first strike, and if you are good, the first strike is all you will need. Invisibility is every necromancer's most important spell." He turned back toward the direction from which he'd appeared. "Every necromancer but me." He started walking. "Be wary of men in black suits."

"Why?" Mason stood up to brush off his jeans. "Am I in danger?"

The stranger stopped, turning to face him this time. "You are a necromancer now, Mason Cross." His thin white hair was thrown sideways by the ocean wind. "You will always be in danger."

He didn't look back again.

Chapter 11

TO MY WIFE, *Victoria, I leave everything: my property, my money, and my passion. I know she will make me proud in this life as I watch on from the next.*
 —The Last Will and Testament of George Westcott

Victoria Westcott became her own woman the day she met Rowland— the day he killed her husband, George. She'd watched him do it. The strangest thing about that night was how weak George had looked. As surreal as everything else had been, that was the most unsettling. George had always been the toughest man she knew, an anchor, not just for her but for all his inquisitors. Under George, the inquisition had grown stronger than ever before. Under George, they were going to win this war and save the world from necromancy once and for all. How quickly their inflated hope had popped.

Victoria had seen her husband die from the hallway, standing still in its shadows like some unwilling spectator, her body frozen from fright. The show didn't last long. Rowland played the butcher, George the chicken, darting around his den, ducking behind chairs, throwing staplers and pens.

In the end, Rowland showed him no mercy. He wasn't a victim, after all— he was his enemy. They were both killers in their own way. George commanded troops, though he seldom ventured onto the battlefield.

She remembered George stumbling in and out of view through the doorframe, Rowland tossing him from wall to wall like a stringless puppet, knocking books and medals off their shelves.

Before long, his head cracked open. Bloodied and bruised, George might have collapsed for good, but Rowland wouldn't release his ghostly grip. She wasn't sure if it was because he was having fun or if he simply wanted to be sure the job was finished.

Victoria figured her husband died before Rowland was done killing him. It was hard to say; he was certainly dead by the time she reached him. She remembered checking his breath and pulse. She remembered how slippery his skin was with blood.

But more than anything else, she remembered that look Rowland gave her. She was still trembling in the hallway when he walked over. She had assumed she would meet her end too, and then she'd see George in heaven. It wouldn't be so bad, really, so long as dying didn't hurt too much, and death was all he had in store for her.

But no. Rowland had no plans to kill or rape her. He didn't even open his twisted mouth to speak. That dismissive look in his eyes had said it all: *you're just the wife*. She was nothing, not even worth killing. He left her to clean up his mess.

Well, fuck him. That would be the worst mistake he ever made. As God as her witness, Victoria knew in that moment that she would get her revenge at all costs. And no one — *no one* — would ever look at her that way again.

Two decades had passed since that fateful night, but her anger hadn't aged a day.

Inside her office, Victoria had a photo of her late husband erected on one side of her desk. George watched her now as he always did. It was a small picture in a modest wooden frame — appropriate for a man who believed in cause over money and luxury. Though they'd always had plenty of that too.

But money brought Victoria little happiness these days. Then again, in her life happiness wasn't supposed to enter into the equation. There was only what needed to be done and what didn't. It required a certain degree of order.

Lately, everything was crumbling under the heavy hand of chaos. Mr. Underwood, one of her best, was dead, and his partner, Mr. Huxley, had gone rogue. Victoria remembered his panicked call well.

He's dead. He's fucking dead.
Who, sugar— who's dead?
Mr. Underwood. He's dead.
What! How?
...
Mr. Huxley?
Rowland. Rowland killed him. He let me live to tell you. To tell you that he's waiting in Terminal City for us. He said... he said he's going to kill you this time. He said he's going to kill all of us.
You should come back, dear. Forget Lester Wright for now. Come on home and we'll figure this out.
No.
What do you mean no?
I mean no. I'm not coming back. Not now. I have a job to do, necromancers to kill. This is war, damn it. I'm not... I'm not abandoning my brothers.
You're not mentally sound, Mr. Huxley, and you have no partner. You know how we operate. You know the rules.
Fuck the rules.
Miles—
It's Mr. Huxley.
We need to be careful.
Don't tell me what I need.
Click

Two weeks had passed since the phone call. Victoria hadn't heard from Mr. Huxley since he'd hung up on her, and she was growing worried. Of course, it wasn't just Mr. Huxley that worried her. Far from it. Sure, this had been the moment she'd been waiting for — Rowland's return — but that didn't make it any less terrifying. Even after twenty years of thinking long and hard, she hadn't the faintest clue how they'd stop him. Only that she needed to, more than she needed anything. Plus, it was him or them— he'd made that much clear.

Still, this was personal. Victoria prayed that her feelings wouldn't cloud her judgment. She was also worried about what she didn't know. Where had Rowland been all these years, and just what the hell was he doing? He'd disappeared a few months after killing George, and they hadn't heard so much as a peep from him since. No one knew where or why he'd gone, not even his fellow necromancers from what she could gather. It wasn't the first time he'd stepped off the scene, but two decades? That was new. One could almost be forgiven for forgetting he was still out there. In fact, some of the younger inquisitors had, but not her. Not for a second. She knew he was biding his time, that he'd come back. But that's all she knew. Was she really ready to face him?

It didn't matter. Her time was up. Rowland had made the first move, declaring all-out war. What choice did she have now? She had to fight back.

Victoria punched three numbers into the phone on her desk. It rang just once.

"Hello, Ms. Westcott." It was on speakerphone. "What can I do for you?"

"Mitchell. Come see me." She hung up before he could reply.

Not a minute later, her assistant, Mitchell, stepped into the room. "Good afternoon, Ms. Westcott."

"Good afternoon, Mitchell."

Behind Victoria's skeletal silhouette, Houston's blocky skyline shone through the window in all its entrepreneurial glory. It was a new office; their last one had been in Dallas. They changed locations often — paranoia was part of the profession — though Victoria always insisted on Texas, her home.

The high inquisitor — that was her official title — pushed herself up from her seat and stepped around her desk. As a point of pride, Victoria said what she needed to say face-to-face. She was dressed in all black: a black skirt, a black blazer, black heels, black nylons. Her usual attire. Victoria could be mistaken for a woman coming from a funeral any day of the week. Around her neck hung a large silver crucifix, a gift from her husband and a promise to God, George, and herself— her holy trinity.

It wasn't a promise the Church officially sanctioned, but there were enough men and women (well, mostly men) who supported their cause, always in secret. Victoria knew well that it wasn't the number of supporters you had that won wars— it was the number of dollars. Luckily, many of her backers were wealthy people who understood that the price of fighting evil was a high one. They kept the inquisition afloat, but sometimes only barely. If there was a silver lining to Rowland's return, it was that news of it had opened a few more wallets.

And then there were men like Mitchell: broke but relentlessly devote. It always seemed to go that way. He was waiting like an obedient dog for Victoria to tell him what to do, what to think. He looked just as he had the first day she'd hired him: soft-faced, neatly groomed, his posture perfect, his eyes expectant. Young and determined, Mitchell was. But too small to be a tough inquisitor and too naïve to be a smart one, though that didn't discourage him. Victoria had come to realize he'd never stop trying to join their ranks. He idolized them and her especially. Maybe Mitchell should get his shot. Desperate times and all that.

Victoria paced back and forth for a good minute, Mitchell's gaze following her each way like a slow pendulum. She was trying to assure herself that the order she was about to give was the right one. The wise one, not the emotional one. She wondered how George would have played this. Not that he'd known better than she did now, not after all these years. It was simply something she always asked herself, a step in her thought process. But the time for thinking was over; she'd made up her mind the second she invited Mitchell up here.

"I have a task for you," she said finally. "Clear whatever is on your plate and do this first. I need you to get a hold of every inquisitor on the continent."

"Every single one?" asked Mitchell.

"That is what every means, sugar," she replied. "Yes, every one you can, and tell them this: wrap up whatever assignment they're on and head to Terminal City. I want everyone there in two days tops. Further instructions will follow."

"Sure thing, Ms. Westcott." Mitchell nodded sharply. "Is there anything else?"

Victoria measured him with her eyes, from feet to face, squinting pensively. "Yes. Just one more thing. Do you still wish to be an inquisitor, Mitchell?"

"More than anything, Ms. Westcott." He was trying not to smile, trying to look serious. "More than anything."

"It'll be dangerous," she said. "Very, very dangerous."

"I'm not afraid of danger." He was so sure of himself. "I've trained for this. I know the protocols. Mr. White has been an exceptional teacher."

"You should be afraid of danger, darling," replied Victoria. "You're young. Danger is what kills young men. But if your heart is set on this, well, we need all the help we can get right now."

"It is, Mr. Westcott."

"Very well." She nodded. "But I still need you to make those phone calls. That's your first priority."

"I'll get right on it." Mitchell nearly saluted her.

And here Victoria had thought he couldn't possibly get any keener. "That's everything, Mitch— I mean, Mr. Crosby."

Mitchell nodded once more before marching out of the room like some Monty Python-esque caricature of professionalism.

Victoria made her way to the window, far less sure of herself than Mitchell. Her steps were slow and cautious. She grabbed a cup of lukewarm green tea off her desk and breathed it in before taking a sip. She stared out at Houston, but her mind was already in Terminal City. Soon, the rest of her would be too. Rowland wanted a war, and she would give him one. But first, she had dinner plans.

"Hi, Mom."

"Sarah." Victoria hugged her daughter, her purse dangling from one hand, keys jingling in the other. "Sorry, I'm late, darling. Busy day at the office." She unlocked the front door. "Have you been waiting long?"

"Fifteen minutes maybe," she replied. "It's fine."

Victoria suddenly felt even worse. Sarah had wanted to cancel tonight, but Victoria had insisted. They had these dinners once a month— at least, that was the idea. They were busy women, both of them, Sarah at the law firm where she articled and Victoria— well, she didn't tell her daughter what she did. As far as Sarah knew, she managed a corporate headhunting firm. That was the official lie, told by all inquisitors when asked what they did for a living. The headhunting part was sort of true.

They stepped inside Victoria's townhouse.

Sarah dropped herself onto the leather sofa in the living room, exhaling. "My boss, Larry, is creeping me the hell out," she said. "I keep catching him staring at my ass."

"In this gentleman's defence, my daughter has a marvelous ass." Victoria was flipping through her mail over the kitchen counter. "I would know." She looked up. "I gave it to you."

"Do you want to just order in?" asked Sarah. "I don't really feel like cooking."

Neither did Victoria. "How about Chinese?"

"Sure." Sarah was reading emails on her phone. "Get that lemon chicken stuff."

Victoria made the order and then brought over two glasses of wine. It was a French Pinot noir, about four hundred bucks worth. She'd been saving this bottle, not for any particular occasion—just the right time. She wondered if her daughter would notice.

"This is really good." Sarah set down her glass on the pine coffee table between them.

Victoria smiled, sliding a coaster underneath. Sarah rolled her eyes. There were some things they would never agree on.

"Did you go on another date with that guy?" asked Sarah. "I forget his name. Phil?"

"He prefers Philip," replied Victoria, "and no. He asked, but I didn't think we had much in common."

"Mom, you always say that." They'd had this conversation too many times. "First dates are like job interviews— people don't let you see the real them. You gotta give these guys a few chances. I mean, look at you. You're fucking gorgeous. I hope I look as good as you do when I'm your age. Don't waste that."

"I don't do it for them, hun." Though she certainly appreciated the compliment. "The thing about this world, daughter of mine, and this is especially true when you're a woman, is that everybody judges you. All the time. If I let myself go, folks would see it as a weakness. They'd think I couldn't take care of myself and wonder what else I couldn't handle. You can't give them an inch, darling. Men resent powerful women. You can't give them anything."

Sarah nodded knowingly. "I just want you to be happy is all."

"I have you. That's enough." Although Victoria wasn't sure that was true.

Sarah didn't look convinced either. "I have this friend, Jill. Her mom's a widow too. She said she changed her last name back, said it helped her reclaim some of her identity and move on. Maybe that would help. You still talk about him a lot, you know. I can barely remember Dad."

Victoria repositioned herself onto the couch beside Sarah. "I'm a Westcott, just like you, and proud of it," she said softly into her daughter's ear. "The way I see it, I was born with a man's name until I adopted another's. Difference is, I prefer the man

I married. I know you're just worried, and God bless you for it, but believe me: I'm already the woman I need to be."

Sarah nodded. "Okay, Mom." She wasn't going to push the issue further.

Victoria took her daughter's hand and kissed it. "The food should be here soon. Lots of lemon chicken, I made sure. I'm glad you came out tonight."

"Me too." Sarah finally looked relaxed.

It made Victoria happier than she let on. She couldn't tell her daughter the truth, after all. She couldn't tell her that this might be the last dinner they ever shared.

CHAPTER 12

MASON WAS PROCRASTINATING. It was the middle of the week, and he'd barely touched the homework in front of him. His laptop was flipped open, his notes stacked to his left, books to his right, but an hour had passed and he'd only typed up a single sentence, which he was probably going to delete anyway. That damn blinking cursor wouldn't shut up.

It was due tomorrow, his homework, but instead of working on sentence number two, Mason was trying to cast the invisibility spell over and over again, each attempt lamer than his last. He'd found the spell in his father's library, just like Rowland had said he would. *The Miraculous Necromancer* — that's what the book was called. They definitely weren't talking about him. He'd so far managed to make his arm a little translucent, like a piece of him was holographic. It was neat — but not exactly life-saving in a pinch.

Mason's cell phone rang. It was Asha. They hadn't spoken in days. He let it ring twice before answering.

"Hey, Asha."

"Hi."

"What's up?"

"Umm. Can we go for a walk or something?" She didn't sound quite like herself. "I just want to talk."

"Yeah," he said. "Of course. Do you want me to drop by?"

"Actually, I'm pretty much at your place already. I was going for a walk anyway, so yeah."

"Okay," replied Mason. "I'll grab my coat and meet you out front."

"Kay."

"All right."
"Yeah, bye."
"Bye."

Downstairs, Lester was making dinner in the kitchen. "It's almost ready," he said.

Mason told him not to wait up, that he might be a while.

Lester shrugged. "More for me."

"Leave some in the fridge. I'll have it when I get back."

"No promises."

"Whatever. Your cooking sucks anyway." Mason was only half-joking.

Lester didn't take it personally.

Mason put on his shoes and coat and grabbed an umbrella, not bothering to say bye or lock the door. Asha was waiting at the end of his driveway, this time with her own umbrella. Damn. He walked down to meet her.

"Sure has been raining a lot lately." She was looking at the sky.

"Yeah, most days it seems," he replied. "That's what we get for living in Terminal City, I suppose."

They started walking. No one immediately said anything. Perhaps they needed to get the silence off their chests first, let the gravity of everything sink in. Meanwhile, it was coming down hard.

After a block of silent meandering, Asha spoke first: "I broke up with Josh."

Mason focused intensely on not smiling. "Oh," he said.

"And it wasn't because of, you know, what happened between us or anything like that," she said. "It's what I told you before—we just weren't right for each other."

Mason nodded. "How are you feeling?"

"Fine, I guess." She looked it. "Actually, I feel pretty good, but then I feel guilty for feeling good. I know he's crushed, but I can't help it. I'm relieved."

"I think that's a pretty natural feeling," said Mason, although he wasn't speaking from experience. In the past, he'd only ever been the crushed one.

"Yeah, my mom and sister said the same thing," replied Asha, "but I still feel, I don't know, sick. Like, not physically sick. Existentially sick, I guess."

"It'll get better. It always does."

Her smile was a bittersweet one. "How have you been?"

"I've been fine," said Mason. "Busy with school and stuff." And busy thinking about her, but he left that part out.

"That's good," she replied. "Yeah, I've been pretty busy too."

They strolled past Sherwood Hall, where they had philosophy together with Alicia Rutherford. Inside, they saw the silhouette of a studious student. Either that or a procrastinator, like Mason, with a looming deadline and a long night ahead. Probably the latter.

"How are you liking philosophy?" Asha nudged him gently with her elbow.

"Quite a lot," replied Mason. "I think I might make it my major. Well, that and a few other things, but it's on the list."

"You should," she said. "You seem to really get it. Definitely more than most of us."

"Maybe, though sometimes I'm not sure I even agree with half the shit I'm saying."

She laughed. "Then where do you get the confidence to say it?"

"Don't know." He shrugged. "It doesn't feel like confidence, I guess. When I'm focused on something, I sort of forget about everything else. I think that's the trick to confidence— forgetting."

"Maybe you should write a self-help book," replied Asha. "I know how much you love those."

"Yeah, right."

"What about when you can't forget?" she asked. "Where do you get your confidence then?"

"Good question." Mason smirked. "Booze, maybe."

"Speaking of which." She bit her lip; he loved it when she did that. "I think we should talk about, you know, what happened between us."

"Ah. The kiss."

"Yeah. The kiss."

"That one was all booze," said Mason.

Asha chuckled. "You don't give yourself enough credit," she replied. "Anyway, I'm sorry for lashing out at you like that. But after you said those nice things, I don't know… something came over me. I was a bit tipsy, I guess, but it's more than that. I mean, it was a pretty big deal, me kissing you."

It certainly was to Mason.

"And I do like you," she added. It was music to his ears. "Else I wouldn't have done that. But it's complicated, even still. I'm single now, but I'm not ready for anything yet, and I feel like

I've led you on. I'm not saying I'm not interested in something eventually, but I can't dive into anything right this moment. I need to come up for air first."

Mason nodded, unsure if he was being rejected or given the green light in a roundabout way. Still, he said, "I understand." It seemed like the right thing to say.

Asha looked him in the eyes. "I appreciate it. I know I'm not being entirely fair. I know I'm sending mixed messages." She paused for a second. "If you don't want to hang out or whatever, I understand."

"Of course I want to hang out." Mason said it like it was the most obvious thing in the world. "Take all the time you need. I've got nowhere better to be." That was certainly true.

She hugged him. It felt more like a friend's hug than a lover's, but he'd take what he could get. After all, it signaled that he meant something to her, and that meant something to him.

"Like I told you before, you're a good a guy," she said.

If wanting her made him good, then sure— he was Mother fucking Teresa. "If you say so," he replied.

"Walk me home." It was an invitation, not a request.

"All right."

It was a fifteen-minute stroll to her place. Their conversation veered into trivial territory — school, upcoming movies, and tentative weekend plans — until they arrived at the front door of her apartment building, a white stucco low-rise. Asha lived on the opposite side of campus, where there were more students and fewer houses like Mason's. She kissed him on the cheek and said thanks. He nodded, feeling more or less pretty good about the whole situation.

"See you tomorrow?" he asked.

"Yeah," she replied. "Let's go see a movie or something."

"Sounds like a plan." But did it sound like a date? He wasn't sure; she probably wasn't sure either. They both said goodbye, and then Mason headed toward home.

Once he was around the block — and Asha out of view — Mason pulled out a cigarette. There were five left in the pack. He thought maybe he'd take a stab at quitting when he ran out. All the more reason to enjoy this one. Mason inhaled deeply and tuned into the sound of rain drumming on his umbrella. Twenty minutes later, he was out front of his house. He walked up the driveway, up the porch steps, and then inside. The door was still unlocked.

"I'm back," said Mason, "and hungry." He could smell dinner from the hallway. Spaghetti again, not that he minded.

But there was no answer from Lester. Mason stepped into the kitchen and then stopped in his tracks. Tomato sauce and pasta were splattered on the floor like a puddle of bloody intestines. There were bits of broken glass too— Mason's favorite plate.

"The fuck?" said Mason. "Lester?" Still no answer. "Lester?" he said again, a little louder this time. Nothing.

Mason checked the living room. The TV was on, muted, but no Lester. He headed down the hall and noticed the basement door was open— as a rule, it generally wasn't. He pushed it fully ajar, its brass hinges creaking, and then stepped inside. He was reminded of the first time he'd walked down these steps. The air was hot and heavy with dread.

"Lester?" Mason's voice was half a whisper. Step by step, he made his way down. The light was on, its dim halo reaching up the stairs. Finally, he lumbered off the last wooden step onto the cold cement floor, and there was Lester.

He was face down, lying in a growing pool of dark blood and something else— it smelled like gasoline.

If Mason had any words to say, he would have choked on them, but he didn't. He just stood there, dumbfounded, waiting for the world to make the next move, and then it did. He felt a thin metal barrel poking into his back, squarely between his shoulder blades.

"Don't move," said a man from behind him. "Who the hell are you?"

Mason didn't reply. He had to think. He had to keep his shit together. But his heart was beating so hard he felt as if he might throw it up. Mason swallowed it back down and almost answered the man's question, but then he stopped himself. His brain was working again, like a computer that had just been rebooted. He should lie.

"Josh," said Mason. He honestly didn't mean to use the name of Asha's ex, but it rolled off his tongue.

"Josh, is it?" The stranger pushed his gun deeper into Mason's back. "Well, Josh, you can call me Mr. Huxley."

Chapter 13

THE LIGHT BULB hanging from the basement ceiling flickered as it always did, swaying, adjusting their silhouettes.

"Mr. Huxley," repeated Mason. "That name doesn't mean anything to me. Who are you, and why the hell did you just kill my friend?" Mason's voice, no longer lost to shock and awe, now trembled with rage. "Who the fuck are you, man?" He growled his words this time, shaking with fear and fury— the pistol pressing into his back only made him angrier.

"I'm Mr. Huxley. That's all you need to know." The inquisitor — Mason had determined quite quickly that's what Mr. Huxley was — sounded equally on edge. "And who the fuck are you, Josh? How do you know Lester Wright? Who is he to you?"

"He's fucking dead." Spit flew from Mason's mouth. "Dead because you fucking killed him."

"Yes," said Mr. Huxley. "He is dead because of me. I bear that burden." He twisted and pushed the barrel of his gun harder into Mason's spine. "Your name isn't Josh, is it?" It wasn't really a question.

And Mason didn't offer an answer, too busy searching for his own. What was the plan here? There was a gun stabbing his back. How would he ever get the upper hand? Then he realized he was thinking like a layman, not a necromancer. Mason considered what he had in his repertoire, what he could do that others could not, what would turn the tables on Mr. Huxley, a man Mason thought he might be ready to kill— if, in fact, he was ready to kill men. He racked his brain for something, anything, that might catch this stranger off-guard.

There was one spell, he realized. He'd performed it only once before, and rather poorly at that. It induced a sort of burning pain. Of course, Mason didn't fancy himself a sadist or a masochist, so he'd only burned himself a little. Could he really make this man burn a lot? There was only one sure way to find out.

"What's your real name?" asked Mr. Huxley.

"My name..." Mason trailed off.

"Well? Speak." Mr. Huxley spoke to Mason like he might a misbehaved dog. "No? Turn around. Let me see your face."

Unfortunately for Mr. Huxley, he realized too late what his captive was doing, perhaps because he'd been facing the back of his head. In the same moment Mason turned around, chanting, eyes blazing crimson, the burning sensation struck Mr. Huxley's hand. "Shit!" He dropped his pistol.

Mason wasted no time. He took a leaping swing at his disarmed captor, pounding Mr. Huxley's ear. The inquisitor stumbled backward, one hand cupping his new bruise, but not for long; he dived for his gun, which Mason tried to kick away, to no avail (he'd never been very good at sports). *Shit*. Mason ran as Mr. Huxley armed himself again; by the time he was able to take aim, the younger man was halfway up the stairs.

Mason didn't want to run, but he also didn't want to get shot. He went out the basement door, closing it behind him— anything for an extra second. He didn't know where to run, so he flew into the kitchen and armed himself with a sharp steak knife. *I don't suppose this will deflect bullets.*

Mr. Huxley was up the stairs and on his way; Mason could hear his clunky footsteps. "Damn it." Mason was shaking and sweating. Mr. Huxley appeared around the corner, gun held out. Mason dove from the kitchen, dropping his knife. A bullet splintered the doorframe a foot from him. Guns were louder in real life than in movies, thought Mason, scrambling to his feet.

He bolted for the front door. As he slammed it shut behind him — *cling!* — a bullet indented its metal facade. He tripped down the wooden porch steps before quickly picking himself back up, desperately like a drowning man, his knees burning and shaking. He ran down the driveway, his enemy emerging from the yellow-lit doorframe behind him. Mason dived through a line of hedges, out of view, and then kept his head down.

As he sprinted across his neighbors' lawns, discovering just how quickly his legs could move him, Mason wondered where he should run. To other people, perhaps, where he would be safer? Or away from them— somewhere dark, somewhere he could kill the man who had killed Lester. In the end, Mason picked fight over flight and headed toward the forest.

He wasn't just some bystander, after all— he was a fucking necromancer.

If he hadn't been faster than Mr. Huxley, who was running behind him, Mason might have been dead already. But his heart was still beating, and quickly, as the forest came into view. He bolted into the brush, beneath a high canopy of evergreens, where the blackness of night became all but all-consuming. Mr. Huxley quickly lost sight of him.

Mason tripped again, this time over an exposed root, landing elbow-first in the dirt. "God-fucking-damnit." He'd cut himself, or at least it felt like a cut; he didn't have time to deal with blood. Mason could hear footsteps kicking through the foliage not far from him. He picked himself up and ducked behind a large tree stump. Through a screen of branches and blackness, he saw Mr. Huxley pushing forward, careful with each step. He was maybe twenty feet away, but he hadn't yet seen Mason, who still had that advantage— but how to use it?

He tried casting the same spell again — tried to burn Mr. Huxley — but it was too difficult with a moving target at this distance. He'd have to take him out the old-fashioned way, somehow without getting shot. He scanned the dirt near his feet for large rocks and found a jagged stone about the size of a baseball. Now came the hard part: not missing. He bided his time, knowing it was all over if he missed. He waited until Mr. Huxley was a bit closer. Once he was maybe ten feet away, Mason arched his back and focused on Mr. Huxley, aiming with his good eye at the back of his target's skull. Figuring this was the best shot he'd get, Mason flung his rock.

For the second time that night, Mason hit Mr. Huxley square in the ear. "Gah!" Mr. Huxley fell to one knee, his gun-hand cupped over his bleeding ear. Mason charged and pummeled him like a football player. The two men rolled like logs, the pistol flying from Mr. Huxley's hand. Quickly, Mason pinned his enemy down with both knees and punched his nose. It hurt Mason's hand more than he'd thought it would, but he punched again, and then once more. This was life or death, after all. The fourth time, Mr. Huxley grabbed Mason's wrist and — with every ounce of adrenaline he had — pushed Mason off him.

Mr. Huxley stood up before Mason could pin him down again. "You little shit." He spat out blood. Mason stood up too. Now they were eye-to-eye. Mr. Huxley scanned the ground for his gun and found it five feet away, closer to him than it was to Mason, but only barely. Mason saw him see it, and Mr. Huxley saw that in turn. Both men jumped for the pistol, bumping shoulder-to-shoulder, but Mr. Huxley's arms were longer. Desperately, Mason made one final grasp for the gun now in Mr. Huxley's hand, but it flew from him like an opposing magnet. Mason fell onto his bloodied forearms— for one second too long.

The shot rang through the forest like a sin on nature. The bullet had gone through Mason's stomach. He tried to get up, in case reality had been wrong, but vertigo got the better of him. He collapsed onto his face instead. Mr. Huxley was now back on his feet, six feet over Mason. It was all the distance in the world.

This was it. He was going to die.

Mason hoped it was a dream. It was all he could do at this point. But both men knew it wasn't.

"Who are you?" growled Mr. Huxley. "What's your name?"

Mason didn't answer. He didn't want to and couldn't anyway, too dizzy and too hurt.

Once it became clear that Mason wasn't going to say anything, Mr. Huxley answered for him: "I know who you are," he said. "A necromancer. Nothing else matters." With that, he lifted his gun once more and put a bullet through Mason's heart.

This really was it.

Mason didn't feel it, the second bullet— only its vibration. Instead, he felt hot and cold at the same time. And then he couldn't move. And then he couldn't breathe. And then, suddenly, none of it mattered anymore. And then Mason felt nothing.

The white light of death shone for an immeasurable stretch of time — the last hurrah of a brain shutting down — gradually growing dimmer, flickering like that light bulb in the basement.

Flickering until it went out completely.

Chapter 14

THE PROVINCE OF MASSACHUSETTS BAY, 1695:

The path was framed in blooming hardwoods. In their midst walked a tall young man with tousled brown hair and a leather bag slung over his shoulder. His name was Rowland. He was seventeen and now motherless.

She'd died a month ago, his mom, taken by a sudden illness. He'd done all he could — he really had — but that didn't account for much. Anyhow, she was dead. That's all that mattered now, and it meant he was on his own.

Streams of sunlight decorated the road ahead of him. The air was warm, finally, after a week-long stretch of wind and rain. Spring had arrived. It was certainly nice— if not warm enough to melt the cold that coursed through him.

"Rowland."

At first, he thought it was the wind or his mind playing a trick. Then he heard his name again.

"Rowland."

This time, the voice came clearly from behind. Rowland turned around and saw a slender man standing in the middle of the road— a man he'd met only once before. Rowland couldn't remember his name. The man approached him, taking his time, and then, when they were nose-to-nose, smiled before he spoke.

"Hello, Rowland," he said in a very Irish accent. His voice was soft and kind, as were his eyes, but there was an undeniable strangeness about him. He was equal parts calming and off-putting. The last time they'd met, Rowland had wavered between doubting everything he said and trusting him completely. *What was his name again?*

"Uilliam," he said, as if having read Rowland's mind. "My name is Uilliam."

"Right," replied Rowland. "I remember now."

"I heard about your mother." The smile flew from Uilliam's handsome face. "I'm so sorry, Rowland. I cannot imagine how you must feel. If there is anything I can do, anything at all, you need just ask."

Rowland nodded. "Thanks." Sympathy made him uncomfortable, as did generosity — though he still wasn't convinced of this man's sincerity. But perhaps that was Rowland's problem. Perhaps he needed to start trusting people.

"I bet you feel quite lost right now," said Uilliam.

Rowland shrugged. Uilliam was right, of course. He felt completely lost. He didn't even know where he was going, let alone how to get there. He was just... walking. Just staying alive.

"Where are you headed, Rowland?"

Rowland answered honestly: "Nowhere in particular. East, I guess. Maybe to the ocean."

"I'm headed east too." Uilliam gazed off in its direction. "For the time being, why don't we walk together?"

Rowland shrugged. "Sure." He felt cornered into the decision, but it had been a while since he'd had company. Maybe it would be nice to talk to someone. Lonely minds lose perspective: that was something his mom used to say. And so they began walking together, side-by-side at a leisurely pace, a soft breeze against their backs.

"There's a town about, oh, ten or eleven hours from here," said Uilliam. "Georgetown. Ever been?"

"Just once," replied Rowland, "when I was young."

Uilliam smiled. "You're still young, Rowland."

It was dark when they arrived in Georgetown. The town brought with it a sigh of relief; Rowland's feet were killing him, but he didn't want to complain. After all, Uilliam seemed so unbothered. Whenever he'd asked if Rowland wanted to take a break — it had been a near ten-hour walk — the younger man had replied, "I'm fine." Rowland hadn't said much else to Uilliam, though Uilliam had regaled him with stories from his past. From these,

Rowland had concluded that his companion was either an interesting man or an interesting liar.

Uilliam claimed he was a traveler, said he helped people along the way and somehow made a living at it. He wasn't too specific about what he did for them, though. "A range of things," he'd said. That answer didn't make trusting him any easier. He was hiding something, Rowland suspected— and though some secrets are noble, most are not.

Uilliam led Rowland to Georgetown's only inn. The pub on the main floor was packed with locals, but the rooms above were all vacant. Uilliam, charming as he was, swung a bit of a discount. Rowland told him he didn't have any money to help pay. Uilliam shook his head and waved his hand, dismissing even the thought of it. Rowland was forced to accept his companion's generosity, which he supposed was preferable to sleeping in the woods.

They had dinner and a couple pints of ale before calling it a night. Rowland wasn't much of a drinker, so it was enough to get him tipsy. While it wasn't a feeling he was accustomed to, it also wasn't the worst one in the world. Finally, about when Rowland could barely keep his eyelids from falling, they both headed upstairs. There were two beds in one room, a few feet from one another; nothing special, but when Rowland sat down on his, he realized it was softer than anything he was used to, and that he might just sleep well tonight. It was something small to look forward to— the most he could ask for these days.

They undressed. Rowland slid under his sheets first. Uilliam smiled at him — he was always smiling — before slipping into his own bed and blowing out the lantern on the nightstand between them. The blue darkness of night set in, accompanied by the sound of crickets through the window. It was perfectly relaxing. Rowland anticipated a good night's sleep. God knew he needed one.

Howling. At first, the sound played into his dream. It was Rowland howling and crying. Adulthood was a permanently open wound, and for the life of him, he couldn't stop the bleeding.

He'd wandered too far into the woods, into a deep place where dark branches and roots overtook the forest floor and hid the stars. Rowland couldn't find his way back out, couldn't return home, lost to nature's whims.

But he could feel God watching him. And so he howled louder and louder, howled for help — for God or Mom or even Dad, wherever he was — but God didn't care, as cruelly apathetic as he was omnipotent. God only watched. Watched him cry, watched those black roots overtake Rowland, crawling up his limbs like snakes, rough bark ripping into his skin. Until finally, Rowland howled so loud that the whole world fell to pieces.

He woke to the sound of a dog crying in the alley. Outside, it was still dark. Rowland let out an exasperated sigh. Once again, a good night's sleep had evaded him. He rolled over, onto his other side, and saw Uilliam in the second bed a few feet away. Like Rowland, he was awake.

"Very noisy dog," said Uilliam, sleepy and raspy.

"Yeah."

Uilliam sat up and wiped his eyes. Then he shifted his body until he was sitting upright on the bed, his feet on the floor, facing Rowland. "Suppose we can chat for a while."

Aaarrrooooooooooooo! Rrrooo, rrrooo, rrrooooooooo!

Rowland nodded and sat up too.

"I'm curious, how old are you, Rowland?" asked Uilliam.

"Seventeen," said Rowland. "How old are you?"

"Older than seventeen." Uilliam smiled. "Older than I look too. Remind me, what's it like being seventeen? Is there some fair, supple damsel you fancy?"

Rowland blushed and shook his head — there wasn't.

"None pretty enough for you?"

Rowland chuckled uncomfortably. "I guess not."

"Aye," said Uilliam. "You're a good-looking lad. You shouldn't settle."

"I suppose so."

"Have you ever been with one — a woman?"

"How do you mean?" asked Rowland, who understood the question perfectly and was stalling.

"You know what I mean." Uilliam called him on it. "Have you slept with a lady yet?"

Rowland shook his head. "Not yet."

"You're young. It's nothing to be ashamed of," said Uilliam, handsome and wise. "What about a man?"

"What?" This time, Rowland really was confused — though not entirely.

"Have you ever slept with a man?" asked Uilliam, as non-threatening as he was serious. He always struck just the right balance.

"No." Rowland cleared his throat. It was the truth, and yet he could sense Uilliam looking right through him, as if he saw something in Rowland that even he himself couldn't see— yet felt. It showed on Rowland's face, which was red even in the dark.

"It's okay," said Uilliam, moving himself onto Rowland's bed. He sat down beside him, as close as he could, resting a hand on Rowland's leg. "You don't have to do anything you don't want to."

Rowland didn't get any more sleep that night, nor did his companion, now lying naked beside him. He wasn't sure how he felt about what had just happened, although Uilliam seemed perfectly content. And ever-perceptive.

"You're restless," said Uilliam. "Don't be. Relax. You're safe with me."

Rowland nodded but didn't make eye contact.

"What do you know about Ancient Greece?" asked Uilliam.

Rowland shrugged. "Not much."

"In Ancient Greece, it was common for men to sleep with other men. In fact, there was a great Greek philosopher by the name of Plato who thought that love between two men was something special, something beautiful. Did you know that?"

Rowland shook his head.

"Aye, he did. Of course, nowadays most people wouldn't agree with Plato. But Plato had a theory about that. You see, Rowland, there will always be men who want to rule over you, control you. These men don't want you to experience beauty. Beauty gives you more to live for. And the Christians, they don't want that. They want the world to be a cold, dark place from which only their God can save you. In the end, it's all about power— for them."

Rowland pondered for a moment, but he knew — as he'd known for some time now — that Uilliam spoke the truth. God, the Church, all of it: a lie. The one woman in his village who might have been able to save his mom, a healer, was hanged in Salem three years ago. Hanged because she could do something beautiful: help people. Hanged because she could do what a non-existent God could not.

"I know," said Rowland. "I know it's all a lie."

Uilliam smiled and nodded, brushing Rowland's hair out of his eyes with his fingers. "Then I will show you true beauty, Rowland," he said, "and true power. I will show you power that can actually save."

Uilliam lifted one hand above his chest, cupping the air over his palm. His lips began to move, and his eyes— they were glowing. And then... red. Emanating from his palm, soaking the walls and sheets, slipping out the window into the blue night. Everywhere, red.

Chapter 15

MASON AWOKE.
Rather, it was something not unlike awaking. He saw, yet he saw nothing; he felt his eyes open, but the world was all black. He pushed his body upward, shifting onto his feet, and somehow it felt too easy, standing did. His body felt too light, and when he took his first step, that was too simple as well. But Mason didn't bother wondering why; questions are born from answers, and the unyielding darkness that encompassed everything around him offered none.

Aimlessly, he walked and walked — there was little else for a man in the dark to do — and more and more he thought about things. First and foremost, he thought about the events that had just transpired— the final moments before the darkness. He guessed he was dead, and he was right. Then this must be the Spirit Realm. He hadn't imagined it would be so... empty. Still, he marched on, unsure if he was even really moving. The darkness also offered no landmarks.

Mason wondered what being dead meant to him and quickly concluded he wasn't a fan of death— that he'd rather be on the other side of the great divide, as he had been only moments ago. He lingered on that last part: had it been only moments, or had it been hours now? With no objective reality in which to ground things, space and time were suddenly as superfluous as his own damned existence in this cruel place. Just like Lester had said. Still, it felt like moments.

Speaking of Lester, he must be here too, thought Mason. He wondered about the other dead people he knew, like his dad.

Were they as lost as he was? Would he ever find them? Would they find him?

Right foot.

Left foot.

Never-ending darkness.

On the plus side, he wasn't growing tired, not even a bit— so apparently there was at least one perk to being dead. Right foot. Left foot. He could do this forever, and perhaps he would. That was a depressing thought.

Mason stopped. He had an idea. Maybe walking wasn't the best way to navigate the Spirit Realm. Perhaps moving meant something else here. If that were the case, he figured he should have an advantage as a necromancer— should be more adept at whatever the hell he ought to be doing. But what did this place require of him? Well, what had necromancy required of him?

Think, think, think.

The first step, he decided, was figuring out where he wanted to go. That part was easy. He had to find his father, assuming his dad still existed as the man he'd known. Could you lose yourself in the Spirit Realm in just ten months? Maybe. Probably. Mason hadn't a clue.

The next step, getting there, proved a little more difficult. He searched for that familiar feeling — the one he knew from necromancy, the one that signaled success — but down here, without his library, he didn't have the words to weave. He didn't have the pieces for this particular puzzle.

But perhaps he had all the time in the world.

Mason kept trying, pushing the limits of his intelligence, until finally he felt the Spirit Realm map onto his mind. He couldn't quite explain it, but he could feel it, just barely, flickering, on the verge of being lost again. He had to stay focused. He couldn't lose this feeling. He wasn't sure where he'd found it in the first place, and he was too smart, too determined— he would find his father. The Spirit Realm had the answer, and goddamnit, he'd have it too.

Truth be told, Mason couldn't say how exactly he'd found him, but there he was— or at least some part of him. His dad. Mason moved toward him like a feeling bubbling to the surface.

A bright flash, a dull sting, vertigo. Mason flinched, closing his eyes and clenching his teeth, then fell to his knees. A moment later, the world calmed and felt... warmer.

Mason reopened his eyes. At last, some light. And more— so much more. Everything around him glimmered and shifted like a monument to lawless physics. There were houses here, but they existed as broken 3-D renderings, each wall refusing to conform to the next. Translucent chunks of earth floated overhead in lieu of clouds, light shining through them from seemingly nowhere. Above him, the sky was purple, but as Mason trekked down the neighborhood's winding brick path — as Dorothy might, with a little less pep — the clouds cycled through colors like an ocean changing reflections.

His father was in one of these houses, he knew, though his eyes couldn't find him. His mind might, however. Then a door opened behind him, and out stepped a ghost. *Dad.*

"Son," said John; he'd never called him that before. "You shouldn't be here." He paused. "When?"

"Just now." Mason turned to face his father. "I think."

John approached his son and hugged him. Hugs weren't as warm or firm down here, but there was no shortage of love in his father's embrace. In that regard, it was probably the best one they'd ever shared.

John looked down at his feet. "How long has it been since I—"

"About ten months," said Mason.

"How's your mother?"

"Lonely. And more religious."

John cracked half a smile. "Oh well. I suppose religion could use more people like her." He sighed. "And you... Mason?" Suddenly, he sounded embarrassed, frustrated, as if it had taken him a few seconds to remember his son's name.

"Well, I'm dead, Dad, so... you know. I guess things were going pretty well before that, all considering."

"Right, right." John had never been very good at consoling people. He was much better at fixing things, but some things couldn't be fixed, and men like John weren't built to deal with that. His son was the same way.

Indeed, Mason was equally at a loss for words. The two of them were left staring at one another in stunned silence. They both had lots to say, but neither knew where to start. It gave Mason a second to observe his father's new form. He looked mostly the same— but not entirely. He was different in a way Mason couldn't quite put his finger on, just like he himself had been in the mirror Lester had shown him.

Oh yeah. That reminded him: Lester was somewhere down here too. Maybe that's where he should start.

"I wasn't the only one," he said, breaking the increasingly awkward silence. "Who died, I mean. They got Lester too."

"They?" John raised an eyebrow.

"The inquisitors."

John didn't take that well. Mason could tell from the tense expression on his father's face. John never fumed — he was better than that. Rather, he turned into human steel, jagged at every edge. "That makes three of us, then," he said.

"What do you mean?" asked Mason.

"I mean me."

"But you died in a car accident. You drove into a tree."

"Who do you think drove me into that tree? I was trying to escape them. You know what, it doesn't matter now." Yet even as he said the words, John sure as hell didn't look like a man who thought it didn't matter. "But" — he bared his teeth — "you… why you? I can't fucking believe it." His anger was visible, a red aura that intensified around his fists and eyes and heart. "No. I can't let you die like this."

Mason looked sympathetically incredulous. "Dad, I'm already dead."

But John wasn't listening. "You said it just happened, right?" he asked. "Your… crossing over?"

"I think so," replied Mason. "It feels that way."

"Good." John was pacing, lost in thought, looking very much like the man Mason remembered him to be. Then he stopped, shifting his gaze back toward his son, and said, "We need to move fast."

Mason didn't like being left in the dark. "For what exactly?"

"There may be a way to bring you back." His dad approached him. "There's no time for details. Grab my hand." He extended his right one until, somewhat reluctantly, his son took it. John squeezed tightly.

The red aura around Mason's father intensified again, this time reaching around both of them. John stood up straight, eyes shut, his chin dropped to his chest. And then the world blurred and faded, bit by bit, until eventually everything was gone. They both lost their balance at the same time. Mason quickly realized he'd just traveled again.

John was first to his feet. Mason took in his surroundings before standing; ahead of him, a steep staircase reached upward — at least a hundred feet — to a large archway. Red emanated from the entrance, spilling onto the top steps, but the rest remained obscured in darkness. Indeed, the world around him was back to black, save for the path ahead.

"Come on," said John.

The two of them started up the steps.

"Where are we going?" asked Mason.

"You'll see. Easier seen than said — that's a saying down here."

"Whatever." Mason was growing annoyed with his father — it never took long — but maybe he was right this time. After all, what did Mason know about this place? The logic that governed reality here was still freakishly foreign to him.

They reached the archway together, and then John led the way. Inside was even more impressive than outside: a sea of see-through pillars reached upward into what looked like a star-studded sky. They stretched left and right, row after row of them; the single pathway of light Mason and John traveled on was all that broke the repetition. They followed the lone trail, pillars popping into then falling out of view, until finally something appeared on the horizon. At first, it was unintelligible — a bright ball of light that should have been visible when they'd first walked in. That is, if physics made any sense here. It didn't. Now, the orb towered over them, twenty, fifty, a hundred feet high. It grew and grew and then morphed into a giant genderless face that stared down at both of them at once. The face spoke a single word, its booming voice like a choir carried by a million versions of the same man: "Yes?"

John stepped forward, craning his neck to look up into the giant eyes peering down at him. "I have a request," he said. "My son, Mason, beside me here: he's been dead for maybe an hour. As I understand it, there's still time to send him back to the Living Realm. His body, his brain — they should be intact enough for a proper resurrection."

The giant face had more words this time: "We do not send people back. We have not for hundreds of years." The voice filled the endless chamber, echoing off walls Mason couldn't see. "You should know this," it continued, "so why is it you think your son ought to be the first exception in centuries?"

"The inquisitors killed him, an innocent twenty-one-year-old," replied John. "He didn't deserve that fate."

"Every minute, people who don't deserve their unfortunate fates end up here, but we do not send them back. Not even the necromancers."

As his father brainstormed better rebuttals, Mason interjected. "What are you exactly?" he asked the towering entity.

"We are the Spirit Realm," it answered. "Just as you are now. You are new here and thus perceive yourself as an individual, as you were in the Living Realm, but everyone here fades, eventually. We are the collective consciousness of all who have faded, of billions, and we have learned from many past mistakes. That is why we cannot accept your father's request."

Mason nodded. "Dad, it's okay." It wasn't, really, but what could be done?

"No." John shook his head. "It's not fucking okay." He took a deep breath, calmed himself, and then continued a little more eloquently. "Things in the Living Realm are getting out of hand," he said. "This war between inquisitors and necromancers is not what it used to be. Even you must see that. It's the good necromancers who are dying disproportionately— the ones who just want to learn things and play no part in this war. Necromancers like my son. And the ones least likely to be killed by inquisitors? Necromancers like Rowland. Necromancers who want and come prepared for a fight. They're the best survivors. Are they to be the torchbearers of necromancy into the future— our most violent, our most selfish?

"Necromancers are the living connection to the Spirit Realm," John finished. "You of all — whatever the hell you are — you must care about the future of our kind."

"We do," said the Spirit Realm. "Let us think."

Mason faced his father, admittedly impressed, but John didn't look back, too busy analyzing the ponderous inflections of the giant face looming over them.

"We have considered your request," it said after only a few seconds, "and have decided to grant it— but only under one condition. And it is a heavy one."

"Anything," John answered for his son.

"The last time we sent someone back to the Living Realm was hundreds of years ago, and that someone is the reason we have sent no one else since," explained the Spirit Realm. "We see that you are aware of him, but you know little about his history. Like Mason, Rowland was murdered by inquisitors when he was still young, still relatively innocent. Certainly, he was not the man that he has become. The most powerful necromancers are those who have been to the Spirit Realm. Those who have died. They inherit a closer connection to us than could otherwise be achieved. So you see, we are partly responsible for Rowland. While his choices have been his own, by sending Rowland back to the Living Realm, we enhanced his power— power that kept him alive and ultimately corrupted him.

"This is where you come in." The Spirit Realm moved its gaze from father to son.

"If we are to release you from us and send you back to the Living Realm, Mason, you must do everything in your power to return Rowland to us. I assume you know what that entails. Promise us this — we will know if you are lying — and then, only then, will we revive you, assuming that is still possible."

Mason nodded. "If Rowland is as bad as everyone says he is, then I suppose someone should stop him. Having said that, I'm a novice. What chance do I have of actually succeeding?"

"A small one," the Spirit Realm admitted, "and it may take you a lifetime. But you will be the only other necromancer in the Living Realm who has been here, to the Spirit Realm, and already you show more promise than most. We believe you have the potential to one day compete with Rowland. We just hope you do not become anything like him in the process. It is a calculated gamble."

"I wouldn't," said Mason. "Never."

"We believe you are sincere in your conviction, but time warps people. And while you are a good man, Mason, your contrarian nature could lead you astray. In fact, it is a quality you share with Rowland— and your father. You fear acceptance. You fear it will compromise your intellect. You feel you must remain an outsider to see the world for what it really is."

"I guess," said Mason.

John looked more offended by the accusation.

"But that's because I want to do the right thing," added Mason. "I can't do the right thing if I don't know what it is. Every action begins with knowledge, or ignorance, or some combination of the two."

"In this you are correct, although you are not without emotion," said the Spirit Realm. "Your noble intentions are what separate you from Rowland. Rowland saw himself as a victim when he arrived here. He believed the whole world had wronged him. He believed humanity was essentially rotten. And so he fights against the world rather than for it. But you are less cynical, Mason. That is why we are giving you this chance."

"Thanks." Mason didn't know what else to say.

"Do not thank us yet," said the Spirit Realm. "Before we send you back to the Living Realm, there is one more thing you must know. You will never be as you were, Mason. It is not only increased power that you will bring back. Because you have been to the Spirit Realm, death will weigh heavily on you for as long as you live. Physically, you may never look quite the same. Worse, your capacity for happiness will be marred. It will be even harder for you to find contentment, which has never been your strength. Life is a far, far heavier burden than death, and yours will be exceptionally heavy. But you must not fall into despair. You must not isolate yourself as Rowland did. In your endeavour to kill him, you will need to find balance. Everyone has a breaking point. Even you, Mason."

"I understand," said Mason.

"Then we are ready to begin," replied the Spirit Realm.

Mason looked to his father, whose red anger had dimmed with sorrow and relief.

"I'm proud of you," said John. "I wish I could do more. I wish I could be there. But you don't need me, never did. You've always been your own man, Mason. You can do this. I know you can."

John was fighting back tears and failing; they dangled from his eyelids like clear gems. "I'm so sorry I brought you into this mess," he said. "I asked Lester to teach you, to help turn you into a necromancer. That's on me. Had I not, you'd still be alive."

"Dad, it's not your fault I'm down here," said Mason. "You didn't kill me. You let me see the world in a way I never would have otherwise. Don't ever apologize for that."

John forced a smile and gave his son a second, final hug. "We shouldn't waste any more time. I love you, you know that?"

"Yeah," said Mason, "I know. I love you too, Dad. When you find Lester, tell him... just thank him for me."

John nodded. "One more thing." He said it under his breath, said it like a secret. "Rowland is beyond hope, but he's not evil.

He's just wrong about a few things — a few big things. Do what you must, Mason, and be careful. I don't want to see you back here tomorrow."

"We must begin," interjected the Spirit Realm with its booming, impersonal voice.

"Okay." Mason stepped away from his father. "I'm ready."

The Spirit Realm bowed its giant head. "This may... sting."

Mason hadn't thought he could feel pain down here. But soon, he wasn't just here anymore. He was there too, in the Living Realm, but not entirely, not yet. He was stretched between this place and home, like an elastic band pulled across the universe — and it hurt more than anything on Earth. His senses screamed, his world blurred, but then...

Then came the moment of truth.

Chapter 16

MASON WAS SCREAMING before he realized it, before it dawned on him that he was alive again, back in the Living Realm.

A raindrop fell through the distant evergreen ceiling looming high overhead, landing on his cheek. It was still night time. The overbearing pain had stopped, but now he felt a new sting in his chest. The bullet, he remembered — it had pierced his heart. Mason rolled off his stomach onto his back, lifting his head to look down; his shirt was encrusted with dried blood. He reached under the torn cloth and touched his chest and then his stomach, where the first one had gone, but couldn't find a bullet hole anywhere on his body. Grunting, he rolled onto his side. The blood on his skin was still wet, still a bit warm.

After a few minutes resting on his elbow, Mason made the effort to stand. He nearly lost his balance in the process but ultimately prevailed. Oddly, straightening his spine was the hardest part, or at least the most painful. "Fucking ouch." He barely recognized his own voice. It carried an uncharacteristic rasp of dehydration.

He looked down toward the ground he'd fallen onto, his untimely deathbed. The dirt was soaked in blood, a dead man's worth. He knelt to get a closer look, but it was hard to see much in the dark forest. He pulled out his cell phone — it was 11:47 p.m. — and used it as a light. Shining it downward, Mason noticed a thin, blood-filled hole where his stomach had been. He reached inside with his index finger and felt something smooth at the bottom — something solid. He yanked it out. A bullet, red with blood. It had gone right through him, he realized.

Mason dropped the bullet and got back to his feet. Now what?

He couldn't remember which way was which— more importantly, which way was home. Mason walked for a while before finding a dirt trail he recognized and then followed it back to the street, back to civilization. Moving still hurt, though increasingly less so. His body was in shock, but as far as he could tell, it was also completely healed. Even the scratches and bruises from his fistfight with Mr. Huxley were gone.

He wondered if that son of a bitch was still close by.

Mason spotted a group of students heading in his direction. He crossed the street to the other sidewalk, trying to look normal, which for some reason was difficult when you sure as hell didn't feel it. He lingered behind a car until they passed. Mason may have been healed, but he was still covered in blood. He didn't want to involve anyone else in tonight's affairs— especially the cops.

With his fellow students far behind him, Mason scurried home feeling naked. Thankfully, he managed to make it back without having to hide again. It was a quiet night. Must be the rain. It was still pouring— though not enough to wash him clean.

The front door was open when he arrived. Everything inside was as it had been when he'd burst out of here only an hour ago. The lights were still on and splashes of spaghetti sauce still stained the kitchen floor. But what about Lester's body? Mason closed the front door and walked uneasily toward the basement.

He stepped inside. The light bulb dangling from the ceiling was still on too, still flickering. Halfway down the stairs, Lester's foot came into view, and then, step by step, so did the rest of him. He hadn't been moved since Mason saw him last, though the pool of blood underneath him had crept further outward. Somehow, he looked even deader. At least Mr. Huxley hadn't returned to the scene of the crime.

Mason stopped at the end of the staircase, Lester's body ten feet in front of him. He seated himself on the bottom step and sighed, as stressed as he was saddened. What the fuck was he going to do now? He couldn't call the cops. They would never catch Mr. Huxley, and they'd think Mason was mad if he told them the truth— necromancers and all that. He could lie to them, but he was a terrible liar. They would probably think it was *he* who had killed Lester. No. He couldn't involve the police. He had to clean this mess up himself, starting with his mentor's dead body.

Easier said than done, of course. His first thoughts were of mobster movies. Those mafia guys were always getting rid of bodies, but he wasn't about to dump his friend into the ocean. He would show him some respect, however he could, and there were others who deserved that opportunity too. Indeed, that's where Lester's body should go, he realized— to the people who loved him. The problem was Mason knew very little about them.

He knew they were necromancers, so he wouldn't need to lie or involve cops. He also knew there were a dozen or so of them, if he recalled correctly, and that they all lived in a big house up north in the mountains. Lester had never been more specific than that, but considering the time it had taken him to get down here, they were probably a day's drive away.

Mason had the workings of a plan now, but two things remained: a car and an address. He could take his own from his mother's place, but he'd have to insure it for a month— wouldn't want to get pulled over with a body in the trunk. As for his destination, Mason would just have to look through Lester's stuff and hope for an address, or at the very least a clue. If he couldn't find anything… well, he'd cross that bridge if he came to it. For now, he was hoping for the best in the worst of situations.

First, he needed to clean himself. Mason was still covered in dirt and blood. He closed the basement door on his way out and headed to the upstairs bathroom. He flicked on the light and gasped, actually gasped — like a B-rate actor in a slasher movie — at the sight of his own reflection.

It wasn't just the dried blood, or the dirt smeared up and down his cheeks, or his newly swollen lip— the face underneath all that had changed too. He ran the faucet and splashed himself with two handfuls of water. He dried his face with the nearest towel— a white one that would probably never be quite white again. Speaking of white, he looked almost albino, his skin paler than it had ever been, the red hues that once gave life to his cheeks faded. The palete of his complexion had changed completely. He looked like a new man, like some twin brother he never had.

His eyes too, they were redder, as if he hadn't slept a night. He wondered if it was all permanent. The Spirit Realm had said he'd look different from now on; perhaps he was looking at the new Mason Cross.

He could mull it over later. Mason ditched his clothes and took a long, hot shower. Afterward, he put on a different pair of jeans and a plaid shirt from his bedroom closet and then headed to the kitchen, ravenously hungry.

Mason stepped around the spilled spaghetti sauce — he would clean it tomorrow — and toward the stove. A pot of dry noodles rested on one of the elements. They were edible, but for some reason, he couldn't bring himself to eat Lester's last meal. He made a quick turkey and lettuce sandwich instead and then poured himself a glass of water. It wasn't enough. Even after scarfing down every last crumb, Mason's stomach growled for more. He checked the pantry for something even quicker and found a bag of chips. He took out a handful and turned around, bag in hand. Immediately, the foil sack slipped from his fingers and hit the floor with a crinkle. There was a man standing calmly on the other side of the kitchen.

Mason recognized him, though he'd never learned his name. They had crossed paths on the beach two days ago when he'd shown Mason how to take control of a dead bug. There was no mistaking him— tall, even whiter than Mason, and ceaselessly enigmatic. He'd found Mason once before and it appeared he'd found him again, although his reason for being here was as elusive as the man himself.

"Hi again," said Mason uncomfortably.

"Hello, Mason Cross."

"Can I help you with something?"

The tall man peered around the room appraisingly. "I am looking for an inquisitor," he said. "Miles Huxley. It would seem I have just missed him."

The kitchen had the look of a warzone, and Mason didn't see the point of lying to a fellow necromancer. "He was here," he told him. "He killed… he killed my mentor. He killed Lester."

"Unfortunate." But the stranger didn't look upset, or even surprised. "Why did he not kill you as well?"

This time, Mason decided to lie; the truth would have been a hard sell anyway. "I wasn't home when it happened," he said (well, technically that was true). "I was out for a walk with a friend. When I came back, the front door was open. I found this mess in the kitchen. Then I found his… his body downstairs." Mason felt like he was being interrogated— it was the way this man looked at him.

"I see." The stranger took one step forward. "You look different from when I last saw you, Mason Cross. Are you sick?"

Mason considered forcing a couple disingenuous coughs, but he was even worse at acting than he was at lying. So he went with a different lie: "I think maybe it's the shock. I've never... I'm a bit overwhelmed." The best lies were also true.

"Perhaps."

Mason couldn't tell if this man believed anything he was saying. He recalled the stranger had ways of finding other necromancers, that he was able to find him on the beach with only his mind. He'd told Mason he could detect necromancy from afar. Maybe he could detect lies too.

"What is your plan for Lester Wright's body?" the stranger asked. "I assume it is still downstairs."

Mason nodded. "I was going to drive it up north, bring it — *him* — back to his friends, back to where he lived. Only I don't actually know where that is. I still need to find his address."

"I possess that knowledge."

"His address?" asked Mason. "You have it?"

The stranger nodded once. "That is what I said."

"Can I... could I have it?" Mason looked desperate. "I'd really appreciate it, if you don't mind."

"Do you have a car? It is a day's drive."

"I do. It's at my mom's house. I just need to go back and get it."

"Hmmm.... No." The stranger retreated a few steps into the hallway. "I will take you instead. I will take you where you want to go. To Lester Wright's commune. My car is outside. We will leave immediately. There is room in the trunk for his body. He will fit. He is small."

Mason would have preferred going alone, but the necromancer mulling in his living room wasn't offering him a choice— he was giving orders. Still, Mason made a bid for his independence: "I don't mind going alone. You know, if you're busy or whatever."

"It is better if I take you." The stranger offered no explanation. "I assume Lester Wright is down here?"

Mason stepped into the hallway and saw his uninvited guest pointing toward the basement door. He nodded. "Yeah."

"Wait here." The stranger disappeared into the basement.

Mason did as he was told, collapsing onto the nearest couch. He was partially relieved this man was helping him. He seemed pretty capable, after all, but his presence invited as much concern. Mason couldn't bring himself to trust him. He was still a stranger and an odd one at that. Hell, Mason hadn't even learned his name yet.

He sighed, wishing he could sleep. Man, he was *dead tired*. Hah.

For a moment, all Mason could hear was the rain outside. Then came the sound of footsteps on the basement's wooden staircase, each one a little louder than the last, until the door swung back open. But it wasn't the stranger who emerged— it was Lester, and he was walking.

Not in his usual manner, mind you. His steps were staggered and his footfalls heavy. The rest of his body hardly moved, apparently just along for the ride. Blood dripped from his shirt, leaving a dotted trail behind him. Not that he would have noticed; his dead eyes registered nothing.

Lester's puppet master emerged from behind. This was clearly routine for him. He looked bored and apathetic, like an aged accountant punching the same old digits into a calculator— only his was a human body. "It is not unlike the beetle you yourself controlled," he said to Mason. "Just another dead animal, only bigger."

"He was my friend." Mason was a little insulted.

"Not anymore," replied the stranger. "We will be gone for two days. Grab whatever you need. I will be waiting in my car."

More orders, thought Mason, who wasn't accustomed to following them. But right now, he had little choice. He headed upstairs and packed a change of clothes and his toothbrush into a grocery bag. He pocketed his father's notebook before hurrying back down— it might come in handy. More than anything, he just wanted to get this all over with. He wanted to get back to his normal life— if any of it was still waiting for him. He wanted to get back to Asha.

The stranger's car was parked in the driveway. It was an old black Cadillac, dark and imposing like the man inside— almost comically suitable. But Mason didn't laugh. He opened the passenger door and slipped inside, looking a little defeated. The car was already rumbling and ready to go.

The stranger looked down at the grocery bag resting on Mason's lap. "You have everything you need, I take it," he said.

"Yeah." Mason clicked in his seat belt. "Is Lester in the trunk?"

"He is."

"Well, I'm good to go, then."

The stranger backed out of the driveway, not bothering to look over his shoulder.

"I never got your name, by the way," said Mason, watching his house — his desecrated home — disappear in the rear-view mirror. "Apparently, you already know mine."

The stranger kept his eyes on the road ahead.

"Rowland," he said.

Chapter 17

LOCAL COP SURVIVES LIFE-THREATENING INJURIES
by John Ryan

A local police officer who was shot Tuesday evening during a drug raid in East Terminal City is now in stable condition, Police Chief Roger Chin told reporters Wednesday.

Detective Constable Clayton Stark, 32, was shot twice in the stomach inside a suburban drug home, which police say housed a "sizable" crystal meth lab in its basement.

The shooter, identified as 17-year-old Charlie Reese, was gunned down by two other officers shortly after the shooting and died on the scene, police say.

According to Chief Chin, Det.-Sgt. Stark had tried to reason with the teenager and was shot for his effort.

Det.-Sgt. Stark has been with the Terminal City Police Department for eight years and is described by Chief Chin as intelligent and kind.

"He's a model detective," Chief Chin said. "It was a tragic day for all of us on the force, but his doctor tells us he's going to be okay. It was music to our ears, I can tell you that."

Chief Chin wouldn't speculate on when Det.-Sgt. Stark might return to work. "It's far too early to say," he said. "Whenever he's a hundred per cent— not a moment sooner."

Little is yet known about his deceased shooter, Charlie Reese, but police say his family was notified of his death Wednesday morning.

—*The Terminal City Chronicle*

♦❖♦

Clayton Stark stepped out of his car and scanned the forest across the street. He couldn't see any of his colleagues, just two blue and white cop cars. He was probably the last one to get here, often was. He took a slow sip of coffee before locking the car door.

With his free hand, Clayton wiped his bloodshot eyes then ran his fingers through his close-cropped brown hair. "God." He shook his head like a wet dog. "All right, let's do this."

He walked up the street until he spotted a small trail burrowing through the brush, jaywalked, then made his way down the dirt path. Clayton could hear ocean waves crashing in the distance. It was pleasant, but he knew only too well that nothing stayed pleasant for long in his line of work.

At least his coffee had cooled down enough to swallow in swigs, which was good because, boy, he really needed this one. He hadn't slept well last night, still not used to another person sleeping in his bed— at least, not that often and not when he was sober. But she was staying over every other night now. Of course, it was a worthy trade-off. Until recently, Clayton hadn't been happy, truly happy, in years. Alicia was great. They'd been dating for almost a year, just long enough that he no longer felt as if she were always on the verge of leaving him (his problem, not hers). She even appeared to be as happy about the situation as he was.

Clayton wondered what she was doing right now. He couldn't remember if her class had started. She taught here at Carwin University, the location of this morning's crime scene, but he wouldn't be seeing her. There were no classes among the trees that bordered Carwin.

But there was a pretty big pool of blood, apparently. He still couldn't see it, but the shoulders of a couple officers about fifty feet off the beaten path popped into view. He made his way toward them, pushing back the twigs and leaves that got in his way with his free hand, holding up his half-empty coffee cup in the other.

"Hey, Clayton."

"Hey, Bernard." Clayton spotted four officers, all guarding the crime scene perimeter from no one in particular. "Any other detectives here yet?"

"Just James," said Bernard. "And you. James is interviewing the witness. A young woman, a student here. She was going for a jog through the forest, noticed a bit of blood in the dirt over that way." Bernard pointed southward, where the trail Clayton had walked down eventually curved. "She thought maybe someone or an animal had been hurt, so she veered off the trail looking and... well, that's when she found this."

The pool of blood had sunk into the soil, but the reddish-brown stain left behind was about the size of a man's torso. Clayton knelt down to get a better look. There were glaring signs of a scuffle: kick marks in the dirt, broken twigs, and smaller splotches of blood all over the clearing. Plus, two sets of footprints, both men's by the looks of it. There had definitely been a fight here, a rough one, and things had ended very badly for at least one of the combatants.

"Yo, you see the game last night?" It was Bernard.

Clayton nodded. "Yeah. Real nail-biter, that one."

"I'll say." Bernard always brought up hockey because, frankly, it was all they had in common. "Man, that fucking kid they have in goal— he's like one of those Buddhist monks, you know? Always calm, always focused." He was talking with his hands.

"I hear ya." Clayton forced a smile. "Maybe the NHL should send a few recruiters to Tibet, eh."

"Yeah." Bernard chuckled. "Maybe."

Clayton looked back toward the blood stain, the centerpiece of this mess. Blood, or at least this much of it, still made him a little queasy. He'd only just joined homicide last month and it took some getting used to, but the work, at least in his opinion, was the most important a cop could do. He hadn't been as passionate about narcotics— drug busts and all that. In homicide, the bad guys tended to be more unambiguously bad. Then again, he was still new to all this. What did he know?

Clayton spotted a bullet.

It was lying right beside his foot, obscured under a veil of dirt and blood. He couldn't see it well, but it looked like a 9mm, a handgun bullet. Certainly not used for hunting, but then these weren't hunting grounds. Indeed, the evidence was starting to suggest what he already felt in his gut— someone had been shot.

As he often did, Clayton unconsciously touched the wounds on his stomach, neighboring scars left behind from the two bullets that had entered his body a couple years back— a permanent reminder that he didn't know when to pull the trigger. And of Charlie Reese, the kid who didn't survive his bullets. Clayton thought about him every day, sometimes like he knew him, like he was a younger brother who'd taken a wrong turn in life.

The memory, up until a point, remained vivid to this day: Charlie lifting his gun, Clayton pleading with him not to do it. He'd seen it coming and let it happen, for which he'd nearly died. Lessons don't come tougher than that. And yet he still wondered if he'd have the nerve to shoot at the right time now, if ever he were put in that situation again. Or perhaps he would overcompensate and shoot too quickly. For some reason, that frightened him even more.

In any event, Clayton suspected that whoever had been shot by the bullet in this clearing hadn't been as lucky as he'd been that day. Then again, nothing was certain yet. This was a strange crime scene.

James, the other detective on site, stepped out from behind a tree. "Hey, Clayton."

"Hey, James." Clayton stood up. "Get anything useful from the witness?"

James shrugged. "Nah. She didn't see anything. Just rambled on about this being a safe neighborhood, the same shit you've heard a million times. What about you? Find anything interesting? I haven't poked around yet."

"A bullet." Clayton pointed near his feet. "Right here. It's a bit hard to see."

"That is interesting," said James.

"It's sort of strange too," added Clayton.

"How so?"

"Well, whoever shot this bullet took the time to remove the body, but he made no effort to conceal the crime scene," explained Clayton.

"You're saying it was an amateur," replied James.

"Perhaps, assuming he was trying to get rid of the evidence." Clayton knelt back down and examined the bullet from two feet away. "Or maybe the victim lived. Maybe he was carried away kicking, or maybe he played dead until the shooter left, used his shirt to stop the bleeding then stumbled on out of here."

"I don't know." James didn't look convinced. "That's a lot of blood. Plus, if someone went to the ER with a bullet wound, we'd know. I didn't hear anything this morning."

"Perhaps." Clayton kept his eyes on the ground. "If he went to the ER, but not everyone wants to involve the police. Or maybe our guy just didn't make it far enough. I know it's a long shot, man, but stranger things have…" He trailed off.

"What is it?" asked James.

"Another bullet," said Clayton.

"Two bullets. You still think this guy lived?" James walked past him. "I'm going to look around the woods a bit, see if I can find anything else."

"All right." Clayton looked around too, but he didn't find any more clues— or bullets.

His cell phone vibrated. It was a text message from Alicia: *Dinner tomorrow?*

Clayton's smile emerged. He texted her back — *What are we having?* — and for a few seconds managed not to think about bullets or blood.

Chapter 18

DAVID,
I miss you, you beautiful bastard. Just a few more weeks then I'll be home. Promise. This kid, I tell ya... what an arrogant little know-it-all. I like him. Reminds me so much of John.
Lots of love,
Lester
PS. That is what "LOL" stands for, right?
—lesterwright@nmail.com

Mason couldn't fall asleep, but he wasn't quite awake either. He lingered somewhere in between, just conscious enough to know he was conscious. It wasn't only the bumpy car ride that kept him up; it was as much the man sitting beside him, Rowland, whom he was tasked to kill. The situation was rather unnerving, to say the least. And yet he was more exhausted than he'd ever been before, more exhausted than he had known was possible. Death, it seemed, sucked the life right out of you.

Mason felt the car slow down and opened his eyes. "Are we there?"

"No," replied Rowland. "Not yet."

Mason peered out the window. They had stopped along the side of a winding road, two lanes barely wide enough for passing cars. The concrete was a web of cracks and neglect, just some skinny line of humanity cutting through the mountains around them. He hadn't been paying much attention to their journey thus far and was a little surprised by the snow outside. They must be pretty high up.

"Why did you pull over?" asked Mason.

"A cop," said Rowland.

"What?"

A man's knuckles knocked on Rowland's window.

Ah, a cop.

Rowland had to roll down his window by hand — it was an old car. "Yes?" he said, making no effort to mask his annoyance.

The cop hunched over to get eye level. "Do you know how fast you were going?" He was a portly man with a generation's-old moustache.

"Yes," replied Rowland. "I do."

"And do you know what the speed limit is on this road?"

"Get to your point."

"Don't give me lip," the cop warned. "You were doing 'bout twenty kilometers over the speed limit, on a dangerous road no less. Not to mention it's snowin' pretty heavy. What if you'd slid into a car coming 'round that bend up there?" He smacked his palms together, mimicking a crash. "Or flew off the mountain side and killed you and your friend." He shook his head. "You can't be speeding through these mountains, mister."

"My senses and reflexes are superior to yours," explained Rowland. "I will be just fine. As will my... friend."

The police officer scoffed. "Famous last words." He stood up straight, metal clipboard in hand, and began filling out Rowland's speeding ticket. "Now I better not catch you speeding again," he said. "Don't think I won't haul your ass into jail."

"Oh," said Rowland. "I do not think that."

The cop walked to the back of their car to double-check the licence plate. Rowland eyed him through the rear-view mirror. Mason eyed both of them, unsure which one he should be more worried about.

The police officer stepped back into view and hunched down again. "There's a strange odor coming from your trunk. Mind opening it up for me so I can take a look inside," he said.

Mason's heart sank.

Rowland, on the other hand, didn't look worried at all. "Yes," he said. "I do mind."

"I wasn't really asking." The cop had one hand on his holstered pistol. "Open up your trunk, *sir*."

They stared at one another for only a few seconds — though if time were measured in tension, it might have lasted forever

— before Rowland made his move. He did so without so much as a peep. In fact, it was the cop who gave it away, and it wasn't pleasant. The noise he made— it seemed like the only noise he could make. It was half a cough, half a scream, and wholly unexpected going by the expression Mason saw in his eyes. He knew what came next.

The police officer collapsed to the ground, bouncing off the side of Rowland's Cadillac on his way down. Rowland put his foot back on the pedal, not wasting any time. Mason felt a bump as the car accelerated, but he didn't look back to see what part of the cop they'd just run over. Frankly, he didn't want to know. He already knew enough— he knew the man was dead.

He asked anyway: "Did you… did you kill him?"

"Of course," Rowland said matter-of-factly. They were driving at full speed now— or rather, about twenty kilometers over the limit.

Mason made a fist and pounded the air like a gavel. "Why?" For a moment, his anger toward the man beside him outpaced his fear of him. "Couldn't you have just, I don't know, knocked him out or something?"

"He had my licence plate number," explained Rowland. "I like this car. And he had seen our faces. Had I let him live, we would have become fugitives. Then I would have had to kill many cops. This way, it is just the one. Surely, you can see the logic in that."

Mason gave him a cold shoulder, gazing out his passenger window at the trees, trying to find the furthest one from the man beside him. "People are not… math," he said quietly.

"Oh, but they are," replied Rowland. "More so than you think."

"How's that?" asked Mason, regretting the question immediately.

"They are predictable," said Rowland, "variables stuck in the same old equations. They never learn. They never change."

"What the fuck are you talking about?" Mason was still mad.

Rowland took a deep breath and leaned forward in his seat, keeping his attention on the increasingly snowy road ahead; they could no longer see the asphalt. "Most people fear what they do not understand," he said. "They fear anything different, anything new."

Suddenly, the car skidded, only for a second, but there wasn't a lot of leeway up here. Rowland slowed down. Mason thought he looked a little embarrassed.

Rowland continued, his anger slipping through the cracks of his pragmatic facade: "Outsiders, for example, are invariably met by the masses with hostility." He enunciated each consonant like gunfire. "Foreigners, heretics, men who love men— it plays out the same way each time. The outsiders are persecuted, killed, made scapegoats for whatever ails society. The masses do come to accept them after a time, but only as society evolves, only as they are normalized. Not because these people have learned anything, Mason Cross— there is a difference.

"When the next set of strangers steps off the boat or out from the closet, the masses will treat them just as they treated outsiders before them. Even those who were victimized in the past, even those who continue to be victimized— they will join right in, ensuring the cycle never ends.

"You see, people are stupid." Rowland had regained his perfect composure. "They accept what they are told like dogs memorizing tricks. They like to think they are more moral, more enlightened than their ancestors, but they are not. They benefit from hindsight but do not see the big picture. That would require them to think for themselves, to be like you and me. Most people are not like us, Mason Cross. And thus society, at least as it exists today, is doomed to repeat the same mistakes over and over.

"Like I said, variables in the same old equations," said Rowland. "Equations people are too ignorant to see, which is why they are stuck in them. They see only the other, the enemy. Imagine they saw necromancers." He lingered on that for a moment. "I am much, much older than you, Mason Cross. I have seen firsthand how history unfolds. It frustrated me when I was younger. Now it bores me."

"So, people are predictable," said Mason, who didn't altogether disagree. "That doesn't justify killing them like fucking flies. That cop probably had a family. And how do you know he fit your stereotype? Not everyone gives into mob mentality, and even those who do… don't always. Ignorance comes in degrees, and no one escapes it completely. Your math only works when you generalize, when you imagine there are two types of people, smart and stupid, us and them, so how are you any better than the people you despise for thinking the same way?"

"Because I *knew* he was a fool," said Rowland. "What makes me different is the fact that my judgements are born from knowledge. I can see people's spirits. I can see who they are, how they think. I could see what kind of man he was, that cop, and what I saw was a fucking fool." Rowland was tensing up; it reminded Mason of his father. "Do not presume to know the limits of my power, novice."

After that, they didn't speak for another half-hour. By the time Rowland broke the silence, the snow on the road had piled high enough to force them well below the speed limit. It was an agonizing situation for both of them: Rowland wanted to go fast, and Mason just wanted to go home, to get this nightmare of a road trip over with.

"Someday," said Rowland, "when you are older and wiser, you will see the world as I do."

Mason shook his head defiantly. "Never."

This time, the silence lasted the rest of the way there.

There was nothing particularly necromantic about the wood-paneled house they drove up to — at least not from the outside — although it was certainly isolated. And big. Mason couldn't tell where the property ended and the forest began, but the last house he'd seen must have been about a kilometer back.

They reached the end of the driveway and slowed to a stop. "Go. Knock," said Rowland. He kept one hand on the steering wheel and the car engine humming.

"Fine." Mason unsnapped his seat belt and stepped out into the biting cold. He was still dressed for Terminal City weather, not the mountains. He zipped up his jacket on the way to the front door and then knocked twice.

Half a minute passed and no one answered. Mason looked over toward Rowland, who was waiting impatiently in his idling Cadillac, and shrugged. That's when the door swung open.

"Hello?"

Mason turned on his heel.

The voice belonged to a middle-aged woman with bushy black hair. "Can I help you?" she asked.

"Hi," Mason said and then hesitated. "Do you… are you a friend of Lester Wright?"

"Yes," she replied, eyeing him suspiciously. "What is this about?"

It struck Mason then that he hadn't prepared himself for this. He didn't quite know how he should deliver the news, in spite of the fact that he himself had been on the receiving end before. He'd been so caught up worrying about Rowland that the gravity of this moment had all but evaded him. Until now.

"What do you want?" she asked again, peering over his shoulder distrustfully at Rowland's car.

"I'm afraid I have some bad news," he said. "It's about Lester."

She returned her gaze to him, and now Mason could see dread in her eyes, in the way her body shifted. "Who are you?" she asked, even more accusingly than before.

"My name is Mason Cross. I'm John Cross's son. My father was a friend of—"

"I know who your father was," she interrupted him. "I knew him quite well, in fact. I'm sorry for your loss." And just like that, her defences had come down. "And for my bad manners. We don't get a lot of visitors here." She cleared her throat. "You can call me Clarissa. Now, what's this about Lester?"

"Lester, he..." Mason stalled for a moment, but he knew there was no point in beating around the bush; he'd always preferred clarity when it came to his dad's death. He took a deep breath and told her, unambiguously, "Lester's been killed."

Clarissa closed her eyes and grasped the edge of the door, as if to keep herself from falling. "How?" she whispered.

"Inquisitors."

"Of course."

"I'm sorry."

When she reopened her eyes, they were red with tears. "Who's that waiting in the car behind you?" she asked.

"Another necromancer," said Mason. "You might know him. His name is Rowland."

Clarissa took a step backward. "Rowland? As in *the* Rowland?"

"He really does have quite the reputation," replied Mason. "He was hunting the inquisitor who killed Lester, but he arrived too late and found me instead. He helped me find this place. Do you know him personally?"

"We've spoken once or twice before," she replied. "I'd heard a rumor that he had returned, but I didn't really believe it myself. I'd always figured he'd gotten bored with life after all these years and ended his. Wishful thinking, I guess. You should know he's bad news, Mason. If your father knew you were—"

"I know, I know," he interrupted her. "Believe me, but there was no other way to get here. I didn't have an address, and I thought Lester's body should be brought home to you, to the people he loved. Rowland said he knew how to get here and insisted on driving."

Clarissa nodded sympathetically. "Thank you, Mason. That was very thoughtful. You're a good man, just like your father— just like your mentor." She wiped a tear from her cheek with the butt of her palm. "It was only a week ago when we last talked, Lester and I. He told me you were very bright, very talented for someone so young. He was quite fond of you, you know, even if he wasn't any good at showing it. That's just how he was."

"I think we had that in common," said Mason. "His body… it's in the trunk of that car. I can help bring it inside if you need." He sure as hell didn't want Rowland moving it his way.

"No, no. You've done enough." She touched his arm affectionately. "I'll get Pat and Roger to carry him in. But please, stay for the night. The funeral will be in a few hours."

"So soon?" Mason didn't mean to sound judgemental.

"We're necromancers, Mason." A sad smile reached across her face. "We see life and death in a different light, so we celebrate them differently too. In private. Besides, I want you to be here for the ceremony. You don't need to say anything. I just want you to hear what a great man your mentor was from the people who knew him best."

Then Clarissa nodded to the car idling behind him. "He can stay too," she said. "If he must."

As they often do, preparations took longer than planned, and it was almost midnight by the time Lester's funeral started. It was also freezing cold. Mason had borrowed a winter coat from Pat, who was much larger than he was, and now had his hands tucked away in its long sleeves.

Everyone was outside, hushed and waiting for a man named David to speak. Everyone but Rowland, who was nowhere to be found, though it was rather dark. The area around Lester's body — resting nobly on a simple stone bed with its arms crossed and eyes shut — shone softly beneath a sprinkling of small orbs hovering in the air like fallen stars. But little could be seen beyond the reach of their red aura.

It was snowing too, a light dusting. The setting was as surreal as it was beautiful. Mason counted eleven people, himself included, all standing, some shivering. Then finally, as the murmuring subsided, the slender man Mason recognized as David trudged through the snow toward Lester's still body and turned to face the living. He was middle-aged guy, maybe Filipino, and he would have been handsome any other day. But right now, he looked utterly defeated.

David cleared his throat and began. "I consider you all family." He spoke softly. "But Lester will always hold a unique place in my heart." The wind was picking up, blowing the ends of his scarf sideways.

"I first met Lester nearly two decades ago," he continued. "I was twenty-four and quite the strapping young lad, if I may say so. Lester was, oh, about my age now and not nearly as strapping."

Everyone laughed. It's funny how people laugh the hardest at funerals, thought Mason. Any excuse to silence the sorrow, he figured, even if for only a few fleeting seconds.

"I was on a beach in Terminal City," said David. "I remember it was one of the first days of summer and absolutely gorgeous out. There wasn't a cloud in the sky, and the breeze was just right— everything you could ask for, and everyone was smiling. Everyone except me. I had my back against a log, my knees up to my chest, my head burrowed in my arms. I was bawling my eyes out and, despite my best efforts, not doing a very good job hiding it.

"I heard Lester's voice before laying eyes on the man himself. 'Cheer up,' he said. 'It's a beautiful day.' That's when I looked up toward him, this unassuming little guy with a big toothy smile, and I didn't know what the hell to say back. But Lester, he sat right down beside me anyway and introduced himself. I told him my name, and he asked what was wrong. At first, I wasn't going to open up. After all, I'd just been cast out of my home for doing exactly that. But something about the way this man looked at me— I just knew it would be okay, that he wasn't here to judge me.

"So I told him what had happened, that I'd come out to my parents, and that they'd responded by kicking me to the curb. I told him how I'd convinced myself they were going to love me no matter what, even if they couldn't understand that part of me. But in the end, the only person who showed me unconditional acceptance was Lester, a man I'd only just met.

"Needless to say, we became immediate friends. He introduced me around to the community, and soon I had more new friends than old ones. Some of these friendships lasted years, some months. Some were quick flings, a couple turned into relationships. But nothing ever lasted— nothing except Lester. He was always there for me and never expected anything in return. I always knew he liked me, but he never let that come between us.

"But then something clicked. I had an epiphany, you might say. I'd just been through a rough breakup and Lester was— well, he was there for me, like he always was. I remember he came over to cook dinner. Nothing fancy— just some pasta, which he overcooked."

Some more chuckles. Mason was reminded of all the nights Lester had cooked for him too, including his last. He was reminded of spaghetti sauce splattered across the kitchen floor. And of his last words to Lester: *Your cooking sucks anyway*.

"And then it hit me." Now David's voice was cracking. A tear fell from the point of his chin as he struggled to continue. "I realized I would never love anyone... as much as the man who had always loved me." He wiped his cheeks with the coarse sleeve of his winter coat and turned to face Lester's pale body, unembalmed and unmistakably dead as it was. "I don't know how" — his voice broke into a keening falsetto — "I'll go on now."

Clarissa stepped forward and hugged him from behind, reaching under his shoulders to his chest. David embraced her hands in his.

Three more people spoke after David, including Clarissa, and each speech resonated with a similar theme— that of a man who undersold himself and earned his love through deeds. He was a complainer, sure, but in the end, he was the friend who never let you down.

When all was said and done, Pat and Roger once again lifted Lester's body, this time carrying it to a freshly dug grave about a hundred feet away. Mason watched them from a distance. He spotted four neighboring tombstones, all aligned in a row. Once Pat and Roger started shoveling dirt onto Lester's plain wooden coffin, which Pat had finished building only an hour earlier, people began filing into the house. Despite the stinging pain in his fingers and the cold wind blasting his ears, Mason lingered a while before wandering back alone.

On the way, he slipped off his right glove and fetched his cell phone from his pants pocket. The damn thing was nearly dead. He hadn't charged it in a couple days, though it hardly mattered considering he couldn't get a signal up here. He really was in the middle of nowhere. Just like Lester had said. Mason wondered if Asha had tried to reach him.

As he pocketed his phone, Mason heard footsteps crunching in the snow behind him. He whirled around and saw Rowland— for the first time in hours.

"Where were you?" asked Mason.

"Wandering," said Rowland. "And thinking."

"About what?"

"About you. About what I should do with you."

Mason took a step back. "I don't understand."

"Sure you do," Rowland said casually. "You have been tasked to kill me. Why else would the Spirit Realm send you back? I know they want me dead. And I know not a single necromancer has been sent back to the Living Realm since they sent me. Until you, of course, which is why I offered to drive you here."

Mason knew he couldn't lie to him. "I made a promise," he admitted, "but I honestly don't know what I'm going to do. I'm a little... in over my head."

"You think?" Rowland cracked half a smile— it didn't suit him.

"So, what are you going to do with me?" asked Mason.

"Nothing," said Rowland. "For now. You could not kill me even if you tried a thousand times and I did not kill you first. But you will be more powerful someday, perhaps even a threat. After all, you are like me: you have been to the Spirit Realm and back. You are smart as well, maybe too smart for your own good.

"No— I do not wish to kill you, Mason Cross," continued Rowland. "Not yet, anyway. But I do want to leave you with something to think about. Your mentor, Lester Wright, was killed by an inquisitor. So was your father, I expect. Throughout my long life, I have killed over two hundred inquisitors — significantly more than any other necromancer in history — and in doing so have undoubtedly saved hundreds of necromancers from an untimely death. Now, ask yourself this: would the world truly be a better place without me in it?"

Mason shrugged. "I don't know," he said. "Either way, it doesn't justify you killing that cop. It doesn't make you a good person."

Rowland scoffed. "So-called good people rarely make a difference, Mason Cross. They like to show off, but it is people who see the world for what it is and do what must be done— they are the ones who leave a mark. Think about that. Think about my question. And above all else, do not let yourself be a tool for the Spirit Realm. You have a mind and will of your own— use them."

Before Mason could reply, Rowland stepped past him, in the opposite direction of the house. "I will return in the morning," he said and then disappeared, his black overcoat bleeding into the night.

Mason couldn't help but think he'd caught a spark of sorrow in Rowland's eyes.

Chapter 19

"SIT THE FUCK DOWN."

The inquisitor sat. There was just the one wooden chair, old and rickety, a relic of some 1970's dining room set that, four decades later, had somehow found itself in an interrogation room deep underground, located God-knows-where. Anton Leroy had been unconscious for at least a day and, like the chair he was sitting on, had been taken far away from where he ought to be.

There wasn't much light in this windowless room, but somehow it seemed to be all directed at him. He was hot, sweating even. He could feel his dress shirt clinging to his skin. He hated that, but right now it was the least of his worries. In all likeliness, he'd be a dead man before he got out of here. Guess that's why he was sweating so much. His body knew what was coming, whether or not he wanted to admit it to himself.

Anton took a deep breath and stared disdainfully at the two men standing over him, both necromancers, one of whom he recognized. He was the necromancer Anton and his partner, Mr. Wallace, had been assigned to kill. Clearly, things hadn't gone as planned.

It had been a trap. Anton and Mr. Wallace were in Toronto at the time, and their target, Jack Ross, must have spotted them first. They found Mr. Ross at night — he walked right past them in a restaurant — and so, of course, they followed. He led them back to his home. That's where they would make the kill; they knew he lived alone, in a quiet place out in the suburbs. But Mr. Ross wasn't the only man waiting for them — and waiting he was — when they arrived. There were four necromancers in all.

Mr. Wallace had his spirit ripped clean out and died on the spot; Anton, meanwhile, was immobilized, beaten, and finally sedated.

That was yesterday. Presently, well, he didn't know where the hell he was now, nor the identity of this other necromancer.

The only door to the room squeaked open. Two more people walked through, a tired-looking man, probably in his fifties, and a middle-aged woman. She shut the door behind them.

"Hello, Mr. Leroy," said the man, stepping in front of him. "My name is Samuel Benedict, but you can just call me Samuel. Or Sam, if you prefer. Unlike your colleagues, we don't go by last names here. Beside me is Joan Worthington."

"Just Joan is fine," said Joan. They were mocking him.

"What do you want?" asked Anton, immediately embarrassed by the obvious tremble in his voice.

"We'll be asking the questions," said Joan. "I know you're used to it being the other way around, but bear with us."

"Just don't kill me," said Anton, "and I'll tell you whatever you want." He wasn't lying. Anton had been on the fence about his work as an inquisitor for at least a year now, and this was just the push he needed to get on with his life. "I swear. I don't even want to do this anymore."

"Do what?" asked Samuel.

"Be an inquisitor," replied Anton.

"I see. Why did you become one in the first place?"

Anton shook his head. "I don't know. I guess I thought you were bad people. They said, the inquisitors, they told me you were murderers. I thought I was doing a good thing."

"Do you still think you're doing a good thing?" asked Samuel.

"I'm not sure," admitted Anton. "I think maybe it's more complicated than I was led to believe."

"Life usually is," said Joan.

"Indeed," agreed Samuel. "Now let's see if you can help us out, Mr. Leroy. Tell me, does Victoria Westcott have any big plans in the works that you're aware of?"

Anton nodded obediently. "I'd say so," he said. "She's going after Rowland."

"Then I take it he's made his comeback known," replied Samuel.

"He killed one of our guys and sent his partner back to deliver the message."

"What message?"

"A message to come and get him."

"And Ms. Westcott listened?" Samuel raised an eyebrow. "She thought it would be a good idea to go after Rowland when he's most expecting it?"

"I don't know, to be honest." Anton shrugged. "But pretty much every inquisitor on the continent is flying to Terminal City at this very moment to confront him. I figure she wants to end this once and for all. Otherwise, he's just going to pick us off one by one. He said as much. Better to strike him together, no?"

"You have no idea what he's capable of, do you?" Joan was shaking her head.

"I've heard stories, you know," replied Anton. "We all have."

"Well…" Samuel sighed. "To be fair, I don't think anyone quite knows what Rowland is capable of these days."

"Now, please," begged Anton, "that's all I know. I don't have the details. I just know everyone is going to Terminal City, even Ms. Westcott. I was going to fly out last night. If you're after inquisitors, that's where you'll find them."

"You're a hundred per cent sure that's all you know?" asked Samuel.

"Yeah, like I told you, that's it. I swear to God."

"God isn't here, Mr. Leroy," said Samuel. "It's just the five of us. And not for much longer."

"What do you mean?" The blood drained from Anton's face.

"You didn't think we would let you go, did you?"

"But I told you everything I know!"

"Maybe you did, maybe you didn't," replied Samuel. "But that hardly changes the fact that you've killed, tell me, how many necromancers?"

Anton shrugged and shook his head. "I… I don't know, but please, I'll change, I swear. I want to change!"

"What a convenient epiphany." Samuel, who was already tall, straightened himself until he towered over him. "Only just yesterday you were willing to kill another necromancer. Now you tell me you've killed so many that you don't even remember the number. Is that possible? Most people can tell you at the drop of a hat how many people they've slept with, and you can't tell me how many you've killed? That's worse than any number, wouldn't you say?"

Anton was shaking, sweating, and sobbing all at once. "S-Seventeen," he stuttered. "I helped kill seventeen, but I only ever pulled the trigger twice. I let my partner do it. I n-never liked killing them. But I know that doesn't make it any better." He sniffled. "I know what I did was wrong." His plea had turned into a confession. "Maybe I deserve this. I don't know anymore.... I don't know." The desperation had faded from Anton's voice; now he sounded depressed and defeated, a lost cause even to himself.

"You do deserve this, Mr. Leroy," said Samuel, "but I will show you a degree of compassion. I won't make you suffer. I could, believe me, but I won't."

Anton nodded, tears streaming from his eyes, accepting his death as much as any man in his thirties could. "Okay," he whispered.

Samuel nodded. "Close your eyes. You won't feel a thing. I promise."

Anton dropped his head to his chest and prayed silently to whatever god would listen. He heard Samuel muttering a spell, and then he grew too tired to remember reality. The chant became the sound of a crackling fire.

In the seconds before he died, Anton dreamed he was home again— his real home, not that condo he slept in. Mom and Dad were in the next room, preparing dinner. And there was Misty, warming herself in front of the fireplace, her paws stretched out as far as they could go. She looked so comfortable. God, he'd strayed so far from comfortable. But not this time. Anton joined her, slipping off his chair and landing belly down on the cold cement floor.

They were back at Samuel's place, lying naked together in his king-sized bed.

Joan sighed. "I guess we're heading to Terminal City."

"Perhaps we should think about it some more first," replied Samuel.

"What's there to think about?" She leaned into his broad chest. "We're guardians. There's a war brewing between our worst enemies and the worst necromancer the world has ever seen. It's a recipe for the apocalypse. The whole reason we exist is to prevent something like this from happening."

"But what can we do, just the two of us?" Samuel kissed the top of her head. He liked doing that; she liked it just as much.

"There's no time to gather the others. Abah is back in Lagos. Camila is in São Paulo. Hiroshi is— who knows."

"You're right," admitted Joan, "but it's still our duty to show up, even if it's just for damage control. In this case, I don't know what that entails. I suppose we'll see when we get there."

"I still think we should weigh our options," said Samuel.

"There are no other options." She didn't like it any more than he did, but it was the truth. "What that inquisitor just told us is all we have to go on, and if he's right, and I sensed he was telling the truth, then there's no time, like you said. We need to leave tomorrow. At least Jack and Victor can come with us. Four is better than two."

"Not much." Nonetheless, Samuel nodded grudgingly. "Very well."

"I wish we didn't have to, believe me, but—"

"I know," said Samuel. "You're right. Goddamnit, you're right."

"Goddamnit, indeed." She burrowed her head deeper into his chest, face-first, and made a whining moan. "This was supposed to be my vacation."

Chapter 20

"ONE DAY, YOU will have to kill someone." More words of wisdom from Rowland, who was sitting beside Mason in his Cadillac.

"I'm not like you," replied Mason.

"Well, you will have to be more like me. That is, if you want to live long enough to see your hair grey. They know who you are now— the inquisitors. Once they realize you are not dead, they will come back for you. You can count on that. Understand this, Mason Cross: Even if I killed every inquisitor on the planet tonight, the spirit of the inquisition would live on. Ignorance and fear are simply human nature.

"In other words," concluded Rowland, stiffening his spine, "one day, you will have to kill someone."

"What's your point?" Mason supposed he might be right.

"My point," said Rowland, "is that if you have to kill someone, and you will, although it will not be me, then you will need to know how to kill. What I did to that bug on the beach… to that cop— that is what you need to learn. Necromancy allows you to take life, to tear a spirit from its body. In more ways than one. Some necromancers are better at it than others. But you will be one of the good ones because, like it or not, you are like me, touched by death, an expatriate in the Living Realm. As you will soon find out, that comes with both benefits and drawbacks. You will live a cold life, always as an outsider, even more so than now, more so than you can yet imagine. But you will also be one of the most powerful necromancers on this planet, if you choose to be."

Mason hadn't thought of it that way before, but he acted uninterested. "What are you getting at?"

Rowland reached into his jacket pocket and pulled out a perfectly folded piece of paper. It was yellow from age. "Learn this spell," he said. "Learn it soon. Learn it well. It is the quickest of its kind. When your life is on the line, timing is everything."

Hesitantly, Mason accepted the gift. Rowland, he realized, was trying to win him over; it wasn't working, but it wasn't not working either. "I take it this is every necromancer's second most important spell," he said.

Rowland didn't entertain mockery.

"Why are you here anyway?" asked Mason, tucking away his new spell.

"I do not follow," replied Rowland.

"In Terminal City, I mean. Why here? Why now?"

For once, Rowland took a while to find the right words. "The mountains, the ocean," he said, "they remind me of a place in which I spent a considerable amount of time."

"Where's that?"

"New Zealand."

Mason had always wanted to go to New Zealand.

"There are also a lot of necromancers here," added Rowland, "in Canada. Privacy is key to our existence. There is no shortage of unoccupied space north of the cities— space to practice, space to hide, space to be ourselves."

"I guess that makes sense," replied Mason.

"I need to get gas," said Rowland, spotting a station at the intersection ahead of them.

They had just re-entered Terminal City after another day's drive, and the first signs of evening were showing. In about twenty minutes — that was Mason's estimate — they would part ways. He couldn't wait. And not just because he wanted to rid himself of Rowland's company. He also wanted to call Asha, but his cell phone had died before he was able to find a signal. Although, after all this, he might need a second to himself first.

Rowland turned into the gas station. "Wait here," he told Mason, who didn't need to be told.

Mason still felt exhausted. Not sleep-deprived — he'd gotten a good night's worth — just drained. He needed a break from all this. He needed to not feel like the weight of the world was pressing down on him, and yet he knew it was. The pressure he felt wasn't just in his head. His responsibilities were real, and he couldn't escape them. Still, he would try to relax when he got home.

Rowland finished filling the tank and went inside the store to pay. Mason, meanwhile, was sort of surprised that Rowland sometimes paid for things.

Or maybe not. Mason watched from inside the car as the door Rowland had just stepped through flew back open at the behest of a dishevelled, horrified-looking man. Mason recognized him immediately. It was Mr. Huxley.

After nearly tripping over his own feet, Mr. Huxley picked up his pace and bolted toward the black SUV parked directly in front of them. He stopped for a second when he saw Mason, a stunned expression on his face. Then out came Rowland, not exactly running but stepping briskly and with deadly determination. It took Rowland a couple seconds to spot Mr. Huxley, but as soon as the inquisitor's van started rumbling, he found his mark.

Rowland might have killed him then too, but Mr. Huxley got off the first shot. A bullet whizzed past Rowland's head. He ducked instinctively and then conjured what looked to be a barrier — an opaque, red sphere that encapsulated his body — in the same second Mr. Huxley sped out of the station.

This time, Rowland ran. He slipped into the driver's seat, started the ignition, and slammed his side door shut as the car began to roll. He tried to peel out of the parking lot as Mr. Huxley had done, but the light down the road had just turned green and the traffic against them.

"Shit." Rowland punched the steering wheel with his palm. The car honked.

"Did you know he would be here?" asked Mason.

"Sort of," replied Rowland, his eyes locked on the stream of cars barring their path. Finally, a small break— Rowland took it. They flew out of the gas station, nearly scraping the front end of an oncoming car as they turned sharply into the far lane. There were angry honks. Mr. Huxley was two intersections ahead of them now, but Rowland was accelerating fast, his Cadillac roaring like a rocket.

"You *sort of* knew he would be here?" said Mason. "I don't understand."

"I sensed him," replied Rowland, "not unlike how I sensed you back on that beach."

"But he's not a necromancer."

"No, but I met him once before. Everyone's spirit is unique. You can learn to recognize them like you would someone's face, only you do not need to be looking at them. You just need to be close enough to sense it."

The light ahead of them turned red, but Rowland tore through it anyway. He'd closed the distance between him and Mr. Huxley to one block, but there were still three cars in his way.

"It is an imprecise art," continued Rowland. "Had I known exactly where he would be, Miles Huxley would already be dead. Instead, I am chasing his fucking van through the fucking streets of Terminal fucking City."

Mr. Huxley made a right a second before the next light turned red, leaving Rowland locked in between idle cars. But Rowland wasn't playing by the rules of the road; he spun his steering wheel clockwise and drove up onto the sidewalk. A passer by stopped in her tracks as Rowland ripped down the pedestrian path in his roomy Cadillac, nicking off someone's side-view mirror as he went. He made a sharp right turn at the intersection, off the sidewalk and onto the road with Mr. Huxley, who was now in clear sight. Rowland revved his engine. Mason clung to his seat belt.

There weren't as many cars on this street, and Rowland accelerated to double the speed limit. But so did Mr. Huxley, who was about a hundred feet ahead of them. Still, Rowland was going just a bit faster, and they were catching up.

A siren started wailing from behind them. "Fuck," spat Mason, peering over his shoulder. "It's just one."

Rowland didn't seem to care. Mason wasn't sure he did either—or perhaps he just wanted to see Mr. Huxley dead as much as Rowland did. Maybe even more so.

Mr. Huxley turned at the next intersection, his tires skidding, onto Granville Street, one of the busiest roads in Terminal City. Rowland followed, hugging the corner, but so did the cop car trailing them. Mason thought he could hear a second siren now.

"He's driving into downtown," said Mason.

"He is trying to get lost in the crowd," replied Rowland, "but I will not let him. I promised Miles Huxley I would kill him the next time we met. I am a man of my word."

"Why the fuck did you let him live the first time?" asked Mason.

"To deliver a message for me."

The way into downtown was over Granville Bridge, which had four lanes, two in each direction; Rowland weaved between them, passing car after car, until Mr. Huxley's SUV was nearly beside them. The sirens were getting closer too.

"Once I am able to see him," said Rowland, "he is as good as dead."

"Got an escape plan?" asked Mason.

"I will do what I must."

Mason didn't like the sound of that. They were close enough now that he could read Mr. Huxley's licence plate, but the man himself was just out of sight, if only for a few more seconds. Perhaps realizing the danger he was in, Mr. Huxley made a move, swerving into Rowland's Cadillac. The car shook, but Rowland didn't lose control; instead, he returned the favour, smashing the front end of his colossal car, which was nonetheless smaller than an SUV, into the inquisitor's back door. Mr. Huxley didn't fare as well. His van started spinning. It was bad news for everybody.

Rowland hit the brakes, but he was going far too fast to stop in time. They smashed into the side of Mr. Huxley's SUV — this time unintentionally. The seat-belt strap across Mason's chest punched him like an anvil as the two vehicles skidded to a halt. But the screeching didn't end there. The car behind them swerved into the opposite lane to avoid the collision, hitting a truck head-on for the effort. Mason watched the pile-up through the window on Rowland's side: car after car, smashing into one another like confused dominoes.

Things had just gone from bad to much, much worse.

At least he appeared to be relatively intact. Rowland seemed uninjured as well, though Mason couldn't decide if that was a good or a bad thing. Without saying a word, Rowland unbuckled his seat belt, cracked his back, opened the side door, and stepped out onto the street, either too angry or too single-minded to speak. Probably both. Mason wasn't sure if he should leave the car too. He didn't want to be spotted, certainly not by the cops he could hear approaching. For the moment, he stayed inside and kept his head low — Rowland was bound to make a scene.

Mr. Huxley's van had tipped over in front of them, and Mason couldn't tell if the inquisitor was still inside. Rowland was on his way to find out; he conjured another red barrier and stepped around the engine like an enraged executioner.

But he became madder still when he realized Mr. Huxley had survived the crash intact enough to flee his vehicle— and was nowhere to be seen. That meant the chase would continue, except now the cops had caught up. It wasn't the police themselves that concerned Mason so much as what Rowland might do to them. After all, he'd already seen him kill one cop in the last forty-eight hours.

Of course, this time there was an audience— and a rather big one at that. Traffic in both directions had ground to a halt, and now people were popping out of their cars to see the pile-up. The cops had also abandoned their traffic-jammed cruisers, and at least six officers were jogging toward them. Surely, more were on their way. Mason could hear the faint beating of a distant helicopter.

An audience, indeed.

"Hold it right there, buddy," yelled one of the cops, a young woman. The others were close behind. They stopped about fifty feet in front of Rowland and took out their guns.

"Oh great," muttered Mason.

Rowland turned around to face them, his barrier still up. It was faint but not invisible, and Mason could see the confusion in their eyes as one asked, "What the hell is that?"

Six pistols were now fixed on Rowland, but he didn't look too worried— just exceptionally frustrated. Mason could hear sirens coming from every direction, growing louder and louder. Backup was on the way.

"Stay where you are," yelled a different cop, "and put your hands up!"

Rowland was not going to abide. He did stand still, however, but with his hands at his sides and his gaze firing at them like shots. After a few seconds, it became apparent — at least to Mason — what he would do instead. Or rather, what he would have these six cops do to one another. Their gun-wielding arms began to move, rotating away from Rowland and toward their colleagues.

"My arm— I'm not doing this! What the fuck!"

He was playing puppeteer with their spirits, six of them all at once, while they were still alive and conscious, something Mason hadn't known was even possible. The realization that it was— it scared him.

Of course, they wouldn't be alive, let alone conscious, much longer, and Mason didn't know how to intervene. Desperately, he screamed at him — "Rowland, don't!" — but it was too late. The six shots went off in unison. The cops fell together at once, like graceless theater performers. The applause followed in the form of panicked screams, but the show wasn't over yet. The backup had only just arrived. Mason needed to get the hell out of there.

With no time to waste, he unsnapped his seat belt and climbed over the driver's seat and out the door. He crouched behind the Cadillac, out of Rowland's view, and then snuck over to the blue car parked behind them. More cops were closing in on Rowland, and no one noticed Mason fleeing the scene.

Once he was far enough away, Mason stopped crouching and started speed-walking, peering over his shoulder at the mess behind him. Unfortunately, it was about to get a whole lot messier.

Now shots were being fired at Rowland, albeit to no avail; the barrier around him bent space and curved the trajectory of every approaching bullet, sending them flying anywhere but toward their target. Still, Rowland retaliated, a little less elegantly this time, ripping out the spirits of two nearby officers. They collapsed like ragdolls. But Mason knew the worst was yet to come. The police helicopter was drumming loudly overhead, and Rowland had just taken notice.

Shots were still being fired at him from a growing onslaught of police, but he'd turned his attention to the sky. He wouldn't want that helicopter following him, which meant it had to be dealt with. Mason knew that all he needed was a line of sight to the pilot. Then the helicopter passed over the bridge and turned back around to face him. The pilot was partially veiled by reflections on the windshield, but for a necromancer like Rowland, it would probably be enough.

Mason didn't see the kill, and for a second thought maybe Rowland had missed, like a sniper with a subpar scope. His wishful thinking quickly faded as the aftermath became far more apparent. The helicopter began flying toward the bridge, tilting awkwardly to one side. Mason started running. Then everyone started running, save Rowland.

Mason first felt the impact. The vibration knocked him off his feet and onto his elbows. He rolled over and saw the fiery explosion, spreading in bursts, from the helicopter and then from cars caught in the chaos. Luckily, he was a couple hundred feet away at the end of the bridge, but even still, he felt anything but safe. The center of Granville Bridge had become a veritable inferno.

The ground shook again. Then the steel beams below began to shriek. The firestorm had stopped spreading, but its reckoning was only now reaching its climax. Just as Mason scrambled to his feet, the middle third of Granville Bridge collapsed into itself. Cars, concrete, and fire fell into the ocean below, splashing and sizzling. Mason kept running, eyeing the destruction over his shoulder. He didn't slow down until he was off the bridge.

Police cruisers, fire trucks, and ambulances were everywhere now. Mason had never seen such chaos. He veered off Granville onto 1st Street to avoid being seen.

He could hear the disaster for blocks and blocks— the screams, the honks, the sirens. But part of him couldn't help but think there might be a silver lining in all this. Rowland had been right at the center of that explosion. Anybody else would surely be dead — and it pained Mason to think that a handful probably were — but, then again, Rowland wasn't anybody else. He was Rowland, and he did have that barrier around him. Could it have withstood all that? Mason hadn't a damn clue. He also wondered whether or not he really wanted Rowland dead, though after seeing him kill all those cops, his doubt was diminishing.

All things considered, Mason figured this ended one of two ways: either Rowland was dead, and his promise to the Spirit Realm fulfilled, or killing him, if that was still the plan, would be even harder than he had imagined.

Chapter 21

ASHA SLID HER laptop into the over-stuffed backpack dangling from her shoulder and joined the crowd of students pouring out of English 120. It was a big class, her biggest, in fact. But they weren't the only students forming a crowd; in the hallway, Asha spotted dozens craning their necks upward at a small TV anchored to the ceiling. It looked like they were watching something on the news. Curious as she always was, Asha went in for a closer look.

"What happened?" she asked the nearest onlooker, a young man with shaggy brown hair.

"Granville Bridge," he replied. "It just, I don't know, collapsed or something."

"You're serious?" She didn't know what else to say.

"Well, not the whole thing," he explained, "just the center."

"How did that happen?"

He shrugged. "I'm not sure. I just started watching a second ago."

Asha turned her attention back toward the television. They were playing an amateur video from just before the bridge fell, shot on a cell phone by the looks of it. Her fellow students watched on eagerly. The footage showed a pile-up at the center of Granville Bridge, at least ten cars, forming a barrier across all four lanes.

"Jesus," said a guy to Asha's left.

But that was just the beginning. The shaky camera shot upward to a helicopter flying over the bridge, trailing the chopper as it swivelled back around. Then it was flying toward the bridge—and it became clear that something was definitely wrong. The helicopter looked out of control, diving awkwardly toward street-level, toward the labyrinth of crashed cars, until finally— boom. People gasped. It looked like something out of a movie. An orange explosion erupted from the heart of Granville Bridge, rolling upward into the early evening sky. That's when the camera was dropped and the footage cut out.

"Oh my god." Asha covered her mouth with both hands.

The news anchor was speaking again, but the TV was muted and out of reach. Still, many stayed watching as Asha left the building, trying but failing to digest what she'd just witnessed.

Outside, the sky had turned a fleeting orange. Clouds were gathering high above the setting sun, never far from sight this time of year. It was supposed to rain tonight, but of course it always did in Terminal City.

A few feet out the door, Asha's phone started ringing. She fetched it from her coat pocket. It was her mother.

"Hi, Mom."

"Just checking to see that you're okay," she said.

"I'm fine," replied Asha.

"Okay. Good. I knew you would be. You saw the news?"

"Yeah, just now on my way from class."

"Your father takes that bridge every day for work," said Asha's mother. "He crossed it half an hour before it fell— that's what he told me. I still can't believe it. The man on the news said twenty people are dead, maybe more."

"That's terrible."

"I'm just glad you're safe."

"I was in class," said Asha. And her mother knew it, or at least she should have. Her parents had a copy of her class schedule. Not because Asha wanted them to have one, mind you. Rather, it was because they paid her tuition, and nothing in this life comes free.

"When are you coming home next?" It was the same question her mother always asked before they said their good-byes.

"I'm not sure," replied Asha. "I'm pretty busy with midterms. Maybe next weekend."

"Okay." She sounded a little hurt. "Your aunt is going to be staying with us that weekend. It would be good if you spent some time with her. We don't get to see her often. It's been a few years. We told her how good you've been doing in your classes, and she's very impressed. You know, your cousin—"

"Okay, okay." Asha stopped her there. She hated being talked about like a commodity, hated being compared with family friends and relatives, as if her accomplishments validated her mother's parenting skills. "I'll come home next weekend. I promise."

"Great." That had done the trick. "I'll let you go, then. Sounds like you have lots of studying to do."

"Yeah." Of course, Asha had no intention of starting tonight.

"Love you," said her mother. "Stay safe."

"You too."

"Bye."

"See ya." Asha hung up first.

With her phone still in hand, Asha jaywalked across University Avenue, a main street that looped around Carwin. She felt her fingers vibrate just as she reached the other side.

It was a text message from Mason.

She hadn't talked to him in two days, not since the night they walked around campus. The night she'd told him she wasn't ready to jump into anything. It seemed then that he had taken the news well enough, but she'd messaged and called him since, and he hadn't replied. Until now, that is. She liked Mason, quite a lot in fact, but she needed a bit more time, at least before she got serious. She wasn't sure he understood that. Maybe he felt rejected. Or maybe he just needed time too.

After a moment of hesitation, Asha thumbed her phone's touchscreen and opened the text message: *Hey, sorry for the late reply. Had to deal with family stuff then my battery died. When are you free next?*

Asha wondered if she was in the mood to see Mason. Her gut quickly provided an answer, but she waited five minutes to reply anyway: *I'm free tonight. Want to come over?*

Mason's response was quicker: *Sure. When?*

In 30?

Sounds good.

Did you see what happened to Granville Bridge?

Yeah... See you soon.

Asha pocketed her phone. She was almost home now, and it was getting dark. What little color that remained in the clouds overhead had turned from orange to a strange crimson. *Neat sunset*. She thought nothing more of it.

Chapter 22

PUNCTUAL AS EVER, Mason knocked on Asha's apartment door twenty-nine minutes after she'd said to come in thirty. She let him in, hesitated, and then hugged him.

"It everything okay?" she asked, closing and locking the door behind him.

Mason nodded. "Yeah. Sorry about the disappearing act."

"I understand," she replied. "Life happens sometimes."

Death too, thought Mason.

"You look pale," said Asha. "Paler than usual, anyhow. You sure you're okay?"

He nodded again. "Just losing my summer tan," he told her. The truth wasn't an option here.

"So that was you tanned?" she said.

"Yeah," he replied.

"You look even more like a vampire than usual."

"I heard they're in fashion right now."

"I didn't say it was a bad thing." Asha perused the fridge before reaching inside. "I have half a bottle of wine left. Do you want a glass?"

"Always." A cigarette would have been nice too; it had been days since his last.

She grabbed two over-sized wine glasses from the cupboard above the sink and poured them both some chardonnay.

"Thanks." Mason took a quick swig from his.

Asha sat herself on a cheap-looking metal stool beside the counter. "I wanted to say I'm sorry," she said. "Sorry that I can't be clearer with you."

"What do you mean?" he asked.

"Clearer about us."

"Right." Mason sipped his wine. "It's okay."

"You're not mad?" She was twirling the lock of hair that dangled down her chest, her arms folded together.

"No, of course not." And that was the truth. Though even if it hadn't been, Mason was too exhausted to be mad right now. Too tired to fight. He took a seat as well, on the stool beside hers.

"So, I was wondering something," said Asha, in a tone that suggested she was changing the subject.

"What's that?"

She set down her glass. "I was wondering what you were like in high school."

"That was a long time ago," replied Mason.

"Not that long ago. Don't you ever get, I don't know, nostalgic?"

"Not if I can help it."

"Was it that bad?" Asha grinned just a little.

"Let's be honest, I'm kind of a strange guy," he said. "Strange and high school don't really go together."

"Were you bullied?" she asked.

"At first," he replied, "until everyone got a little older and stopped caring. I stopped caring too. I actually did this thing in my head when I realized I wasn't ever going to fit in." Mason held up both hands, one over the other, straightening his fingers until they were parallel. "I imagined there were these two lines, and most people, they existed somewhere in between them." He peered through the space between his hands. "But I knew I didn't. I existed somewhere outside them. So the question for me was where to place myself. It had to be either below or above the lines because clearly I didn't fit within them. And, well, I decided I wanted to live above them. But that meant being better than they were, being smarter, holding myself to a higher standard. Even when it was inconvenient. Even when it made me feel like more of an outsider than I already was."

"Do you still hold yourself to a higher standard?" asked Asha.

"I try," said Mason.

"I see. That explains why you're so rational about everything all the time." Asha poked him.

"Well, somebody needs to be." He appreciated her poke. "Your turn now. What was your high school experience like? I bet you were popular."

"Why do you think that?" she asked.

"For the obvious reason." Mason blushed; the color made him look more like his old self.

"Which is?"

"You're, you know... a very good-looking woman."

"Why thank you, Mason Cross." She was teasing him, but he could tell she enjoyed hearing him say the words. "I guess I was pretty popular in high school, but I definitely didn't let it get to my head," said Asha. "Being popular isn't all it's cracked up to be. It was just more... pressure. Pressure to look a certain way, to act a certain way. To be honest, I don't miss it one bit. My parents already pressure me enough, my mom especially. I put a lot of pressure on myself too. The last thing I need is more people expecting me to be someone I'm not.

"Does your mom pressure you at all?" she asked.

Mason shrugged. "Not really. I think she just wants me to be happy. My dad used to. Well, sort of. In a passive-aggressive kind of way. I could always just tell with him, like he expected me to be making all the same decisions that he made at my age. He thought I was wasting time, wasting my intellect or whatever." Mason paused and then chuckled to himself. "If I'm being honest with you, I probably was wasting a bit of time just to spite him. Not because I didn't love him, but I wanted to teach him a lesson, make him realize I wasn't his fucking reincarnation. Bit of a vicious cycle, I guess."

"Men." Asha shook her head, smiling.

"What?"

"That's just such a man thing to do."

Mason didn't take it personally. "Like I said before, we're all clichés— even me."

"Well, no one can be perfect," she said.

"I don't know. I think you come pretty damn close."

Asha visibly recoiled at the very idea. "No. God, no. Why do men think women want to hear that? That we're perfect? It's just another idea no woman can live up to."

"I didn't mean it like that." Mason held his hands out like a shield.

"I know, I know," she replied. "You're just trying to be sweet. I'm sorry. Like I said, I'm not perfect. Far from it."

"We can talk about that if you prefer," he said.

"Talk about what?" she asked.

"All your flaws."

Asha laughed. "I don't think there's enough time for that."

"Well, pick one then," said Mason. "Come on. I've shared personal things with you."

"I don't know." Asha topped up her glass of wine. "It's kind of embarrassing." She turned toward the nearest window, one of only two in her tiny bachelor apartment. "Okay, fine," she said. "I have these panic attacks sometimes. Like when something is really stressing me out, or actually it's usually a bunch of stuff, piling up until I feel like I can't breathe. Sometimes it gets really intense, and I need to stop whatever I'm doing, and… yeah."

"How do you calm yourself down?" he asked.

She looked back toward him. "Sometimes with a couple drinks."

"Cheers to that."

"I also remind myself that I can't be everything for everyone," she said.

"That's true," replied Mason. "But if it were up to me, I still wouldn't change a single thing about you. I don't care what you say."

"You're cute, Mason." Asha brushed his leg. "I don't believe you, but you're cute."

This time, Mason made the first move. He hadn't planned on kissing Asha tonight but fuck it. He'd just been to hell and back, more or less literally, and life felt shorter than it had just a few days ago— since the last time he'd seen her. Between then and now, he'd witnessed so much ugliness and she was so the opposite. Thankfully, the kiss was well-received. She leaned her body into his. There were no regrets this time.

When the kiss finally broke, Asha wore a satisfied grin. Neither of them knew what it meant, but it certainly felt good. It felt right. "That was unexpected," she said.

"Sorry." He wasn't, really, and didn't look it either.

"Don't be." Asha hooked her finger into the collar of his shirt and led him from the kitchen to her bed. Mason didn't resist. She pulled him down onto the sheets beside her. They bounced, and then they kissed again. Slowly, she pushed his chest with her fingertips until he was lying flat on his back. Then she climbed on top.

Mason couldn't think of anything clever to say.

Asha mounted herself on his waist and began unbuttoning his favorite shirt (he always wore one of his favorites when he knew he would see her). But Mason didn't let her finish. He sat upright to kiss her again, and because he could unbutton it faster. Besides, he should take control — even if it felt a little staged on his end — because women liked that. Or at least he'd read something somewhere to that effect. He lifted her up as best he could, kind of awkwardly, and swung her around, planting himself on top. Good enough. She moaned and pushed her pelvis into his. She did indeed like that.

Their kisses became deeper. He cupped one of her breasts, caressing it. She ran her hand through his hair and down his spine. Mason kissed and sucked on her neck. Asha liked that too.

"I knew you were a vampire," she said.

"Oh yeah?" He bit her softly.

She traced his chest with her index finger. "Yeah." Then she moved her hand downward in the space between their bodies, past his navel, past his belt, and into his jeans.

Lying next to Asha's warm body, her head on his chest, Mason wondered about the coldness he now carried with him. He felt rather content at the moment, even when his thoughts drifted to dark places, so there was hope for reprieve. If his present happiness was diminished from what it could have been, he couldn't tell. Even with death weighing on him more heavily than ever before, Mason was the happiest he'd been since before his father died. The feeling was fleeting, he knew, but he'd enjoy it while it lasted.

Asha, meanwhile, slipped in and out of consciousness. She seemed just as content as he was, or at the very least cozy. Her bed's thick comforter had been tossed aside during sex and now covered only their feet, but they kept each other warm enough.

Outside, it started to pour. Mason could hear the soft drumming of raindrops through the window.

"So, when was the last time you, you know?" Asha still had her eyes shut. "Before tonight, obviously."

"The last time I you-knowed?" replied Mason. "It's been a bit."

"You weren't a virgin, were you?" she asked.

"No." He sounded only a little defensive. "I dated this girl for about six months a couple years back. We had lots of you-know. But I guess it has been a while."

"No complaints." Asha kissed his chest. "You were great. And also very, how should I put this, in your head. Not in a bad way. It just seemed like you were thinking about something really intensely the whole time."

"Huh. Is that weird?"

"We're all weird, Mason. So, what were you thinking about?"

"During sex?" he asked.

She nodded, her eyes still closed.

"Honestly, nothing deep," said Mason. "I was probably just thinking about the best way to have sex with you. Like, sex strategies."

"Sex strategies?"

"Yeah, basically."

"Are you sure you weren't unraveling the mysteries of the universe while you were doing me?" She opened her eyes and looked up from his chest to his face.

"Well," he said, "you were pretty stellar."

She smiled. "You too, emo vampire."

"Girls always say that, though," replied Mason, "regardless of whether or not it's true."

"How would you know? You've only been with two of us." She poked his arm.

"I never said that."

"Then how many have you been with?" she asked.

"Two," he answered frankly, "but you still inferred."

"I'm good at inferring." She slid herself up his body and kissed him on the lips. "Want another drink?"

"Sure."

Asha kissed him one more time before getting out of bed. Mason sat upright and eyed her appreciatively as she moved about the apartment naked. Save for her socks. Somehow, those had stayed on. He enjoyed looking at her almost as much as he enjoyed touching her, at least like this.

She poured the rest of the wine, which wasn't much, into a single glass. "We'll share," she said, setting down the bottle.

But two steps out of the kitchen, Asha stopped in her tracks, transfixed by the window in front of her, or more likely what she saw outside it.

"What's the matter?" Mason got to his feet.

The wine glass slipped from her fingers and shattered on the hardwood floor. She jumped but didn't avert her eyes. Mason hurried over and placed a comforting hand on her bare shoulder. Then he followed her gaze to the window, and he understood immediately.

It was the rain. To be clear, not just any rain. This downpour was about as red as blood. Blood that was pouring from the sky and streaming down the window pane.

"What the fuck?" Mason muttered under his breath. He walked over to the window for a better look, scanning a stretch of road from one block to the next. He could see other people standing behind their windows too, scared and confused. He figured they were probably even more frightened than he was. At least he knew it wasn't the apocalypse. Rather, it was... it had to be... oh goddamnit. Fucking Rowland.

Which meant he was still alive. Who else could make the sky bleed?

Mason's heart sank. Of course it couldn't have been that easy. Life had never given him any breaks before, so why should he expect it to start now? Rowland was still out there and Mason's promise to the Spirit Realm still unfulfilled. He almost wished it were the apocalypse— at least no one had made him responsible for that.

And just what the hell was Rowland doing, he wondered? Then it hit him. It was something Lester had once said, back when he first showed him the laboratory underneath the house. Mason had asked about the red lighting. "It's good ambience for doing necromancy," he recalled Lester saying.

Mason figured this rain would be good ambience too. In other words, Rowland had just turned all of Terminal City into a necromantic playground. As to why he had done that, Mason hadn't a clue, but he knew it couldn't be good news. At least, not for anyone whose name didn't start with *R* and end with *owland*.

Well, shit.

Mason returned his attention to Asha.

She finally tore her gaze from the window and looked toward him. "What could possibly make the rain red like that?" She was breathing heavily and hugging her naked body.

Mason consoled her with a hug of his own but didn't offer any answers, even though he had one. "I don't know," he lied.

"Stay here tonight," she said.

Right then, he wanted nothing more in this world than to say yes— and right then, it struck him that he couldn't. He had to go. But it wasn't because of the promise he'd made to the Spirit Realm. Indeed, he still wasn't sure he wanted to kill Rowland, although he was sure he'd have about a snowball's chance in hell if he tried. Rather, he felt responsible because he knew of no one else in Terminal City who could reason with Rowland. Not that he had ever won any of their arguments, mind you, but at least Rowland would give him a chance to speak, which was more than most could say. They had a connection, weird as it was, to death and to each other.

Thus, he had to try. He had to go find Rowland and attempt to stop him from... shit, he didn't even know, but it couldn't be good. He knew it was the right thing to do— his body told him as much. The wretched, right thing to do.

The worst part was leaving Asha behind. "I'm sorry." Mason kissed her one last time. "I want to stay. Believe me. You have no idea. But there's something I need to go take care of."

She didn't look pleased. "You're leaving?"

He began gathering his clothes— his pants and socks from the floor, his shirt from the bed. "I'm sorry." He meant it. "I wish I could stay."

"You're leaving right now?" She grabbed her housecoat from the closet and wrapped herself in it, no longer wanting to be naked in front of him. "I don't understand."

"I'm sorry." Mason slid on his right pant leg.

"Stop fucking saying you're sorry." Asha was equal parts mad and scared. "What is it you have to go do? What's so goddamn important?"

"I wish I could tell you." Mason figured that was probably the last thing she wanted to hear. If only he were a good liar, he might have been able to handle this better.

Asha shook her head. "Whatever."

"I'll make this up to you," he told her. "I swear."

"How do you know it's even safe to go outside?" she asked. "How do you know that red shit won't burn your face off or something?"

"I'll be fine," said Mason. But she did have a good point; hopefully, he wasn't wrong about the nature of the rain.

"You're acting like you know what's going on out there." She nodded toward the window.

He didn't tell her otherwise.

"I want to know, Mason," she said. "Whatever it is, if you know something about all this, tell me. Stop being so cryptic or protective or whatever. I deserve to know."

She wasn't wrong, but that didn't mean telling her the truth was the right thing to do. For a moment, he entertained the idea, mentally tracing the consequences from point A to Z. If he told her he was a necromancer, he'd have to prove it. Once he did that, she'd want to see more. She'd want to know more. Eventually, she'd want to try it herself too— because who could resist? And once she became like him, a necromancer in her own right, she would face the same dangers he did. And that, Mason couldn't allow. He pictured Mr. Huxley cornering her, shooting her— the gasoline. He'd sooner die, again, than let that happen.

And so he said, "I have to leave now," and left it at that.

"Then leave." She stayed a cool distance from him.

"I'll come back as soon as I can."

"Whatever."

"I'm sorry."

Asha shook her head and crossed her arms.

Mason stepped through the front door without saying goodbye, closing it shut behind him. He lingered until he heard the lock click from the other side and then ambled down the dim hallway toward the elevator.

Why now? Why did this have to happen tonight of all nights? Rowland, you son of a bitch.

Mason could certainly feel the coldness now.

Chapter 23

MR. HUXLEY WAS nursing a wound back in his motel. It was a modest room with two beds — but now only a single inquisitor. He didn't want to be here, but a rather serious gash over his left eye didn't leave him with much choice. Every inquisitor kept a first-aid kit (hospitals were always a last resort), though he'd never needed to use his before, save for a bandage or two. But a flurry of shattered glass had rained over Mr. Huxley's face in the accident on the bridge, slicing open his forehead.

The biggest cut was only half an inch, but what it lacked in size, the gash made up for in blood. Mr. Huxley had covered the wound with a torn piece of his shirt on the way here — and gotten into an argument with his cab driver, who insisted he go to the hospital — but now he needed a more permanent solution.

With his head bent over the bathroom sink, Mr. Huxley washed his cut with tap water and disinfectant. Then came the hard part. He'd learned how to stitch years ago as part of inquisitor training, but this was something else. This was backward stitching through a mirror — on himself. To make matters worse, his hand was trembling.

Breathe. Damn it, you can do this. You have to do this.

He was used to pain — that wasn't the problem. God knew he'd handled worse. Rather, it was the needle itself and the suture that followed. He'd never liked them, needles that is, though these were more like hooks. And it didn't matter that he'd seen, and done, a lot of shit in the last decade. He simply hated the feeling of cold metal slipping so easily through his flesh, into his body.

The first suture was the hardest. Mr. Huxley started from the bottom, but he wasn't good enough with tweezers to thread the needle through his skin. He made it bleed more. *Son of a bitch.* He tossed the tweezers into the sink and used his right hand instead, pinching the wound shut with his left. This time, he got the needle in. Mr. Huxley yanked it up through the other side of the gash. He knotted the suture string twice before cutting the excess.

One more should do the trick, or at least be good enough. Mr. Huxley got the second one through quicker, but it didn't hurt any less. Afterward, he cleaned his forehead and slapped on a bandage. Of course, he still looked like shit. That kid had done a good number on him in the woods.

Mr. Huxley collapsed onto the toilet seat, exhaling relief. At least that was over. But now what?

That simple question had plagued him since Mr. Underwood's untimely death. Indeed, it permeated every aspect of his life, every time frame that laid in wait. He didn't know what he ought to do with the next minute, the next hour, the next day, week, month, year, decade. It wasn't that he despised necromancers any less — on the contrary, there was one in particular he hated even more — but now he felt aimless. There was no getting around the fact that he couldn't kill Rowland even if he tried. And though he verged on being suicidal, held back by the sinful nature of the act, Mr. Huxley didn't want to give Rowland the satisfaction of killing yet another inquisitor.

Hence, here he was, without even the inkling of a game plan, and he'd always been such a methodical man. So much so that, absent of direction, he no longer knew who he was. Certainly, he was no longer a father or a husband. Now, with his partner gone, he wasn't even a friend. More than ever before, he was a man empty of everything but his cause. And with that, there was only one question left to ask — what next? — and he hadn't the slightest clue.

Mr. Huxley sat up absentmindedly and wandered out of the bathroom. He strolled past his bed, past a pile of dishevelled clothes strewn across the floor, past his pistol on the nightstand, resting atop his King James Bible. He stopped in front of the window at the end of the room. It was dark, but he could hear rain drumming on the pavement outside. He rested his palms on the windowsill and stared into the night.

It took him a second to register what he saw then, but the moment it clicked, he knew where to lay the blame. Only a necromancer could turn rain into blood, only someone possessed by demons.

Did that mean Rowland had finally found him? Instinctively, Mr. Huxley bolted across the room for his gun— a fat lot of good it would do him. And yet, in the face of danger, he felt naked without it. Much like his silver matchbox, tucked away in his blazer pocket— where it always was. Mr. Huxley clicked off the safety on his pistol and double-checked that the door to his motel room was locked. It was. Then he waited silently for anything to happen, but nothing did. Perhaps he was safe, at least for the time being.

But that would mean the rain really was red, not just outside his window but throughout the city. Mr. Huxley grabbed the remote control from the nightstand and clicked on the television, an old, black tube TV. He flipped to the news and, lo and behold, Terminal City was awash in crimson.

Footage was shown of downtown, abandoned by all but a few cars speeding to get home, splashing through bloody puddles. "As you can see, most people have already taken shelter." The news anchor, a middle-aged woman, came back on screen. "Once again, we strongly recommend everyone stay indoors. We still don't know why the rain has turned red in color, nor if it's dangerous. What we can say is that it has certainly been a strange news day. And a tragic one. With me now is meteorologist Harold Buchanan to talk about this remarkable weather. Thanks for joining us, Dr. Buchanan."

"My pleasure."

"So, my first question for you, the one on everyone's mind: why is the rain… red?"

"The truth is we don't know yet. Having said that, it hasn't even been an hour. It can take days or weeks or even months of research to uncover the reasons behind phenomena such as this."

"Of course," said the anchor, "but can you think of any potential ones? Has something like this ever happened before?"

"Well, sort of." Dr. Buchanan hesitated. "Red rain, or blood rain as it's often called, is a known phenomenon, although a rare one. Usually, it occurs when wind whips up fine grains of sand from deserts like the Sahara. These small grains get suspended in the clouds. Up there, they can travel great distances. Once it finally rains, the sand comes down too, making the rain appear reddish in color."

"Do you think that's what's happening right now?" The anchor leaned forward. "Is this just sand?"

"I'm not so sure," replied Dr. Buchanan. "I don't know of a single recorded case of blood rain occurring in the Pacific Northwest. And this red, the shade of it, is a bit... different. Blood rain is generally more of a reddish brown. What we're seeing tonight in Terminal City looks more crimson— more like actual blood.

"There was an instance of red rain in southern India where the culprit was local airborne spores," he added. "In other words, there can be multiple explanations for phenomena like this. We won't know why it happened tonight, in the way that it did, until we study it, and that will take some time."

"I see. Well, we here at TCN have been advising people to stay indoors," said the anchor. "Do you think the rain could be dangerous?"

Dr. Buchanan shrugged. "That seems unlikely, but it's better to be safe than sorry, I suppose."

Mr. Huxley flipped off the TV, dropping the remote onto the bed beside him. He'd heard enough. They didn't know what they were talking about. They didn't know about necromancers. They didn't know Rowland. Then again, he had never seen anything like this either. Necromancers were supposed to be secretive. But just today, Rowland had caused a bridge to explode and now this— *and why this?* Something was going on, he wagered. Something big.

And then there was that kid, whose real name still eluded him. Mr. Huxley had killed him. He'd checked his pulse as he always did (he was a professional, after all), and there was no doubt about it: he had exited this world, just like the rest of them. Only now he was back, and that had never happened before, unless Mr. Huxley was seeing things.... No. He was stressed, sure, on edge, but he still had his wits about him, and that was definitely the necromancer he'd killed that he saw sitting in Rowland's car. He never forgot the faces of people he'd executed, especially the young ones.

Mr. Huxley lit a cigarette and began pacing around the room.

That kid, he was... important somehow, sent back by the devil for ungodly purposes. There was a connection, Mr. Huxley was sure of it now, between Rowland coming back, the blood rain, which he could still hear pattering outside, and that young necromancer's apparent resurrection. All in Terminal City, no less. Satan was at work here. Come to think of it, this might just be the beginning of the end.

Well, Mr. Huxley sure as hell wasn't going to sit by idly. He was a warrior for God, a man of duty. If he couldn't kill Rowland, then he would just have to find another way to help out, another necromancer to kill. Like the one he'd already killed once before. Only a man beholden to the devil could come back to life— save Jesus, of course, who Mr. Huxley was quite sure was no necromancer (he didn't stop to think about it).

With his wound now stitched, Mr. Huxley was ready to go. He picked up his blazer from the bed and dusted it off with a couple hard slaps. Religiously, he checked to see that his steadfast silver matchbox was where it should be, resting in the inner pocket, and then slid on his jacket and grabbed his gun from the nightstand. He made sure the magazine was full and then headed for the door. He didn't bother locking it behind him, and Mr. Huxley, well, he was a man who locked things, checked them twice even— but right now, he wasn't himself.

Unsurprisingly, no one was outside when he reached the parking lot. That was probably for the best. He needed to steal a car, a sinful but necessary deed. Carwin University wasn't exactly walking distance from here, and he had a young necromancer to stop. And this time, he wouldn't leave a body for him to come back to. This time, that kid would burn.

Mr. Huxley stepped out from under the cover of the veranda, carelessly into the rain. And that's all it was, rain. The red was a necromancer's illusion— he'd seen them before, though nothing like this. But he wouldn't let it scare him. God was on his side. He didn't fear death.

Mr. Huxley reached out with both hands and cupped his fingers together until a red pool formed between his palms. Then he carried the water to his mouth and took a swig.

Chapter 24

DEAR GRAND INQUISITOR,
    It would appear that Mr. Uilliam Collins, the Irish-born necromancer we executed a fortnight ago with your blessing, was not without a protégé. There is no doubt that he too is possessed by the same demons that had overtaken Mr. Collins. The young man, foregoing any family name, calls himself only Rowland and looks to be in his early twenties. Last night, he took the life of one of our fellow inquisitors in a quest for vengeance. The victim was a recent recruit, Mr. Sharpe. There were two witnesses to the deed: Mr. Smith and Mr. Elliott. Both tell the same tale. They say Rowland wandered into our camp sometime after midnight, asking for directions. As Mr. Sharpe offered his help, turning his gaze from the young necromancer, Rowland struck him down with a demonic spell. Mr. Elliott managed to shoot Rowland before he was able to harm anyone else, but the wound was not fatal. For now, we have imprisoned and gagged Rowland to prevent him from casting any more spells. With your permission, however, we would like to carry out his execution.
    Mr. Adams
    3rd of May, 1698

Rowland seldom thought of his father, a man he'd hardly known. Rowland wasn't a bastard, but he often felt like one; his parents had been married, but his dad was the other sort of bastard. He had abandoned him and his mother when Rowland was only five, never to return, not once. And that's all Rowland knew of him. In his mind, his father was little more than a blurry silhouette, towering over his five-year-old self. Little more than a blurry bastard who abandoned his wife and child.

Rowland had a surname once, his father's, which his mother kept because he was still her husband, even after all those years, and because she believed, perhaps out of desperation, that he would come back one day. She believed it up until the day she died. Rowland remembered that better than he remembered his father.

And that was just fine with him. Rowland didn't want to remember his dad, and he sure as hell didn't want to carry on his legacy. The day after his mom died, he forever disregarded his family name. From then on, he was just Rowland. Whenever anyone would ask him about it, he'd say it wasn't their business. It didn't leave folks with a favorable impression of him, but then Rowland was never going to be likable— no matter how you sliced him.

He'd nearly been sliced a few different ways only hours ago. In his heart of hearts, Rowland knew he could have died. In those brief but intense moments, as the fire and rubble was bearing down on him, he had feared for his life. But his barrier held, with no small amount of effort on his part, and he lived, unscathed too, save for a small scratch on his cheek. Nonetheless, the narrative in his mind was already course-correcting, telling him his continued existence was, as it had always been, inevitable. You can't kill a god with fire and concrete.

He'd since emerged from the water, drenched but unseen, and had reached a conclusion. He had decided that tonight he would end this war. He knew the inquisitors would be here now. He had given them enough time. And soon their time would be up.

But first, he'd need to get ready and find a way to draw their attention. Clever as he was, Rowland had mustered up a plan that killed two birds — and a whole lot of inquisitors — with one stone: the red rain.

The benefit was twofold. First of all, it would draw their attention— hell, it would get everyone's attention, but the inquisitors would know it was him. And second, it would turn the tide of battle in his favour. Wherever they fought, so long as it was raining, he would have an edge. Spirit energy would be everywhere, pouring over everything. He would be even more powerful than usual, and all he had to do was infuse the clouds.

Nature would take care of the rest. This was Terminal City, after all; it rarely stopped raining long enough for the ground to dry this time of year.

The only step that remained was finding a vantage point — a place to make his stand. A place to slaughter inquisitors. And Rowland believed he had just found one, right in the heart of downtown.

The Apex was to be the tallest skyscraper in Terminal City. It already was, in fact, even in its uncompleted state. In all, the tower would have seventy storeys, sixty-seven of which had been erected thus far. Although they were not all finished; panes of glass covered the bottom half of the Apex, but the top remained unsheathed, a giant concrete spine.

For Rowland's purposes, the skyscraper was ideal. It would be abandoned at this time of night, and it was the highest vantage point in town — perfect for sending a signal to the many inquisitors down below, no doubt prowling the streets to find him.

To this day, Rowland had still never used a cell phone.

The construction site was locked up, but he found an opening between two chain-link fences that didn't squarely meet. He passed through the foot-wide break shoulder first, stepping in a puddle of mud that had turned red from the rain.

It was pouring even more than he'd expected. Rowland had a small barrier erected over his head, acting as a sort of invisible umbrella, which did little to protect his legs. It looked as if he'd walked through a shallow pool of blood, but at least it wouldn't stain. The redness was only temporary; infused spirit energy left no residue.

If there had been a security guard here, the rain had scared him off. Rowland was all alone, free to scale the tower — or find an easier way up. He was in no mood to climb sixty-seven flights of stairs. Luckily, he spotted a construction elevator around the corner of the tower. He trudged toward it, stepping over concrete blocks and piles of rebar.

Inside the small metal elevator box was a panel. A panel in need of a key. He didn't have one of those, but he did have something even better: just the right spell. He shocked the panel with a jolt of spirit energy, which had a unique, and in Rowland's opinion under-studied, relationship with electricity. His first attempt was a bit off, but one more jolt did the trick. The light on the panel flickered green as the elevator began to hum. Slowly but surely, the lift creaked upward, toward the top of Terminal City and its low-lying crimson clouds.

No one would ever know what Rowland had really done during those twenty years he was gone. He would be sure of that. He hadn't died, of course, as many had speculated — and no doubt hoped for. He had just… taken a break of sorts, or at least that's how he looked at it now.

The truth was more complex and buried in Rowland's past. Some things no one can escape, even after three centuries.

Rowland had felt lost without Uilliam in the years that followed his execution. It wasn't just his guidance he lacked but his love too, though he would seldom admit that, even to himself. But it was the truth. In the Spirit Realm, it was Uilliam who had pleaded for Rowland's life over his own, a favour that Rowland could never repay and would never forget.

He had summoned him once, after he learned how to do that, but it wasn't the same. Uilliam had resigned to fade away quickly. He was hardly himself. The charming intellectual he knew and loved was lost, preserved only in Rowland's memory. And, perhaps, in his son.

Yes, Uilliam had a son back in Ireland. He had even been a good father, or at least he'd always claimed as much. It was never his intention to abandon his child, anyhow, which would have been a point of contention for Rowland.

But Uilliam had been found out. His wife, a good-hearted, homely woman whom he liked more than loved, would have stood by her husband. But not the townsfolk. He would curse them all, they thought, if they didn't burn him first.

In the end, Uilliam killed three of them, people he once thought were his friends, making his escape in the middle of the night. That his wife wouldn't forgive him for, though he'd never know for sure. He left her what money he could and used the rest to buy passage on a ship to America — to start his new life.

The only time Rowland ever saw Uilliam cry was when he told him of Ireland. And after a decade on his own, Rowland had grown determined to find the boy he'd heard so much about. Peter, his name was. The last living piece of Uilliam.

Finding his late mentor's son, however, was not as easy as he'd hoped. Rowland traveled to Ireland with only a name and an age. But he was a necromancer and could see what others could not. Or rather, feel what they could not. Two months into his trip, in a pub in Dublin, a wave of déjà vu hit Rowland from behind, as if Uilliam were about to walk up to him as he had so many times before. Instead, it was a young man, eighteen maybe, and handsome. Rowland struck up a conversation and eventually the kid told him his name. It was Peter.

The two of them didn't have much in common. Peter was a farmer who liked drinking and girls, and little else that Rowland could surmise. But he was Uilliam's son— there was no doubt about that. And he seemed to be doing well, which Rowland was glad for.

Two more times in Peter's life, Rowland returned to Ireland to check on him, though he never again said hello. He watched from afar, nothing more.

Peter died at age forty-eight of pneumonia, leaving behind a widow and two daughters, one of whom moved to America, not far from Rowland. And so, like he did with Peter, Rowland dropped by her house from time to time, but not once did they speak. Rowland only watched. She eventually had children of her own, and Rowland watched them too. It became a habit, something he neither looked forward to nor dreaded but couldn't stop doing— watching over the generations that Uilliam had left behind.

It wasn't until about twenty years ago that Rowland finally felt compelled to introduce himself to one. At the edge of the world, in Christchurch, New Zealand, Rowland found Ethan, a descendant of his mentor who looked more like him than any of the others ever had. Even his mannerisms reminded Rowland of Uilliam.

Ethan was in college, twenty years old, and popular. Rowland didn't approach him at first. Indeed, he'd never planned to at all. But he couldn't get Ethan out of his mind— or was it Uilliam? In his head, they became one and the same. After watching him from a distance for two months, Rowland saw his chance to say hello in a coffee shop downtown and couldn't resist.

Ethan was reading Plato, after all, Uilliam's favorite. Maybe they weren't so dissimilar— or maybe it was just for school. Seeing that he was reading *The Republic*, Plato's most famous work,

Rowland asked him what he thought about the philosopher's view on art— that it was emotionally manipulative, harmful to society, and best used as a tool by those who knew better.

Ethan shrugged and looked taken aback. Of course he did, thought Rowland. He wasn't Uilliam.

None of them were. None of them ever would be.

Rowland didn't bother Ethan again. He also gave up watching him. All of them, he decided. His descendants were no more his mentor than a stranger on the street. Any trace of Uilliam that remained existed in one man alone: the only person who remembered him. The only person who still cared about him. In other words, he was on his own.

Of course, Rowland already knew this. He always had. Yet for some reason, the knowledge stung like never before, even though he shouldn't care. Gods were solitary by nature— inevitably separated by their power, inevitably alone. And still, he fell into despair.

For most of Rowland's two-decade disappearance, he did very little. He wandered, explored, learned a few new tricks, and watched the world change around him more quickly than ever before, but none of it interested him. Nothing these humans did interested him. He was as bored as he was depressed. And for a long while, it seemed there was no going back.

Until finally, he had an idea.

There was something left in this world for Rowland, after all, an idea so bold it seemed fanciful even to him, but he couldn't remember the last time anything felt so... exhilarating. For a man like Rowland, a lonesome god, there was only one thing left to do, he realized. If the world and its people would not change for the better, then he would just have to change things himself.

That was what Uilliam had always dreamed of— a better, smarter world. A world that wouldn't have exiled him from his home, a world that wouldn't have killed him. Rowland couldn't bring Uilliam back, he knew that, but just maybe he could turn their shared dream into a reality. Just maybe he could still find meaning in his endless existence.

The elevator refused to go any higher. Rowland looked out the window, now nearly atop the tower. He stepped off the lift and onto the Apex's third highest floor, a sub-penthouse that would probably look a lot nicer when it was done. He climbed a set of unfinished stairs to the exposed roof. The blood rain was pouring on him now — his barrier had faded — but this time he embraced it. Embraced the water running down his face, dripping from his nose.

He took a deep breath and stared down at the slim glass towers beneath him, shooting skyward like a monolithic crown. For his plan to work, the first thing Rowland would need to do was eliminate his enemies. Once the inquisitors were dead, it would be easier to build an empire of necromancers. Necromancers who would have him to thank for their safety.

It was time to let the inquisitors see where he was. Time to send out a signal. Time to begin this battle and time to start a revolution.

With one hand, Rowland reached toward the clouds, his fingers curling into a claw, crimson running down his forearm. Then he released a burst of red so bright that all the towers down below shone like sirens. They couldn't have missed that.

Patiently, he waited.

Chapter 25

AT FIRST, MASON thought it might be lightning — red lightning in a red storm — but the flash lingered too long. He traced it to its source, a bright spark atop the Apex. The crimson light washed over downtown like a small sun and then retreated, fading back into darkness. No thunder trailed behind.

Rowland.

Mason had left Asha's apartment five minutes earlier, determined but directionless. He was wandering aimlessly across campus, through the red rain with his black umbrella, when he saw Rowland's beacon. Now at least he had a destination, and it was the tallest tower in town. But getting there would prove its own challenge. It was on the other side of the city, and he was in a bit of a hurry, to say the least. Problem was, no cars were on the road. Everyone was in hiding. There were no busses either. No cabs. No way for him to get downtown in a timely fashion.

Well, no legal way. Mason had always been a law-abiding citizen, more or less. Certainly, he'd never broken any of the really serious ones — like grand theft auto. Of course, even if he could work up the nerve to steal a car, it's not like he knew how to hot-wire one. He was smart, not street smart.

But for once in his life, Mason caught a lucky break. Parked crookedly in a driveway not far from his own was a small blue car with its side door half ajar. The light inside was still on too. Somebody must have been in a panicked hurry to get inside the house. Some poor person more worried about safety than security. Some decent fellow human being who, given the circumstances, was understandably forgetful.

Even the bloody keys were still in the goddamn ignition. As he approached the vehicle, Mason sighed with relief and shame. One man's gift from God was another's stolen car. He promised himself he would return it, assuming he could.

Quickly, Mason collapsed his umbrella, slipped into the driver's seat, and slammed the door shut, hoping no one was watching. He turned the key until the car hummed and then rolled backward out of the driveway. With no time to waste, he sped down the street, double the speed limit, and took a sharp turn onto University Avenue— all the while feeling like the worst neighbor in the world.

Mason didn't pass another car until he drove off campus. He had never seen the city so deserted, as if transformed by some apocalypse, only everyone had their lights on. And they were all watching, waiting for it to stop— or for something else to happen.

With no traffic to contend with, Mason was running red lights and zooming toward downtown in record time. That is, until he nearly smashed into another car. Two cars, actually. The intersection at Broadway Avenue and Burrard Street, one of Terminal City's main arteries, was blocked by a violent crash. A grey pickup truck and a small car, red like the rain, were kissing bumper to bumper under a shower of broken-glass confetti. Mason skidded to a halt, just in time. He'd had his fill of car crashes for the day.

Cautiously, he placed his foot back on the gas pedal and circled around them— and then stopped again. Only this time, it wasn't for his sake. Mason had spotted a woman inside the car, unconscious— or worse. Forgoing his umbrella, he ran outside. The driver's door was locked, but its window was broken; he reached through, careful not to cut his forearm. Unlocking the door, however, was not enough. It was stuck. He pondered for a moment, rain bearing down on him, then planted his right foot on the back door and, after a couple failed attempts, successfully yanked open the front one. He leaned inside.

The woman was lying face down on the steering wheel, hidden under a tussle of auburn hair, her right arm reaching desperately across the dashboard, her left dangling limply from her shoulder. Gently, Mason pushed her back into a sitting position. She didn't twitch, or move, or anything. He brushed the bloody strands of hair off her face — they clung to his fingers — and looked for a sign of life. But her eyes were closed, her face covered in cuts and a stream of blood that trickled down from her forehead. It was worse than he'd thought, worse than he'd hoped. And no one else was coming.

But if he could, Mason was going to save her. He had learned a simple healing spell two weeks ago, although he'd only ever used it to mend a paper cut. The spell was easy enough, in theory; he just needed to infuse her wound with spirit energy, speeding up the healing process to a few seconds. If he could seal the gash on her forehead, he could stop her from bleeding out. At least, that's what he told himself.

He chanted the spell, his hand hovering over her wound, but nothing came of it. He tried once more, then again, faster, and again. "Fuck." Once more. "Fuck, fuck, fuck— come on!" But nothing happened, and nothing would happen. She was already dead, and not a thing he could do at this point would change that.

Mason checked her pulse to be sure, but he already knew the truth. He could feel it, in fact: her spirit, it just wasn't there. It was like Rowland had described in the car. Ever since coming back from the dead, Mason could feel the warmth of spirit energy and the coldness of its absence. And she was cold, even though her blood was still warm.

He stood back up and closed the car door. It felt wrong leaving her, but nothing more could be done. At least not for this woman. There was, of course, something he needed to do. He wasn't quite sure what it was yet, but it began with finding Rowland.

Mason walked back to his stolen car, took a deep breath, and continued on his way, circling around the accident and onto Burrard Street. The Apex was just across the bridge. Burrard Street Bridge, that is. He could see the ruins of Granville Street Bridge in the distance. Traffic into the downtown peninsula was already bad enough, save for tonight; Mason couldn't imagine what it would be like going forward. The fire had been put out, but the sight of Granville Street Bridge, broken in two, seemed no less unreal— especially in this weather.

Things got noisier as he rolled into downtown. He could hear people yelling from their balconies, some worried, some entertained. He counted himself among the former. As Mason passed through an intersection two blocks from his destination, he spotted a corner store that looked open. More or less open. The lights were on and there was a clerk inside, but he was probably feeling nothing if not trapped.

Mason decided to park here. After all, it had been a while since his last cigarette — days, in fact — and if ever he could go for one, it was right now. Maybe he would quit tomorrow, but tonight he had more pressing concerns. Although it probably wouldn't be the last one he'd need. Mason turned off the ignition and stepped outside, this time with his umbrella. The clerk eyed him incredulously as he crossed the street and entered the store.

"Hey." Mason approached the man, a portly red-cheeked forty-something who looked equal parts worried and wary. Mason flipped open his wallet to check how much cash he had left. Not a lot. He asked for the cheap smokes.

"ID?" said the clerk, even at a time like this. He was sitting on a stool behind the counter, periodically glancing back at the small TV beside him. He was watching the news, just like everyone else in Terminal City.

"Sure." Mason showed him his driver's licence.

The clerk nodded and fetched the cigarettes. "You should probably head home, buddy," he said, ringing up the sale. "Could be dangerous out there."

Mason nodded. "I'll be careful."

"It's seven-fifty."

Mason handed him a ten.

The clerk gave him his change then peered out the window. The rain was still coming down hard. "Stay safe," he said.

"Thanks. You too." Mason pitched his umbrella as he walked out, the door chiming a goodbye. He headed down the sidewalk toward the Apex, tearing off the plastic wrap from his new pack of cigarettes before reaching for his lighter. The first puff was always the best, but unlike usual, it offered little comfort this time. And to think, smoking and walking in the rain were his favorite meditations. But right now, each step felt heavier than the last.

His smoke was halfway finished when he arrived out front of Terminal City's tallest tower. Before he could find a way up, however, Mason was in for a scare.

A loud thump. The tinkling of shattered glass. Mason jumped backward, dropping his umbrella before falling on his ass. It took him a couple seconds to register what he'd just seen. A man's body had fallen from above, like a vertical torpedo, crushing the roof of the white van parked ten feet in front of him.

"Jesus." Mason scrambled to his feet then fetched his umbrella. He looked up at the sky before moving any closer, but no one else was falling from it, at least as far as he could tell.

The man's torso had crushed the roof of the van. His head, meanwhile, dangled face down through the shattered windshield, a glass spike jutting through his neck. The red rain made it hard to see where the blood began, but unlike the woman in the car, Mason didn't doubt for a second that this guy was dead.

But who the hell was he? All that Mason could tell was that he was wearing a black suit and that he'd fallen from the Apex. He certainly didn't look like any construction worker Mason had ever seen. Then it hit him. The black suit. It was just like Mr. Huxley's. This guy was an inquisitor— what else? If he'd doubted himself before, he didn't now: Rowland was definitely up there. And he was not alone.

That's when Mason noticed three more vans parked behind this one. He might not be alone either.

"Ms. Westcott, over here!"

Mason didn't know who Ms. Westcott was but decided not to risk it. He bolted toward a station wagon parked across the street, dropping his cigarette in a puddle as he hid himself behind the trunk. Peering around the rear of the car, he watched as more men in black suits, carrying equally black umbrellas, swarmed around their fallen colleague. At their helm was a slender woman, older but attractive. Ms. Westcott, he assumed. She moved closest to the body, examining it in grisly detail, never once looking the least bit fazed.

Mason tried to count the number of inquisitors. There were at least twenty, maybe even thirty. The only thing he was certain of was that he would rather remain unseen.

"Poor, sweet Philip," said Ms. Westcott; things were quiet enough that Mason could hear her clearly. "He was a good lad, a good inquisitor. Dutiful and eager to please. He never once shied away from doing what needed to be done, certainly not tonight. He's with God now, but he'll be missed down here."

"What now?" said a voice in the crowd.

"Ain't that the million-dollar question," she replied. "We may not know much, boys, but we do now know one thing for sure. That evil son of a bitch is up there, and we're going to kill him— mark my words."

"But he knows we're coming."

"Shush, Frank." Ms. Westcott strolled through the men around her; they parted like water. "Of course he knows we're coming, but that don't matter. There are two dozen of us and one of him, and I ain't letting him leave alive. I wager there'll be two sets of stairs going up. We'll flank him, make sure he can't escape. I know it's a long way up, but in the bigger scheme of things, darlings, it's little more than a hop, skip, and a jump."

No one looked particularly happy about the plan, but perhaps pleasing them wasn't her job. From his vantage point, Mason got the impression that nothing was more important to their cruel cause than killing Rowland. Or to this woman.

She split the inquisitors into two groups and assigned each a staircase. "You two stay behind and guard the entrance," she said. "And remember, this ain't a race. Pace yourselves. I'll be going with group one."

"Ms. Westcott, maybe you should stay behind. It's too—"

"I said shush, Frank." She raised her voice this time. "I need to see this through. I need to see Rowland die with my own two lovely eyes. Surely, you gentlemen understand."

There were a few grudging nods.

"Good." Ms. Westcott moved to the front of the pack. "Now, let's do what we do best. Let's go kill a necromancer." She looked at them one by one. "All right, then. Leave your umbrellas."

Mason watched the inquisitors file through a break in the construction site's chain-link fence, mud splashing their ankles. They smashed open the Apex's glass front doors and then disappeared into the tower, one body at a time.

Once they were out of sight, Mason emerged from his hiding spot and walked over to the opening. He considered having one more smoke, but screw it, nothing could cool his nerves at this point— and time wasn't on his side. He just had to do this. He hesitated before stepping through the fence, but adrenaline guided him past the mud and metal.

Just get this over with, he told himself.

"Mr. Cooper, go watch the front entrance."

Oh shit.

Mason ran back without thinking, diving behind the nearest car. Of course he couldn't just walk right in. Sure, it took a lot of nerve, but nerve would only get him so far from this point on. Now, he needed something more. He needed necromancy. Indeed, tonight Mason was bound to find out just how good of a necromancer he really was.

Chapter 26

CLAYTON DIDN'T KNOW what to make of the crimson rain. He'd been caught in it initially, walking back from the wine store with a bottle of Pinot noir in hand. When the rain started dotting the pavement, it took him a few seconds to notice anything was off. Once he realized the rain was red, however, he started running. He and everyone else. Good thing Clayton had only been a block from his place.

That was an hour ago. He'd since showered and rinsed the red from his clothing. As far as he could tell, he was okay, although no less confused.

But right now, he was thinking more about his date with Alicia. The plan had been to meet at her place for dinner, only she hadn't made it home. Alicia had been wrapping up her last class of the week when the rain began, meaning she was stuck on campus, waiting for better weather inside Sherwood Hall with her students.

She had told him as much on the phone — and to stay where he was — but Clayton had decided not to listen. He wanted to see her. He wanted to be there for her. And after a day like today, after seeing so many of his fellow officers — his friends — killed on that bridge, he needed her to be there for him too. He was going to down this bottle of wine one way or another, and he didn't want to do it alone.

Plus, he'd already been outside, and he was fine. This time, he had an umbrella and, more importantly, a car, which he was now driving out of his apartment building garage. He was the only one.

Clayton drove up to Broadway Avenue and took the same lane all the way to Carwin University, only ever passing one other car, speeding in the opposite direction. But he wasn't in the mood to pull anyone over, and he'd blown past a couple yellows himself tonight, so who was he to judge? Well, besides a cop.

Like many universities, Carwin was a bit of a labyrinth. He knew his destination, Sherwood Hall, but getting there was another matter— and this wasn't even his first time. As it turned out, the road he thought would connect to the one he needed to be on didn't, and somehow, he ended up in a cul-de-sac surrounded by houses. He wasn't far from the crime scene he'd investigated yesterday, come to think of it, but a good hike from Sherwood Hall.

"Son of a bitch." Clayton circled back around, ready to drive off, but stopped instead. Much to his surprise, there was a man outside, wearing a suit and walking warily toward one of the houses, unbothered by the red rain, or so it seemed. Clayton took his foot off the gas pedal and rolled almost — but not completely — out of sight, watching him from afar.

The stranger stepped onto the veranda then stopped, peering into the living room window, though the lights inside were off. He tried opening the front door, but it was locked, and apparently, he didn't have a key. Next, he tried the window, but that wouldn't budge either. Clayton started to suspect this man didn't live here. But should he intervene?

The stranger eventually took a few steps backward, and Clayton wondered if he was giving up. The answer, it turned out, was a loud no. The man charged back toward the door, kicking it open— something Clayton had only ever gotten to do once in his career, much to his dismay. But at least his reason had been lawful; this guy, on the other hand, was up to no good. And this time around, Clayton had to be a cop.

Once the suit-wearing stranger had disappeared inside, Clayton turned off the engine and grabbed his handgun from the glove compartment and his umbrella from the back seat. He stepped outside, stuffing his pistol into his jeans, and then took his time walking toward the house, carefully surveying the dimly lit cul-de-sac for anyone else. As far as he could tell, there was just one man, though he'd lost sight of him.

As Clayton inched his way up the driveway, his free hand hovering over his pistol, the kitchen light came on. He could see the stranger's shadow through the blinds, pacing past the window. Clayton left his umbrella on the veranda and stepped through the broken doorway. He walked down the hallway and turned into the kitchen, but the man had moved on.

Clayton tiptoed across the room, growing exponentially nervous every second. There was something about this guy, this house. He couldn't put his finger on it, but a sense of danger poured over him like a sudden, cold sweat. He could feel his heart kicking at his chest, his muscles tightening. It compelled him to reach for his gun.

That's when he heard footsteps behind him. Clayton whirled around, clutching his pistol with both hands, and there he was, the man in the suit, pointing his own gun right back like a vengeful reflection. He looked surprised— maybe even more so than Clayton.

"Who the hell are you?" he asked.

"I'm a police officer," replied Clayton. "Now, put your gun on the ground. Slowly."

The stranger peered back pensively and then around the room, breathing heavily, weighing his options like a disgruntled chess player. His face was covered in cuts and bruises, and he had a fresh bandage over one eye. It looked to Clayton like someone had kicked his ass.

"I'm not going to tell you again." Clayton tightened his grip on the trigger, adrenaline coursing through his veins. "Put your gun on the ground. Right fucking now."

The stranger returned his gaze to Clayton, who saw something in his eyes just then. It was a look he recognized. A look he'd seen only once, in that brief second before two bullets nearly ended his life.

But not this time.

Bang!

The stranger dropped his gun and grunted, stumbling two steps backward, a bullet now lodged in his forearm— exactly where Clayton had intended it to go.

"Kick it toward me, your gun," Clayton instructed him. "Try anything else, I shoot again. And next time, it won't be your arm."

The stranger glared at him disdainfully, clutching his bleeding arm with his left hand. But he did as he was told, kicking the handgun with the tip of his shoe. It slid across the white tile floor and stopped a foot in front of Clayton, who left it where it was and made his way across the kitchen, his own gun pointed at the other man's head.

Normally, Clayton would have told him to get on his stomach at this point, but he'd left his handcuffs in the car. That made things a bit trickier. He would have to escort him there— carefully. "Turn around," he said sharply.

"Yeah, yeah," grumbled the stranger. He was a tall, lanky man, maybe a decade older than Clayton, and exhausted by the looks of him— which may have had something to do with his ravaged face. Hesitantly, he turned toward the hallway.

"Now walk. Slowly." Clayton kept his gun and three feet between them.

"Whatever." The stranger stepped out of the kitchen and into the unlit hall.

Clayton followed. But then, just as he turned the corner— *smack!* The stranger had snatched a ceramic dish off the table around the corner, hurling it at him. It hit Clayton like a hard slap to the face, knocking him off balance. He tripped over his own foot and fell onto his back.

"Piece of—"

Clayton let off a shot without looking, but the stranger had already slipped into the kitchen, where his handgun rested on the floor. Realizing this, Clayton ran into the living room and dived behind the nearest couch. "I should have killed the fucker." He was more than a little angry at himself. The next two shots weren't his: one punched the back of the couch, the other broke the TV behind him. Clayton returned fire with a blind shot, keeping his head hidden, and hit the wall. "Shit."

Shit was right. Another bullet whizzed past him, smashing a hole through the window across the room. Clayton squirmed forward on his elbows toward the edge of the couch and peered around it. He could see the kitchen entrance, the only room with lights on, and the tip of a black shoe poking out from behind the doorframe. Carefully but quickly, Clayton took aim. *I gotcha now.*

Bang! The stranger keeled over toward his foot— and into view. This time, Clayton didn't take any risks. He'd had enough. The next bullet ripped through the corner of the stranger's eye, spinning him forty-five degrees and head-first into the kitchen floor. He didn't move again. *Yeah… I gotcha.* Clayton rolled onto his back and exhaled a heavy sigh.

He spent the next few moments staring at the ceiling, absent of focus or thought. Eventually, he got to his feet, double-checked himself for bullet holes — there were only the two that had already been there — and then walked toward the body of the man he'd just killed. Clayton felt dizzy.

There were two pools of blood, one underneath the stranger's arm, the other under his head, growing and eventually converging. His right eye was still open, his left lost to blood and mutilation. Otherwise, he wore only a grimace. For some reason, Clayton felt he ought to look contemplative, as if searching for meaning in his own demise. But he just looked hurt. And dead.

Clayton sat down on the floor beside him, wondering just who the hell this guy was. He checked all his pockets, first finding a silver matchbox engraved with a cross and then a brown leather wallet. He flipped open the latter and looked inside. According to his driver's licence, he was James Harris, a forty-five-year-old man from Ohio. Clayton checked the billfold and found one-hundred Canadian dollars, eighty American, and twenty Euros. It would seem James traveled a lot.

Clayton also found two small photographs tucked behind his credit card. They looked at least a decade old. One was a picture of a woman, thirty maybe and pretty, the other of two young girls, both blonde, just like the woman. Perhaps they were his family, thought Clayton.

(He was right about that, but what he didn't realize was that these faded, unmarked pictures were the only honest pieces of ID on Miles Huxley's body; like every other inquisitor, he never traveled as himself.)

Clayton put the pictures back where they belonged and the wallet on the closest counter. Then he picked himself up and walked out of the room, not wanting to have to see the man he'd killed for a second longer.

Clayton flicked on the living room light and plunked himself down on the couch that had saved him from at least one bullet. Now what?

Obviously, he had to call this in, which meant not spending the night with Alicia. He decided to send her another text message first: *How are you? Is everything still ok?*

She replied almost immediately: *Yeah. A bit scared. A bit bored.*

Her words calmed him. *Do you need a ride home?* Clayton figured he could spare thirty minutes to help his girlfriend.

Thanks, but don't worry about it. A lot of students are still here. I want to stick around and make sure they're safe.

Of course. I hope I see you soon.

Yeah. Me too.

Clayton smacked his phone down onto the coffee table in front of him and then stared out the window across the room — the one with the bullet hole — at nothing in particular. What a fucked up night. And what an unassumingly fucked up neighborhood: that pool of blood and now this. This was supposed to be the safest part of town, for Christ's sake.

But he could ponder on that later. First, he was going to rest. He was going to see Alicia and put this terrible, terrible day behind him— if he could. That was the plan for tomorrow, anyway. Unfortunately, the night was still young and pouring red.

Chapter 27

VICTORIA COULDN'T REMEMBER the last time she felt this tired. By the looks of her inquisitors, she wasn't alone. She had stopped counting floors a while ago, preferring to remain oblivious. It was always so many more, too many more, simply more than she could handle, at least if she thought about it. So she didn't. Instead, she forced herself to think about other things — like how she would kill Rowland when the time came — as her legs marched on mindlessly, one after the other. Each step, she told herself, was one less step to go. Eventually, she grew so exhausted that even thinking became too much for her.

Then finally, Mitchell placed one of his small hands on her shoulder. Or Mr. Crosby, rather. She kept forgetting to call him by his new title; in her mind, he was still her dutiful assistant. "Wait here, Ms. Westcott," he said. "We're almost at the top."

"Good riddance," she replied between pants.

A handful of inquisitors poured out of the stairwell and onto the floor above her. Victoria couldn't see them from down here, so she listened, half expecting to hear the worst — shots, screams, especially screams — but the only sounds were of footsteps. After about two minutes, the men returned, unharmed.

"There's only one way up from here on," reported Mr. White, a grizzled veteran of the cause. "One stairwell. It's a two-storey penthouse."

"Shoot." They just couldn't catch a break, thought Victoria. "Suppose that means we can't come at him from both sides."

"No, ma'am," added Mitchell, still standing beside her.

"He'll knock us down like dominoes if we all come out from the same stairwell," said Mr. White. "That's assuming he's even up there."

"Where else would he be, sugar?" Victoria was thinking. "Believe you little ol' me, he's up there all right. Waiting, just waiting, because he's old and patient. Waiting for us to file in, one after the other, like sheep. Exhausted sheep. No doubt that's his plan."

"Then what's ours?" asked Mr. White.

Victoria didn't like his tone. "Perhaps you could learn something from our enemy. A bit more patience would suit you well, Mr. White, or did your mother not teach you that?" She let them chuckle before continuing. "Let's regroup with the others first, down on this here floor" — she pointed to the exit beside her — "so as not to be overheard."

Before she could step through, the same handful of inquisitors scanned the floor to make sure it was safe. They returned with nods of assurance. "It's clear," said Mr. White.

Victoria walked ahead of the others to the biggest room she could find. Everything was still metal beams and concrete, dimly lit by the city lights outside. All two dozen of her inquisitors formed a circle around her, standing shoulder to shoulder, as she placed herself in front of a window. Or at least where a window would be; without any glass, it was just a gaping hole into the red storm.

The men's eyes were all on her now. Their oppressive gaze, always a few inches north of hers, just enough to look down at her. She stared back bravely, as she'd gotten good at doing. Appearances were everything.

"All right, fellas," she began. "Here's what we're gonna do. We can't catch him by surprise, but we can make ourselves invisible. Even Rowland needs to see his targets before killing them, so we ain't gonna let him. What we will do is throw a smoke grenade up those penthouse stairs. Because we have something our necromancer friend does not." She paused for a second. "We did bring two pairs of thermal goggles, correct?"

"We did, ma'am."

"Wonderful. Now who are our two best shots?"

Nobody spoke up. While not faint, the praise would certainly be damning — a possible death sentence, and they all knew it. But Victoria followed their eyes, and most of them landed on Mr. White.

He seemed to notice too. "Yeah, yeah," grumbled Mr. White. "I'll kill the fucker."

"I certainly do hope so," said Victoria. "And in your opinion, Mr. White, as you are apparently our foremost expert on the subject of shooting, who among your brothers in arms is our second best?"

Mr. White shrugged. He clearly didn't want to volunteer anyone for this either. "I'm not sure. Maybe Mr. Reid or Mr. Jackson. Mr. Banks is good too."

"I see. Well, are there any volunteers?" She moved her gaze between the three of them.

"I'll go," said Mr. Banks, a little too confidently. "It would be an honor to kill this piece of shit." He was the youngest among them, eager and violent, vices that, in this instance, could prove themselves virtues.

"It's settled, then," Victoria confirmed. "Mr. White and Mr. Banks will, as you so elegantly put it, Mr. Banks, have the honor of killing this piece of shit. Indeed, Rowland is our worst enemy, the most evil necromancer of our time. Maybe of all time. It really is an honor. I'm proud of you boys, and I'll be prouder still when I see him dead. But don't savor it, ya hear me? Kill the bastard the second you see him. You might not get two seconds — not with Rowland. In this instance, you're encouraged to be impatient, Mr. White."

They chuckled again, but this time uneasily. The silence took over quickly, save for the faint rhythm of wind and rain drumming the tower's jagged edges.

"We won't let you down," said Mr. Banks, arched upright like a soldier.

In her heart, Victoria didn't believe him, but she wouldn't let it show. She never did. "Now then, where are those fancy goggles?"

"Just don't shoot me with that thing," said Mr. White, taking the lead.

"I'll be careful, sir," replied Mr. Banks.

Mr. White felt responsible for the young man. It wasn't because he was the better shot or the more experienced inquisitor. It was his face: Mr. Banks looked like a kid to him. He couldn't have been older than twenty-five. He was a big man, sure, but fresh-faced, unwrinkled, unscarred. Mr. White wanted to keep him that way, at least for the rest of the night.

The two of them were alone on the bottom floor of the unfinished penthouse. From here, there was only one storey above them. Ms. Westcott was convinced Rowland would be up there, but Mr. White was less sure— hell, a good part of him hoped he wouldn't be.

He'd caught a glimpse of Rowland once before, way back when he was still green. Rowland had ambushed their headquarters in Dallas, and Mr. White had been one of three inquisitors to make it out alive. Now, two decades later, he was the most senior inquisitor among them. Some of his colleagues said it was a sign, said God was watching over him. But not Mr. White. He'd lasted this long precisely because he didn't think like that, because he knew he could die. All it meant was that he was getting old and pushing his luck. If only he knew how to retire.

Mr. Banks, meanwhile, displayed no hesitation, like he was impersonating a robot or something. Was he truly that brave — that ignorant — wondered Mr. White, or was his confidence only for show? Perhaps he'd find out soon enough.

Mr. White approached the rough, wooden stairs at the north end of the floor— the only way up. With one foot on the bottom step, he peered through the opening above, his gun matching his gaze. Mr. Banks stood right beside him, waiting to hand over the smoke grenade. After examining all that he could, Mr. White gave him the nod. The younger inquisitor smacked the grenade onto his palm. It was time to roll.

Being a good shot didn't make Mr. White a good pitcher, unfortunately, but he figured this shouldn't be too hard— so long as he got the damn thing up there. He flicked on his thermal goggles, signaled Mr. Banks to do the same, took a deep breath, and then tossed the smoke grenade upstairs. It landed with two hard bounces and a roll, spewing out grey smoke wherever it could.

Wasting no time, the two inquisitors sprinted upstairs into their misty veil. Mr. White led the way, Mr. Banks covering him from behind. He scanned the room, stepping slowly now. And then he spotted him through his goggles: an orange and red silhouette of a man, standing idly amid the smoke some thirty feet away. Mr. White recalled Ms. Westcott's sound advice: don't waste a second, or it could be your last. He took aim with his pistol and shot the ghostly figure through its head.

But Rowland didn't fall— or even move, for that matter. He stayed perfectly still and statuesque. Did he miss? Mr. White fired again, and this time something did happen, but not what he was expecting: the silhouette dissipated like steam, fading to nothing. That was not Rowland— the realization settled in like cancer. That was Rowland's illusion.

Mr. White whirled around to check on Mr. Banks, but the young inquisitor was nowhere to be seen. *What the fuck?* It didn't make any sense. He was there a few seconds ago, right beside him. Mr. White's heart was racing now. Realizing that he was no longer the predator, he started making his way back to the staircase. Not that he thought he could actually get out of here alive, but his body was bent on trying.

And then he found him, or at least it looked like him— it was hard to tell through the goggles. Mr. Banks stepped out from behind a concrete wall, almost too casually. Mr. White waved to him. The two stepped forward to meet, Mr. White with his gun aimed and his skepticism loaded. Once they were close, he flipped up his goggles to get a better look at — yes, thank God — Mr. Banks. And for a brief second, he sighed relief.

It was short-lived.

Now, the smoke no longer obscured Mr. Banks, who was bleeding in no small amount. Blood poured from his nostrils, his mouth, his ears, his eyes— his red fucking eyes. In all his years of service, Mr. White had never seen anything like it. Rowland had made Mr. Banks his puppet— or at least the shell of him. The big, young, stupidly eager inquisitor who'd followed him up here was dead. Some protector he was.

This time, Mr. White hesitated, but he still got off the first shot, putting one right through the zombie's heart. It staggered backward, but only from the force of the bullet. Mr. White fired again, his hand shaking now, tearing off a piece of the puppet's ear.

The third shot came from a different gun.

Mr. White's heart, it turned out, was not as resilient. The elder inquisitor fell to his knees, still in shock, his fresh-faced killer towering over him apathetically. And it struck him just then, in his dying seconds, a thing he'd known all these years but could never admit. Mr. White couldn't be more certain of it now. Wherever he was going, it sure as hell wasn't heaven.

◆❖◆

The last gunshot had gone off five minutes ago. Neither Victoria nor her inquisitors had heard or seen anything since, save for their own uneasy glances, bouncing between them like guilty secrets.

"It's been too long." Victoria was staring at her thin silver wristwatch. "They should be back by now."

"What should we do, Ms. Westcott?" asked Mitchell in almost a whisper.

"The only thing we can do, fellas," she replied. "Take Rowland by storm. After all, we still have strength in numbers."

Victoria could tell they liked that plan even less than her last one, and she couldn't blame them. She didn't like it either. "Let's head up one floor and take another gander, boys. All of us now. Maybe we missed something before." She doubted it, but they looked in need of a little false hope.

This time, Victoria headed up with them. They scanned the penthouse floor thoroughly, but it seemed all for naught. There really was only one way up. False hope, indeed. But then, finally, she had an idea.

The thought was interrupted. "They're back!"

Everyone turned their attention north, toward the stairs. Grey smoke still billowed over the top steps — as if Satan himself had conquered the stairway to heaven — but now two pairs of legs had emerged. Mr. White and Mr. Banks walked out of obscurity, slowly and heavily, either exhausted or considerably worse. When the moment of truth finally came, at least one thing was certain: they were not themselves.

Mr. White had a bullet hole in his chest, pumping out blood, and Mr. Banks didn't look any better. They were a gory sight, but it was their eyes that frightened Victoria most. They were solid red. She knew it was the necromancer's witchcraft that made them this way. She knew Mr. White and Mr. Banks were dead.

Still, Victoria hesitated. They all did — but it was Mitchell who paid the price. Victoria was standing right beside him when the bullet from Mr. White's gun flew through the young inquisitor's thin, pasty neck. He seemed not to realize for a second. Then he tried to stop it — all the blood — but the bullet had struck an artery. It was a god-awful sight, Mitchell choking his own neck, red squirting from between his wiry fingers.

And as he collapsed to the ground, unambiguously done for, the bullet storm began.

A hand grabbed Victoria's bicep from behind and pulled her backward. She resisted until she saw it was Mr. Trent, whom she'd always liked. "We need to get you into the stairwell— right now," he said sternly, shielding her body with his. She peeked past him and saw Mr. White and Mr. Banks still standing, riddled with red splotches.

"They're not going down!"

"Shoot 'em in the fucking head!"

That seemed to work. Mr. Banks fell first, but he was joined by at least four more of her inquisitors, she realized— four more bloodied suits, all family men, all her friends. All faithful until the end. She didn't have time to process it. Though she did notice one more thing before Mr. Trent led her into the stairwell. It was Mitchell, poor, sweet Mitchell, pushing himself off the ground, his eyes glimmering red.

Chapter 28

DEATHSPEAK: WITHOUT IT, *necromancy would not exist. It is what links us to the Spirit Realm. Even then, only those who have died can truly understand its meaning. It is, after all, a language intended only for the dead, given to them by the Spirit Realm. It therefore resonates with power and purpose. You see, the dead do not move about as we do. The tools of travel in the Spirit Realm are intention and comprehension— in effect, Deathspeak. Its words have the power to weave spirit energy, even here in the Living Realm.*

Stories are told of necromancers sent back to life, necromancers who truly understand Deathspeak— so much so, they need not even speak it aloud to cast spells. I know of only one man still living with this ability. For the rest of us, Deathspeak is a necessary means to an end.
—Samuel Benedict, *The New Necromancer*

Mason was looking for a way in. The smashed front door wasn't exactly welcoming, blocked by a rather big inquisitor. Hell, he was big in every possible way someone could be— tall, fat, muscular. Just a lot of man. His suit didn't fit him particularly well, and no suit probably ever would. He had the body of a bear.

The bear-man was rotating his gaze from left to right, rhythmically like a slow-motion sprinkler. No doubt he was on the lookout for— well, someone like Mason.

But Mason preferred not to be seen. Problem was, he couldn't find any other way to get inside the tower, which meant he needed a plan to deal with its oversized gatekeeper. At first, he considered throwing a rock to distract him, but the big man might see where it came from— and probably wouldn't be in the mood to play fetch.

Mason pondered some more. Come on, he was a necromancer. He could do better than a rock. Finally, he had an idea.

Mason had experimented with light before, having conjured up more than a few red orbs, but he'd never manifested anything from a distance. For his plan to work, he would need to create a bright point of light at least a block away, something to encourage the inquisitor to inquire away from Mason.

Finding spirit energy at a distance is like finding anything from afar— it takes a bit more effort. But not this time. It might have been the rain, but more likely it was Mason. It struck him then, staring out at his radiant red creation, that he was a very different necromancer now than he had been before his death. The Spirit Realm had told him it would happen. He had a special connection to it now, a connection that would make him more powerful than before, more powerful than other necromancers— well, save for the one he was on his way to meet.

The distraction seemed to be working. The husky inquisitor lumbered away from the building toward the next intersection, squeezing his thick body sideways through the thin break in the fence, his gun held ahead of him like a bowsprit. Mason moved the red orb further and further away. He wasn't sure how long he could keep it up, but the bait had done its job well enough. Now he needed to do his. He stepped out from behind the car shielding him and then hopped the chain-link fence barring his way.

"Fuck." He had cut his hand in the process. The wound was bleeding, but this time his healing spell worked. A little impressed with himself, Mason tiptoed through the mud, as quickly as it would let him, toward the Apex's fancy marble lobby, looking over his shoulder once more before slipping inside.

Bits of broken glass crunched under his heel. It was dark in here. Mason stepped carefully. He could barely see where he was going, but he didn't want to risk drawing attention to himself, so he kept it that way. His shiny distraction had likely faded by now, and he didn't want to give the big guy another target to chase.

Now, to find a way up.

"Hey! You there. You can't be in here."

Shit.

Mason spun around. It wasn't the same inquisitor, but an inquisitor it was. This one was ugly and bald and about his height. He was carrying a flashlight in one hand and a gun in the other— pointed right at Mason.

"Why are you here?" asked the inquisitor.

"Just trying to get out of the rain," replied Mason, hands raised. "What are you— security or something?"

"Or something." He was stalling, wondering what to do with Mason.

Mason was wondering what to do with him.

Before either of them could decide, his heftier colleague stepped into the lobby.

"Find anything?"

The big one shook his head. "Nah, but it looked like necromancy. That light... it was the right shade of red, ya know?"

"Indeed, I do," said the bald one. "And what about you?" He turned his attention back to Mason. "Do *you* know?"

"Know what?" Mason forced a shrug.

"What he's talking about."

"No."

His captor looked torn. "What to do with you," he wondered aloud.

"He's one of them," said the big inquisitor, grimacing like a dog. "I can tell."

"Now, now. We have a process." The bald one fancied himself the voice of reason. "They're all innocent until proven guilty."

"Then let me go," said Mason, "if I'm innocent."

"I didn't say that."

"Yes, you did. Literally two seconds ago."

"You misunderstood me." He sounded flustered.

"Do I at least get a lawyer?" replied Mason.

The inquisitors exchanged a glance. "He's a smart-ass," said the big one. "These fuckin' Canadians, I tell ya."

"We'll wait for Ms. Westcott," said the other with a calming hand wave.

"Can I go?" asked Mason.

"No. Turn around."

Mason did as he was told. There were still two guns pointed at him, after all. The bald inquisitor stepped forward, grabbed Mason's wrists, and then bound them together with a zip tie as tight as he could.

"Sit down." He pointed to the nearest wall. "Over there."

The big one wandered back outside to his post.

"I'm pretty sure this is illegal," said Mason, sitting uncomfortably on the hard marble floor, wriggling his wrists to no avail. The plastic bond wouldn't budge, but it did bite.

The situation wasn't good. He knew what these men were capable of, what they would do to him given the opportunity. He'd already died once finding out; he doubted the Spirit Realm would give him another shot at life. But he couldn't talk his way out of this predicament, not at this point. Technically speaking, they were right about him— he was a necromancer.

But they weren't doing their due diligence. The big one was outside, and the bald one looked lost in thought. Mason could make a move, if only he had the right spell. That's when he spotted the yellow piece of paper poking out of his inside jacket pocket. Rowland's gift.

Craning his neck downward like a hyena, Mason snapped up the small slip of paper with his front teeth. It wasn't easy, but unfolding it proved even harder. He rubbed the paper — and his face — against his leather-clad shoulder over and over until finally it flipped open. Then he dropped the note face up onto his lap and checked on his captor. So far, so good.

He stared down at the note without really reading it. Written in coarse black ink were two lines of Deathspeak, nothing more. They were words that could kill— Rowland had been clear enough about that. If Mason used this spell now, he would be a murderer, just like the man upstairs. And yet what choice did he have? It really was him or them, and he didn't want it to be him. Besides, they probably deserved it.

"What's your name, kid?" The pensive inquisitor had finally returned his attention to Mason.

Mason looked up. "Josh." He said it almost automatically. Maybe this time it would work.

"I go by Mr. Lee. My colleague, Mr. Cooper, the big guy out there, he can be a bit brash."

"I noticed."

"And I apologize," said Mr. Lee from across the room. It surprised Mason. "But understand, Josh, that his heart is in the right place."

Mason had his doubts. "You don't say."

"I know you don't believe me, but the world needs people like Mr. Cooper. We all play our part— in different ways."

"So, what about you?" asked Mason.

"What about me?"

"Why does the world need people like you?"

Mr. Lee smiled. His teeth were stained and crooked, as neglected as the rest of him. "The world needs people like me," he said, "to temper people like Mr. Cooper."

Mason almost laughed. "And me? What purpose do I serve?"

Mr. Lee shrugged with false humility. "Only God knows for sure." And with that pearl of pseudo-wisdom, he returned to his thoughts, pacing around the unlit lobby with his hands folded behind him like a philosopher.

Back to the task at hand. This time, Mason focused on the text. It was hard to read in the dark, but he managed. In fact, he was surprised how easy deciphering it was. He'd memorized how to pronounce Deathspeak, but never before had he truly understood the language. Suddenly, it made sense to him, in a strange but clear way. He probably wouldn't have been able to translate the message for someone else, but he understood its purpose well enough: to transfer life from this realm to the next.

Mason began muttering the chant, more for practice than purpose, but his trial run was cut short. Mr. Lee had noticed something was off.

"What are you reading?" he asked accusingly.

Mason didn't bother to lie this time. The inquisitor was walking toward him. It was now or never. It was him or Mason.

Mason relayed each Deathspoken word more loudly than the last, until he felt their purpose, and then directed them toward Mr. Lee.

The inquisitor reached for his gun and dropped it in the same second. He coughed up a litre of blood, speckling Mason's face crimson. Red dripped from his nose and ears, until finally he fell down face-first, his head thumping the marble floor between Mason's legs.

There was no doubt Mr. Lee was dead. Nor that Mason had killed him.

Mason didn't move for a while, not until the pool of blood spreading underneath Mr. Lee's head nearly touched him. With his back against the wall, Mason rolled his body sideways — away from the dead inquisitor — then scrambled awkwardly to his feet. Standing up was harder than it should have been; he needed to cut the zip tie binding his wrists.

But that would have to wait. Mr. Cooper, the big one, re-emerged from behind the corner, gun in hand. He stared at Mason for two seconds, standing dumbly ten feet away, then shifted his attention to the corpse of Mr. Lee, resting face down behind his killer. Mr. Cooper's eyes widened with realization and then, just as quickly, shrunk beneath a furrowed brow. It was a look that said, *I knew it.* But Mr. Cooper never got a chance to say the words.

Killing him came easy. Automatically, even— like a burnt hand recoiling without thought. Mr. Cooper was dead before Mason even thought to kill him. And yet there he was, dead. Of course, it was a good thing all considered. Mr. Cooper would have done the same to him had Mason given him the chance, albeit via different means. Still, now he had killed two people, the second one before he'd even had a chance to process the first.

But there was little time for that now. Mason had come here for a reason, and killing these men wasn't it. This was just the life he lived these days. Kill or be killed. He fucking hated clichés.

Mr. Cooper had fallen onto his back, his arms stretched outward like a crucifix. Mason stepped over his hand and turned the corner. He went back to the building's shattered front entrance, kneeled, and picked up a jagged piece of glass from the floor. Once he'd cut his bond, he turned back around— back to the task at hand.

And just as he found the stairwell, behind a plain metal door at the end of a hallway, Mason had a realization: he hadn't even chanted the second time. He'd killed Mr. Cooper with hardly more than a mean glance. He'd killed him just like Rowland would have.

Chapter 29

JOAN COULD SEE the frustration in Samuel's eyes. He always got this way when things took too long— intense, irritable. The former, she'd always found attractive. The latter, not so much.

The two of them had been driving through Terminal City and the red rain for the better part of an hour now, looking for a sign, a fluctuation in spirit energy— any clue as to Rowland's whereabouts. So far, they hadn't found a damn thing. Just more empty streets and bleeding gutters. But there was no question he was here— and up to something. The proof was pouring from the sky.

"So many condos." Joan was peering out the passenger side window. "They all look the same, like giant glass blades of grass. Don't get me wrong, it's a pretty city — the mountains, the ocean — but there's something missing here. History, perhaps."

"I like Terminal City," replied Samuel. "I like the newness of it. Maine certainly has history, but Terminal is building toward a future. It feels full of promise."

"And condos," added Joan. She looked tired.

Samuel shook his head, one hand slung over the steering wheel. "This is getting ridiculous. Call Jack and Victor again."

Joan grinded the gum in her mouth, sighing out her nostrils. She'd just phoned them five minutes ago. Had they found something, anything, they would have called back. Samuel, however, didn't know how to wait; he needed to feel in control, to keep scrambling, even when it was futile. Especially when it was futile. But she didn't want to argue with him, not right now. Relationships were about picking your battles. She punched in Victor's number with her thumb.

"Nothing," she reported back to Samuel.

Of course, he already knew that. After a pause, he shook his head. "Even for Rowland, this is... something else," he said. "I mean, look around— he's covered the whole goddamn city. In all my years, I've never seen anything like it. I've never seen such a blatant violation of our laws."

Joan nodded in agreement. Maybe he was finally starting to see things her way. "It can't go unpunished," she said. "We must find a way to reprimand Rowland."

"I still haven't the faintest clue how."

"We'll think of something."

"I can't imagine what," he replied. "We have nothing he wants. Nothing to offer him and nothing to take from him. And he certainly doesn't care what we think. Tell me, how do you exile a man who's already exiled himself?" Samuel turned onto Burrard Street Bridge. "And that, over there." He pointed to the ruins of Terminal City's other downtown crossing. "I know that was him too. What I can't decide, though, is whether he's just being incredibly reckless or if he actually wants to be found out."

"He knows what he's doing," said Joan. "Rowland does everything for a reason. I just wish I knew what it was. What I do know is that he's a threat. To us, to everyone. It only takes one arrogant necromancer, especially in this day and age. Once our secret's out, we're all in danger."

"I wonder." Samuel looked pensive. "Do you think it's inevitable?"

"Do I think what's inevitable?"

"That we'll be found out."

"Not if we do our jobs," she said resolutely.

He didn't look so sure. "To be honest, I don't know anymore. I've been thinking about this a lot lately. I know you really believe in what we do, and I certainly believe in looking out for our fellow necromancers, but just think about how much has changed over the last decade. All those videos being uploaded onto the internet, and smartphones— everyone's recording everything now. How do you keep a secret as big as ours in the information age? One crack in the hull and we all start sinking— you said so yourself."

"You've never been a defeatist, Samuel." Joan racked her brain for a better rebuttal.

"I'm not," he said sternly. "I just wonder if maybe we should be preparing for this. We still work off the assumption that information can be suppressed and controlled, off an outdated worldview. What would we say if people found out? We don't even know. Is it so wrong to have a contingency plan?"

"We don't work in public relations," she replied.

He shrugged. "Maybe one day we will."

"I sincerely hope not."

They were back in the heart of downtown, back in the same intersection they'd driven through thirty minutes ago. Nothing had changed. They were no closer to finding Rowland.

"Maybe it wouldn't be so bad," said Samuel. "At first, yeah, probably. But hasn't history shown us that people change their minds? That they learn to accept new things, new people, new ideas?" He was hand-talking with his free one. "At least, if you give them enough time."

"It's not the same," said Joan. "We're something else. And so far, history has not treated our kind well."

"I'm not saying you're wrong," he replied, "but the world has changed. For the better, I believe. The truth often faces an uphill battle. I mean, Galileo was convicted of heresy, but hey, now everyone knows the Earth rotates the Sun. At the end of the day, the truth won— and aren't we better off knowing?"

She smiled. "I would have never pegged you for an optimist when we first met."

"I don't think I'm an optimist." He almost sounded offended.

"Yes," she said, "you are. And don't change. It's my favorite thing about you."

"You know what my favorite thing about you is?" Samuel looked her in the eyes. "Your amazingly stunning... ass."

Joan spat out her gum and slapped him on the shoulder. They both laughed for the first time in a day, but the smile slipped from her face a moment too soon. "Slow down," she said. "Do you feel that?"

Samuel slowed the car. "Yeah," he said. "I think so. It's very faint."

"Or far away," replied Joan.

"We've already driven everywhere downtown."

"Everywhere but up," she said, her gaze climbing the skyscraper at the end of the block.

"You think he's in one of these towers?"

"I think he's in that tower." She pointed to the tallest one.

"It's still under construction," he replied.

"Exactly," she said. "Think of all the empty floors up there. Lots of room to wage a war. A good place to draw attention to yourself too. I bet he's up top. He could have sent out a signal before we got here, something to attract the inquisitors."

"A light for flies," Samuel chimed in. "Let's check it out."

"It could be crawling with them," she said.

"We'll be careful." He was back to being single-minded. "Call Jack and Victor."

She rang Victor, eagerly this time. "We found something. A fluctuation in spirit energy. Yeah. We think it's coming from inside a tower. Downtown. It's the tallest one. The one under construction. You can't miss it. It's at Burrard and, umm—"

"Nelson," said Samuel.

"Nelson. Are you close? Well, then speed." Joan hung up and turned to Samuel. "They're about ten, maybe fifteen minutes away."

Samuel rolled to a stop along the curb just outside the tower's front entrance. While typically a law-abiding citizen, he was willing to ignore the no-parking sign tonight. Sometimes good deeds needed to be prioritized.

Joan knew that only too well. "I'm ready," she said with a quick exhale.

He nodded and stepped out first. They both knew the rain wouldn't hurt them, but they wasted no time heading to the tower. "Over here." Samuel squeezed himself through a break in the fence that surrounded the construction site.

Joan followed. "This bloody rain better not stain."

He grabbed her hand, enveloping her small fingers in his, as the two of them jogged toward the main entrance. And there it was, their first clue: the glass door leading inside had been shattered, its bits strewn across the floor like ugly jewels. They exchanged a glance, and then Samuel went through shoulder-first, his hand slipping from hers. Joan went in after him.

They walked slowly. The lobby was dark, a contrast to the city outside, like ink spilled over white paper. Samuel pointed ahead— or rather, at a head. The rest of the inquisitor's body was hidden behind the corner.

In her mind, Joan was already reciting a killing spell. She could end a man's life in about two seconds if the situation required it. She always hoped it wouldn't.

Samuel turned the corner, ready to strike. Thankfully, he didn't have to. "There's another one," he whispered. "Dead too."

Dead and then some, thought Joan. Both inquisitors were lying in pools of their own blood.

Samuel brushed her back with his heavy hand. "Jack and Victor will be here soon."

Joan nodded. "Now we know for sure," she said. "Rowland is definitely upstairs."

Indeed, there were many ways a necromancer could kill a man. Some were gentle, others tortuous. Some were clean, some bloody. And by the looks of it, whoever had killed these inquisitors was a brutal executioner.

"Yeah," sighed Samuel. "Who else?"

Chapter 30

THE SOCIETY WE *have described can never grow into a reality or see the light of day, and there will be no end to the troubles of states, or indeed, my dear Glaucon, of humanity itself, till philosophers become rulers in this world, or till those we now call kings and rulers really and truly become philosophers, and political power and philosophy thus come into the same hands.*
—Plato, *The Republic*

Mason was nearing the top of the tower. One misstep and he would fall over from exhaustion. For once, despite the stress, he didn't want a cigarette. He wanted quite the opposite: more clean air than his lungs could hold— and perhaps a new pair of legs.

Gunshots had been echoing down the stairwell for a while now, growing louder the higher he climbed. He'd heard the first one maybe ten minutes ago and wondered when they would run out of bullets. Probably not before he arrived. Mason wasn't lucky enough for that. He would need some form of luck, however. He'd already killed two inquisitors, sure, but there were a hell of a lot more upstairs. Of course, they weren't his target. Rowland was. They were just in the way, but that wouldn't make getting past them any easier.

Mason stopped abruptly. There were three inquisitors two flights of stairs above him, clutching their guns and ducking for cover around a doorframe. Mason didn't waste any time retreating. He couldn't exactly waltz right past them.

"Shit," he mouthed silently. Now what? As far as he could tell, there was no other way up. Could he kill all three inquisitors at once, he wondered? Surely, that's what Rowland would have done, but Mason didn't want to risk it, plus he still didn't like killing people. Not to mention there were more inside; he could hear them.

Stealth was his best option. He'd never mastered the invisibility spell, but he also hadn't tried it since, well, his return as Mason 2.0. Perhaps he'd perform better now. There was only one sure way to find out, and time was as much his enemy as the men upstairs. He couldn't remember the whole chant, but he knew enough to get started.

As Mason spoke each word, it became clearer what should come next, until finally everything came together, as if he understood what it all meant. This time, he went fully invisible, though it took him a few seconds to realize, to see what could not be seen. He held out his right arm and stared at it, or rather where it ought to be. He couldn't see so much as a mole now— just the stairs underneath him. It was a little disconcerting, yet once again he couldn't help but feel proud of himself. Of course, now was not the time for self-congratulations.

Quickly and quietly, Mason sprinted up the stairs on the tips of his toes. All three inquisitors were still ducking behind the wall, clutching their guns, sweating. A bullet whizzed past Mason's head and into the cement wall behind him. That's all it would take, said the voice inside his head that thought this was all a very bad idea. Just one bullet. He took cover barely two feet behind one of the inquisitors. At least his spell was working.

The inquisitors were taking turns popping around the corner, shooting at whatever they could. They seemed rather confused. When finally they took a quick break, one of them reloading his pistol, Mason seized his chance, sprinting out the door into the open. But not for long. He took cover behind the closest concrete pillar and patted himself for bullet holes. So far, so good.

From his new vantage point, Mason surveyed the battleground. At first, it looked to him like everyone should be on the same team. They were all wearing identical black suits. Then he realized some were not like the others. Some were red-eyed zombies. Rowland had made them his puppets. Of course he had.

The man himself, however, was nowhere to be seen. But there was a staircase, Mason noticed, at the northern end of the floor. The zombified inquisitors appeared to be guarding the way up, meaning Rowland must be on the top floor, above everyone else. Of course he was.

After counting to three in his head, Mason abandoned cover and bolted toward the stairs, keeping his head down and, hopefully, away from bullets. Thankfully, he made it in one invisible piece. He put one foot on the first step and— *bam!*

The blood wasn't his, but one side of Mason's face was covered in it. The zombie four feet in front of him had gotten a bullet to the head and Mason a rather gruesome shower— not to mention a good scare. He'd tripped and fallen onto his stomach, but at least he was alive, assuming his heart wasn't about to explode. It certainly felt that way.

Bloodied and trembling, Mason scrambled up the remaining steps, hoping the hard part was over. Indeed, things seemed comparatively peaceful on the top floor. Then again, he couldn't see much of anything, his view obscured by a thin, dissipating veil of smoke. Until, finally, he saw him, no doubt at the very moment he meant to be seen: Rowland, sitting peacefully on a stack of plywood, staring back at him.

"Hello, Mason Cross," he said.

Clearly, Mason was not invisible to him. Or anyone, he realized; he'd become a sculpture of red splotches. Damn blood was everywhere. He let the spell fade as he walked forward.

"You learned the invisibility spell, I see," said Rowland. "You even managed to slip past the inquisitors unseen. Good work. Of course, I allowed you to reach me. I knew you were coming from the moment you stepped inside this tower. It took you a while to get here."

"I was held up," replied Mason, out of breath.

"I see. I took the construction elevator." Rowland pointed to the tower's eastern wall with his long, skeletal thumb. "It was much faster." He nodded toward a pile of bricks across from him. "Take a seat."

Mason was exhausted enough to accept the invitation, not that he should be getting too comfortable.

"One thing I cannot do, unfortunately, is read minds," Rowland said as Mason sat down.

I wouldn't consider that unfortunate, thought Mason.

"So, do tell me, why are you here?" Rowland conjured up a red light between them, warming the dim space as a crimson campfire might. "Surely, you have not changed your mind about killing me."

Mason shook his head. "I'm not going to kill you."

"No," confirmed Rowland, "you are not."

"I just want to talk," said Mason.

"About?"

"About whatever the hell it is you're doing."

"Since you have risked your life to come see me," said Rowland, "you must think it is something bad. Perhaps you even believe you can change my mind. That is a lot of uncertainties, Mason Cross, and yet here you are."

"Honestly, I don't know what the fuck I'm doing," replied Mason. "This was probably a mistake."

"Nonsense." Rowland shook his head. "You may lack information, but you do not lack purpose. You came here because you believed you could do something good. You came believing you could alter the events of tonight for the better. You came here, young necromancer, for a noble reason."

"Well, when you put it that way…" Mason trailed off.

"There is no better way to put it," declared Rowland. "There is a fundamental difference between great men, men like you and me, and the typical human animal. Men like us do not submit to circumstance. We act, even in the face of danger — especially in the face of danger. In the end, Mason Cross, we are here for the same reason. Only our methods are different."

"I'm not so sure about that." Mason resented the comparison. "You still haven't told me what you're doing, or why the sky's bleeding."

And bleeding it was. The smoke had mostly cleared, and the outside world had come back into focus. Unfinished window frames were dripping red, dripping like gory paintings come alive. But the real violence was downstairs; Mason could still hear gunshots, though there seemed to be fewer now.

"The rain was a signal to my enemies," explained Rowland.

"You couldn't have been a bit more, I don't know, subtle about it?" replied Mason.

"No," he said resolutely. "I am done being subtle. History will remember this night, as it should. The rain is appropriate. Rain washes away yesterday's filth, which is precisely what I intend to do, starting tonight. One must clean before one rebuilds. I have big plans, Mason Cross."

Mason couldn't think of any good way to interpret that.

"You think I am cynical about the world, do you not?" asked Rowland.

"Something like that," said Mason.

"Then you are mistaken. A cynic sees only the bad. I see the good quite clearly." Rowland paused — another gunshot rang out from down below — then leaned forward. "Consider how I came here. Like most people these days, I flew. An airplane took me from Boston to Terminal City, across a distance of four-thousand kilometers, in just five hours. It is easy to forget how remarkable that is when it is all you know, but I am old, unlike you. For most of my life, traveling this way has not been possible.

"In so little time," he said, "so much was accomplished. The first controlled planes took to the skies a little over a century ago. I still remember it quite well. Just two decades after that, the earliest airlines emerged, and by the middle of the century, flying had become mainstream.

"It took inventors and engineers a mere half-century to change the world, and their task was immensely complex." Rowland stressed the last two words. "And yet," he continued, "it took the American people five times that long to end institutionalized slavery, one of humanity's most obvious wrongdoings. The question of slavery is simple, the challenge of flying incredibly difficult. Why then, Mason Cross, did slavery take so much longer to remedy?"

Mason was still trying to figure out how any of this was relevant. For now, he played along. "I suppose because one was political," he said. "And the other, well, people left it to the experts."

"Exactly right." Rowland smiled— the one thing he wasn't very good at. "Exactly right," he said again. "People left it to the experts. In politics, there are experts too, but they are experts in a flawed system. They specialize in winning elections, in mass appeal, neither of which should be the goal of government. The goal of government should be to forward humanity. Yet many do quite the opposite, would you not agree?" It wasn't really a question. "Alas, it is no mystery why this happens. We simply have the wrong type of experts in power.

"Plato realized this over two thousand years ago," he continued. "He also offered a solution. A new system, one ruled by philosophers— by the experts who should be in charge." Rowland paused dramatically. "Imagine if the world were run by people like us. Imagine how quickly foolish laws would be revoked and insightful ones implemented. Policy would be rational, based on evidence rather than mass appeal.

"This new system," he said, "is worth fighting for."

"Fight how, exactly?" Mason furrowed his brow.

"However I must," said Rowland. "My ambitions are lofty, I admit, but my expectations are realistic. I know this task could take decades. I know the costs will be high. But in the end, they will be worth it. Starting tonight, I am rewriting history. I will no longer hide in the shadows with the rest of our kind. Step one is to eliminate the threat downstairs. The inquisitors are a nuisance to me, killing off the men and women I would have take up my cause— my fellow necromancers."

"Well, count me out." Mason waved off the prospect like a referee.

"Perhaps you will reconsider your position in time," replied Rowland, who was patient enough to take no offence.

"No!" Mason objected loudly for once. "I won't. What you're talking about is a violent revolution, and I've seen what you do to people who get in your way."

"Every revolution is paid for in lives, Mason Cross, but history still remembers the great ones fondly. Mine will be one of the greatest."

Mason shook his head as if mourning lives yet to be lost and then, lowering his voice, said, "So, this is why you came back after all those years."

"Yes," replied Rowland. "I came back with a purpose, with a plan."

"I don't doubt you'll succeed in killing a lot of people," said Mason, "but I seriously doubt the rest. The world is too complex for one man's plan." He knew it was true but struggled to find the right words.

"People like democracy, and it works," Mason eventually said. "Not perfectly, but it works in reality. It has a proven track record. Your idea is just that— an idea. And not everyone's going to like it. The world is a better place now than ever before, and things keep improving. Why can't you just accept that? Why must people die because you're fucking bored?"

"I expected more from you, Mason Cross."

Stop saying my full name, you weird bastard. Mason had never felt so frustrated. His dad had nothing on this guy.

"I must admit I am a little disappointed," said Rowland. "You blindly accept one reality over another because it is what you know."

"I accept it— but not blindly," Mason shot back. "My eyes are as open as they've ever been. Not everything needs a goddamn revolution."

"Then it seems we have reached an impasse," replied Rowland. "There is no argument you can put forward that I have not already considered. I have been planning this for years. Therefore, only one question remains: what do you intend to do about it?"

Mason didn't answer immediately. He was no more certain of his intentions now than he had been when he arrived. Indeed, he felt stuck. He couldn't accept Rowland's resolution, nor could he sway him. He didn't care about the inquisitors downstairs — as far as Mason was concerned, Rowland could kill them all — but everything afterward was cause for more than a little concern. It was a strange feeling. This was what Mason considered himself best at: winning arguments. But this wasn't philosophy class, and Rowland had the edge of age.

"I don't know," Mason finally said.

A stretch of silence followed, the two of them looking at the air around one another— as if they might spot something else to say. It was an odd moment, but for more than one reason, Mason realized. It had been several minutes since he'd last heard a gunshot. Were the inquisitors all dead?

"They figured out how to kill my puppets," said Rowland, as if he could, in fact, read minds— despite his claim to the contrary. "A shot to the head." He pointed at his own left temple. "It is no matter, though. They are few in number now. I can sense them. They are standing right below us, weighing their options. If they come up here, I will kill them. If they turn back, I will follow— and kill them."

Mason wondered if he should take cover somewhere.

There was another moment of awkward quiet, the city's usual hustle and bustle muted by fear. If Mason closed his eyes, he might forget he was downtown. There were no honks, no hollers, no laughs, no booming car stereos. Only the rain— the seemingly endless rain.

Once again, Rowland spoke first. "You think we are so different, you and I," he said. "We are not. I am much older, yes, but we both face this world alone."

"I suppose," sighed Mason.

Rowland was still leaning over their pseudo-campfire, staring through it. "Plato believed that people are stuck in a cave," he said, "mistaking shadows on the wall for reality. He believed that only philosophers find their way out, find daylight."

"I know the story," said Mason.

"When I was your age, I had a mentor, a great man." Rowland matched eyes with Mason, almost longingly. "He said something to me once that I will never forget. He said it will always be lonely outside the cave."

Mason didn't know what to say, but before another bout of silence could return, a loud boom erupted beneath him — louder and deeper than any gunshot — and suddenly he was falling. Rowland too. Falling through smoke and cement. And perhaps to his death.

If he'd been sitting there with any other man, it probably would have been. Instead, he was alive and mostly unscathed, Rowland's protective red barrier shielding both of them from disaster at every angle. Mason picked himself up, dust billowing beneath him. He had fallen to the floor below and onto a pile of rubble. Rowland was already standing— hell, he probably landed on his feet.

They were surrounded by inquisitors, maybe ten— not even half as many as he'd seen enter the building an hour ago. The rest were bodies on the floor.

"Nice try," said Rowland, trading glances with the men pointing unsteady pistols at his head. One of them took a shot anyway; his bullet hit the barrier then steered left, into the shoulder of another inquisitor.

"Fuck!" The injured inquisitor stumbled backward.

Rowland smirked then killed the shooter, who seemed more shocked than scared— and then more dead than anything. The only question now was who would he kill next? He seemed to be savoring the experience.

Mason couldn't say the same. He was just standing there, useless. That is, until it dawned on him that he had the opportunity he'd thought would never come. The opportunity to kill Rowland. The barrier was between the two of them and everyone else; the only barrier between Mason and Rowland was trust. He knew that if he thought about it too long, the chance would slip away.

So he didn't.

Facing Rowland's back, Mason began reciting the chant in his mind. The elder necromancer had just killed another inquisitor and was distracted from the only real threat in the room. Mason repeated the spell until his head felt like it might explode and then took that as his cue. He seized onto Rowland's wayward spirit, and not a second later, ripped it from his body.

Rowland fell to his knees, still like a statue, and then toppled headfirst off his podium of rubble. He hit the ground open-eyed, looking not frightened but surprised. Surprised and gone from this world.

It wasn't hatred that drove Mason to do it. He felt no emotional reward— if anything, quite the opposite. There was only math. He had killed Rowland, his idealistic acquaintance, the man who'd just saved his life, because more would die if he had not. And because they were not so different, the two of them.

Chapter 31

NO ONE QUITE knew what to do, least of all Mason. He was surrounded by more inquisitors than he could kill, and Rowland's barrier had died with the man himself. Mason didn't know the spell required to recreate his own. He knew how to take lives, but apparently not how to save his own. Clearly, he hadn't thought this through.

Only a few inquisitors were pointing their guns at him, while others were still staring at Rowland's tall, dead body, sprawled face down in front of Mason. They looked just as confused as he was. After all, he had just killed their worst enemy. But he was still a necromancer — he'd just made that as clear as, well, any other day — and they weren't in the business of overlooking that fact.

The only woman among them stepped forward. Mason recognized her from outside the tower.

"I'm Victoria Westcott," she said. "I don't believe we've been acquainted." Nothing in her voice suggested she wanted to be.

For once, Mason gave his real name, but only his first. "Mason," he said, staring at the exit behind her (he didn't have a hope in hell).

"What is your business here, Mason?" she asked. "And why did you just kill your friend?"

"We weren't that close," he said. "I killed him so that he couldn't kill anyone else."

"Sounds a lot like what we do," replied Victoria.

"No," he said firmly. "What you do is genocide. Almost everyone you kill is innocent. You're worse than he was." He nodded toward Rowland's body.

"Necromancy is a poison, young man," she said. "The longer you let poison fester, the worse it gets. Just look at you. You're young, so the poison is only just setting in. But Rowland, he was an old man. How long before you become like him?"

"You're more like him than I am," replied Mason. "I'm not the one killing people to get my way."

"Honey, you just did."

She had a point. "Well," he said, "I won't make it a habit. It's your goddamn mandate."

"Our mandate is to save people," she replied. "However we must. It's called prevention."

"It's called murder. Give me a fucking break."

"That's what I'm trying to decide, dear, but you're not making it easy for me," said Victoria. "On the one hand, you did kill our worst enemy, for which we and God are eternally grateful. On the other, well, by doing so you've proven just how dangerous you already are... and at such a young age." She sighed. "It's one heck of a big ol' Texas-sized pickle."

Since Mason couldn't say anything nice, he said nothing at all. It was his best bet.

"I suppose we could pardon you this once," she continued, "but not unconditionally. Though I may come to regret it, I will let you walk tonight if — and only if — you swear to leave necromancy behind. Invite God into your heart instead. Fill that void in your soul, son, before it consumes you. Promise me you'll do this, that you'll seek salvation, and against my better judgement... you'll be free to go. But we will always be watching you, Mason."

"That's it?" he asked.

"That's it," she said. "Just give me your word."

It should have been an easy decision. All he had to do was say a few words and get the hell out of here. He accepted this, and yet his mouth stayed tensely shut. *Just say you promise,* he told himself. *Just say those two simple words— you don't have to mean it.* But giving them the satisfaction, submitting to them— that's what he couldn't bear. That's what stood between him and life or death: damn pride. And a whole lot of anger. These men and that woman were responsible for his father's death. For Lester's too. Still, it was an easy decision, and yet even after a night like this, it felt like the hardest one he'd ever faced.

"I don't have all night, darling," said Victoria, eyeing him suspiciously.

Mason was red-faced and trembling, his hands forming fists, every unwise urge bearing down on him like gravity. He would give them his empty promise, though. It was the only rational option. He knew his heart's protests were in vain. Better a lie than his life. And Victoria was right: he would make them regret their mercy, if that's what this was. Finally, he opened his mouth to speak.

"Necromancers!" It wasn't the voice everyone was waiting for. An inquisitor ten feet behind Victoria stumbled backward, his bloody nose dotting the floor with red constellations. He gasped once then fell down dead.

In a flash, all eyes abandoned Mason. He took the chance to flee, finding cover behind the makings of a brick fireplace. He couldn't identify any of the new guests, but they were welcome company as far as he was concerned. Anybody was better than these guys.

The gunshots were going off like popcorn again, chaotically if not aimlessly. One of the bullets chipped a piece of brick by Mason's leg. "Shit." He scooted backward.

He counted four of them, necromancers that is, none of whom he recognized. Two looked middle-aged, the tallest one and the woman beside him; the others were maybe thirty. He couldn't have guessed why they were here, but clearly it wasn't by accident.

Everyone was taking cover now, the inquisitors having retreated to the west end of the floor, the necromancers fortifying their position on the east. Mason, meanwhile, was stuck in no man's land, waiting for the battle to end, once again hoping he wouldn't get shot.

But hiding wasn't always an option: An inquisitor was moving toward him, sprinting from cover to cover along the northern wall, trying to get a better vantage point. Until finally, he was running toward the fireplace Mason was hiding behind, though he didn't see him there— at least not yet. Mason knew he had to act now, to use his advantage or lose it. With his back against the bricks, he twisted his torso and fell onto his forearm, into the open, setting his sights on the inquisitor. Quick as rain, Mason tore spirit from body and watched the latter topple mid-stride, rolling over twice before flopping to a full stop.

He was getting too good at this. Already, his kill count for the night had reached four— and this last one had come easiest. He hadn't even gotten a good look at the man's face. Who was he but a nameless threat, a boulder bearing down on him, an inquisitor?

In any case, he was dead, and he wasn't the only one. Mason could see only five inquisitors left, including Victoria. They were guarding her with their lives. It looked less like a fight now and more like a retreat. The necromancers, it seemed, were winning.

"Stand back," one of the inquisitors yelled, waving his pistol at them — for all the good that would do — as he positioned himself in front of Victoria. The five of them were huddled together, easing their way backward into the stairwell out of here. They fired a couple warning shots and then turned sharply and booked it.

The last one through the door didn't make it very far, however; a necromancer, the woman, marched forward and focused all her might on the man unlucky enough to be trailing behind. The necromancer's eyes were red with rage. It took her a second longer to kill him than it would have taken Mason, but she got the job done. And then she collapsed to her knees.

Two others charged ahead of her.

"Just let them go," she muttered somberly. "It's not worth anyone else dying."

Hesitantly, they heeded her words and stopped the chase. "Where's the kid?" asked the youngest-looking one.

Mason resented the term. *That guy's barely older than I am.* Still, he stepped forward on the assumption that these fellow necromancers meant him no harm. "Hi," he said, drawing their attention, but had nothing to add.

The woman returned to her feet and cleared her throat. She wiped the sweat from her forehead as she approached him, stopping at a safe distance. "Who are you?" she asked. "What are you doing here?"

"I'm... one of you," replied Mason. "I'm a necromancer."

"Are you now? My name's Joan. This is Jack and Victor. What do they call you?"

"Mason," he said. "Mason Cross."

She paused. "You're not related to John Cross, are you?"

"He was my dad."

"I see. My condolences. He was a brilliant man, your father." Her gaze wandered from his toward something or someone around the corner, hidden from Mason's view. "Is that why you're here, then?" Her voice cracked. "Revenge?"

"No." Mason shook his head. "Nothing like that. I came here to talk to someone." He pointed toward Rowland's lifeless body. "Him."

Joan's exhausted expression regained some of its former intensity. "Is that…" She approached the corpse— one of many in the room. "I can't believe it," she said. "They killed Rowland." The others looked no less surprised.

"No, it wasn't them," Mason clarified. "It was me. I killed him."

"I find that hard to believe," she replied. "I mean no offence, but you don't look very… seasoned. And I thought you just came here to talk." She sounded defensive.

"That was the plan," he said. "I thought maybe Rowland would listen to me, which was stupid on my part. Anyway, the inquisitors took out the floor beneath us and we fell through. Rowland conjured a barrier around both of us. He kept me from being crushed. Then he started killing them, one by one, with his back turned to me. I knew I'd never get another chance like that."

"And that's when you killed him?" asked Joan.

"Yeah," he said. "That's when I killed him."

She still seemed skeptical. "Why?" she asked. "If he saved you, like you say, why would you kill him?"

"I didn't want to," replied Mason, "but it seemed like the right thing to do. I hope it was the right thing to do." He caught a glimpse of empathy in her stare.

"I suppose it was," she said, "although I still find it hard to believe— someone as young as you killing the most powerful necromancer in the world."

As Mason considered how to respond to that, he became suddenly aware of just how many dead bodies surrounded him, two of which he was responsible for. It was like those war movies he'd seen. The action flicks never showed the aftermath, but this was the part he would remember. He wouldn't forget those three men piled against the wall behind Joan, riddled with bullet holes, their blood leaking into the same red pool. They were all the same now, all faceless— one of them almost literally.

"I'm like him," Mason finally said. "Rowland, I mean. Two nights ago, I was killed by an inquisitor." He made his hand into the shape of a gun and pointed the barrel at his chest. "I took a bullet right here and woke up in the Spirit Realm. I found my father pretty quickly then told him what happened. Of course, my old man was too stubborn to let me die, even though I was already dead. He took me to some big talking head that said it was the Spirit Realm, and then he pleaded for my life."

Mason couldn't tell if they were buying any of this, but frankly, he didn't care. "At first, the Spirit Realm wouldn't play ball, said that every once in a while some necromancer like me would come along and beg for his life back. And every time the Spirit Realm gave them the same answer: no. You see, it regretted the last time it sent someone back. It regretted Rowland."

"So, I made a promise," he continued, "to kill Rowland. My father convinced the Spirit Realm that things here had gotten so bad that intervention was necessary. I would be a sort of silver bullet. I would do everything in my power to kill Rowland for as long as we both lived.

"That's not why I killed him, though," he added. "I did it because if I didn't, he would have killed a lot of people— more than you probably know. It wasn't because of the promise. It was my decision. Good or bad, it was mine." Mason felt that was important to say. "But it made it easier, coming back from the dead. It made me more powerful, more like him."

"That's quite a story," replied Joan, still skeptical, though now it seemed like she wanted to believe him. "Perhaps it's my turn to open up. I'm what's called a guardian."

"I've heard of you," said Mason. "Not you, specifically, but I know the term." He'd read a paragraph about guardians in one of the books Lester had told him to read.

"Then I'll cut this short," she said. "We knew Rowland and a large group of inquisitors were coming to Terminal City. We wanted to… defuse the situation."

Mason nodded. "That's what I was trying to do."

"In the long run," Joan said after a pause, "I think you did."

But even in death, Rowland still seemed imposing, thought Mason. Still impervious. As if the world itself might tilt ninety degrees so that he would be standing again, making fools of them all.

"We paid a steep price tonight," she added, walking around a corner.

Mason took that as a cue to follow, trailing behind her with Jack and Victor.

"This is Samuel." Joan bent down so that she could touch his face— while it was still warm. "Samuel Benedict," she said. "He was a guardian too and a better person than I will ever be. He believed people like us had a bright future, even when everything seemed dark. I rarely admitted it to him, but some of that rubbed off on me."

Though she remained stubbornly eloquent, tears streamed down Joan's cheeks unchecked. "I loved him very much," she whispered. "I'll miss him. I'll really, really miss him."

Samuel had a bullet in his chest, not unlike the one that had killed Mason, but he looked like the man Joan described. He looked strong, just like her.

"I'm sorry," said Mason. "I know what it's like to lose someone you love."

She gave him a bittersweet smile. "Indeed."

"Is there anything I can do?"

"No, no," she said. "You've done more tonight than we could ever repay you for. We're going to destroy these bodies and take Samuel's with us, but you should leave now. Use an invisibility spell if you can. If it weren't for the rain, police would already be swarming this place."

"Okay." Mason nodded. "It was good meeting you."

"And you, Mason," replied Joan, standing to shake his hand. "Perhaps we'll meet on better terms next time. I've no doubt we'll be seeing each other again."

On his way out, Mason glanced over at Rowland's body one last time. Then he spoke two words in a whisper so quiet that only the dead might hear them.

"I'm sorry."

Chapter 32

CROSS, JOHN

John Cross passed away suddenly on January 2, at the age of 52. John was a professor of Latin and linguistics at Carwin University and the author of seven books. A highly influential man in his field, John will forever live on through his writing, his groundbreaking ideas, and the countless students he taught over the past two decades, always with unwavering passion. John is survived by his wife, Julie Cross, and their son, Mason Cross.
—*The Terminal City Chronicle*

Mason fulfilled a second promise that night: returning the stolen car. He was careful not to be seen, or at least as careful as one could be driving a stolen vehicle back to its owner. The rain had returned to its natural color, and though it was late, people were re-emerging from the safety of their homes.

The red water had mostly vanished by the time Mason rolled up his neighbor's driveway. He made sure all the windows were dark — they were — but didn't waste a second running from the scene of the crime, his head held down as if it made a difference. He stopped trying once he reached the end of the block, meandering the rest of the way home with a cigarette between his lips.

Mason nearly swallowed it turning the corner into his cul-de-sac. Five cop cars were parked outside his house. There was yellow tape too, stretched across his front lawn. He stopped in his tracks and took a long drag off his cigarette. "What the fuck?" His words were laced with smoke.

Mason's heart assumed the worst, but his mind couldn't figure out what that might be. There was no question that he'd broken more than a few laws tonight, but he'd gone unseen. Besides, the yellow tape meant his home was the crime scene. That didn't make sense. Lester's body was gone, his blood cleaned (Mason had mopped the floors before heading to Asha's). This had to be something else. Maybe something that didn't involve him.

If it did, well, he figured they would find him one way or another. Best get the truth out now. At any rate, he didn't have the willpower to run. He was an exhausted shell of himself, sleep his only desire. And so he marched on home.

As Mason stepped onto his driveway, one of a handful of cops approached him.

"Can I help you?" she asked.

"I live here," he said.

"Oh." She took a second to think. "Wait here, sir."

He had nowhere else to be. Two minutes later, she returned with a man in dark jeans and a black button-down shirt. As he neared, Mason spotted a bandage on his cheek; the wound underneath was still red and purple.

"I'm Detective Stark." He shook Mason's hand. "But call me Clayton. Constable Smith tells me you live here."

"That's right," said Mason.

"Do you know what happened here tonight?" asked Clayton.

Mason shrugged. "No idea." It was the truth. "It's been a strange night." That was equally true.

"You're telling me," replied Clayton. "Well, I'll be straight with ya. A man was shot and killed in your house." He paused to let the information sink in.

Mason was more confused than shocked. "Do you know who shot him? Or why?"

Clayton nodded just once. "Yeah," he said. "I did. A gunfight broke out between us after I followed him into your house. It happened about two hours ago. I was turning my car around and saw him breaking in."

"I see." Mason wondered if an inquisitor had come to kill him— but they'd all been after Rowland tonight, not him. "Thanks, I guess. Is there anything I can do to help?" It seemed like the right thing to say.

"You can come down to the station, answer a few questions for us. And if you don't mind, take a look at the body." Clayton checked his watch. "Not tonight, of course. Sometime next week."

"Okay," said Mason. "But I'm not sure how helpful I'll be."

"Even if we just cross off a few possibilities— it's all useful to us. Do you live here alone?"

Mason had to remind himself that Lester was dead. "Yeah," he replied.

"Is there anywhere else you can stay tonight?" asked Clayton.

"Umm." Mason looked down at his feet. His first thought was Asha, but she wasn't exactly happy with him right now. He didn't want to mess things up even worse, which he would undoubtedly do in his current state. That meant he really only had one option. "I guess I could stay at my mom's place, but it's kind of far."

"Where does your mom live?" Clayton scratched his chin.

"Sanford," said Mason.

"Do you have a car?"

Mason wasn't willing to steal one this time. "No, I don't."

Clayton surveyed the scene behind him. "I can give you a ride," he said. "I'm done here anyway. There's no traffic this time of night. Won't take long."

"You sure?" asked Mason. Because he wasn't. Something about being in a cop car on this particular night made him nervous. But what other option did he have?

"Yeah," replied Clayton. "It's no problem. To be honest, I could use the drive too. Need to clear my head."

"All right." Mason shrugged.

Clayton said his good-byes before leading Mason to his car, a cobalt blue Ford. Mason slid into the passenger seat as Clayton started the engine.

"Before I forget." Clayton popped open the glove compartment and dug out a small leather notebook. "Can I get your full name and number?"

"Mason Cross. Spelled like the crucifix. Six, zero, four, five, five, five, seven, seven, five, three."

Clayton read back the number.

"You got it," confirmed Mason.

"Great. I'll call you Monday." Clayton reached into his jacket pocket and then handed him a card. "In case you need to get in touch beforehand."

"Thanks." As he slid the card away, Mason felt his fingers brush against the note he'd used to kill four men only a couple hours ago.

The car began to move. "So, are you a student here?" asked Clayton.

"Yeah," replied Mason, who would have preferred to skip the small talk.

"What are you taking?"

"Not sure yet. Probably philosophy."

"Oh yeah? I majored sociology myself, but I took a few philosophy courses." Clayton flicked on his turn signal. "You know, back when I was going to Carwin. I'm actually dating a professor here now who, believe it or not, teaches philosophy."

"Is that why you were driving through campus?" asked Mason.

"Yeah," said Clayton. "We had a date tonight. Then the rain started being all… weird. She got stranded inside Sherwood Hall with her students. I was coming to surprise her and, well, I guess she'll be surprised when I tell her about tonight." They were leaving campus now. "Alicia Rutherford— you know her?"

"You're dating Alicia Rutherford?" Mason was taken aback.

"For about a year now," he replied. "She's great. She's one of your teachers, I take it? How do you like her— as a professor, I mean? Don't worry, I won't say anything if it's bad."

"Honestly," said Mason, "she's my favorite." He was warming up to this cop. If Alicia approved of him, he couldn't be all bad.

"I had a feeling she was a good one." Clayton appeared genuinely pleased. "What about you? You got a special someone in your life?"

Mason shrugged. "I'm not entirely sure. I mean, there's someone. I don't know where we're at, but I really like her. Although I may have just screwed things up."

"But you really like her?"

"Yeah. More than any woman I've ever liked. Granted, that's not saying much."

"Well, then you gotta unscrew things," Clayton said matter-of-factly.

"That may be easier said than done," replied Mason.

"What I'm saying is don't give up without a fight. You're young, I get that, but believe me, as someone who's got a good decade on ya, things don't get any easier." Clayton had apparently left his police-officer facade back in Mason's cul-de-sac.

"Women that make you feel that way, that make you feel like they're the best thing that could ever happen to you— they're rare, man. Sometimes I think it only gets harder as you get older. You don't meet as many people. You get more... jaded."

Mason watched the downtown skyline shimmer by in the distance, dimmer than it had been an hour ago. "You're probably right," he said after a moment. "I just need to figure out what to say."

"That's the hard part," replied Clayton. "The part I always fucked up."

Mason was surprised by his nonchalance— in a good way. It made him more at ease.

"But Alicia," Clayton continued, "she just kept giving me chances. I still don't know why, but I'm sure as hell grateful. Take tonight..." He struggled to find his next words. "It could have been a lot harder to get through. It's still hard, don't get me wrong. I shot someone. I killed someone. To tell you the truth, man, I haven't quite wrapped my head around it yet. But knowing I have her— it just makes all the dark stuff a little less dark, you know?"

Mason nodded. "I think so, yeah."

"I used to be a pretty fun dude," said Clayton. "I went out a lot, made friends with everyone. Real extroverted and all that. I was one of those guys everyone liked." He paused for a moment, merging onto the empty highway. "Then something happened a couple years back. Something that changed me. Suddenly, I wasn't enjoying the things I used to. I didn't feel light anymore. I felt heavy. I started seeing a shrink, but that didn't do me any good. Then I read a few of those stupid self-help books. You know, *Ten Ways to Heal Your Soul* or whatever— shit like that. And they all said the same thing. They all said that happiness comes from within. And you know what? That's total bullshit."

Mason laughed, something he hadn't thought possible tonight.

"I'm serious, man. Absolute bullshit. There's a limit," said Clayton, slicing the air with his free hand. "You can only help yourself so much. But like I said, it's tough out there. It's not easy finding a good woman, a good man, whatever you're into. A lot of us, we never do, or we lose them. And so these books say it's all, you know, a state of mind. That it's all about you and how you see the world. But happiness, it ain't, uh— what's the word?"

"Subjective?" offered Mason.

"Exactly," replied Clayton. "Happiness isn't subjective. You can't intellectualize your way there."

"That's a good way of putting it." Mason yawned. "I suppose most people want to believe the world is a simple place with simple answers."

A semi truck rumbled by in the opposite direction.

"Ain't that the truth. But look, man, I'm finally happy again," said Clayton. "In fact, I would say I'm even happier than before because now it's a deeper, realer happiness. It's no easy task, happiness, but it's out there. Somewhere. Fight for your lady friend, that's all I'm saying. We're not meant to be alone, we humans— we didn't evolve that way." He looked back toward the empty stretch of highway ahead of them. "Sorry if I'm rambling a bit. I'm in sort of a weird mood right now."

"Makes two of us," replied Mason.

"It's been a strange night, that's for sure."

Mason couldn't argue with that. Or with sleep, apparently. He was struggling to keep his eyelids from calling it a night.

Clayton noticed. "You look tired," he said. "If you want to nap for a few minutes, go ahead. I'll wake you when we get to Sanford."

Mason nodded, sliding deeper into his seat, eyes already closed. God, he was exhausted.

It was the next day (although not technically) and Mason couldn't remember the last time he'd slept so long. Twelve hours, uninterrupted. His mother told him he was partying too hard. In her defence, this was because he'd lied to her.

Mason had said he was in town for a friend's party. Someone from college— she didn't know him. Sure, he was a crummy liar, but the truth would have seemed far more unbelievable. Of course, that's not why he lied. He just hated worrying her. And she would worry— boy, would she ever. She might even be justified this time. A man had been shot and killed in his house, after all.

But she didn't need to know that. Besides, she seemed happy to have him home. Why ruin that? It was the first time he'd returned since moving out. She had even cooked him afternoon breakfast: scrambled eggs, toast, and black coffee— all made to perfection, at least in his biased opinion.

"I need to buy groceries," she said, walking through the kitchen, keys jingling between her fingers. "Will you still be here when I get back?"

Mason nodded, his mouth stuffed with food. He swallowed. "Until tomorrow, I think."

She looked happy to hear that. "Stay as long as you'd like. This is still your home. Always will be."

He nodded again, muted by another forkful of eggs and toast. She left smiling.

Mason returned his attention to his phone, resting on the counter beside him. Like most men his age, he checked it rather compulsively. Last night, however, its battery died once again— he'd only charged it partially. Of course, he'd been too distracted to notice, but now it bugged him. What if Asha had tried to call?

After scraping his plate clean, Mason headed upstairs to his mother's bedroom. Her phone was not unlike his, and he was hoping it used the same type of charger.

Lucky for him, the plug snapped in perfectly. His phone began booting up within seconds, and Mason felt more relieved than he probably should have. He had one missed call from his mother and a text message from Asha, sent three hours ago. He clicked open the latter.

I'm sorry about last night, it read. *I was scared. You don't owe me anything. I haven't exactly been clear about us.*

It could have been a lot worse, thought Mason, feeling relieved. She hadn't ruled him out, or so he hoped. Quickly, he typed up his response: *I'm sorry too. I'm at my mom's place, but I'm coming back to campus tomorrow. Can we talk about it then? (PS. My phone died again.)*

He took a seat on the bed and waited, not that there was any reason to think she'd reply anytime soon. And yet, not a minute later, the phone in his hand beeped and vibrated at once. She had sent back a single word: *Okay*. It was all he needed to hear.

On that note, Mason abandoned his phone so that it could charge and he could shower. He flicked on the bathroom light and locked the door, even though no one else was home. And for the first time that day, he caught a glimpse of himself in the mirror.

It caught him off guard, his own reflection. He stared at himself for a full minute. But not in vain. He stared because the man staring back was exactly that— a man, not the kid he saw a mere month ago, the last time he stood here.

It wasn't a physical thing, though in some respects he did look different. He was paler— not as pale as he'd been yesterday, mind you. His eyes too, there was a new darkness, a tiredness, that surrounded them. But that wasn't it either. No. It was this: Somehow, in some way he couldn't quite explain, Mason had lost his youth.

And that's when he began to cry. It snuck up on him without warning, without precedence. He just... cried. Cried for the first time since his father's death. Cried like he had never cried before, his head bobbing up and down, tears tracing his cheeks, snot slinking over his lips. He cried like an idiot, falling onto his forearms, and then cried some more. He couldn't have stopped even if he wanted to.

And then he laughed. Mason slid down onto the tile floor, his back against the cupboards, laughing his ass off. Laughing and crying, crying and laughing. "Stupid fucking emotions." He wiped his tears with both hands, still chuckling.

Mason picked himself up and took his shower.

Once he was clean, he left the bathroom with a towel around his waist, yesterday's clothes crumpled on the floor behind him. He crossed the hall to his father's library, Mason's favorite room, feeling refreshed, feeling lighter.

Still dripping from the shower, he stood and stared mindfully at the familiar details around him. The classic books lining each wall. His father's old oak desk, as regal as any desk ever was. The sunlight slipping through the blinds, blotting the floorboards with faint golden hope. He stared and soaked it all in.

Then finally, Mason exhaled.

Chapter 33

I THINK, THEREFORE I AM.
   —René Descartes, *Discourse on the Method*

He'd been here before.

A black sea of chaos: that was the Spirit Realm. Down here, a million stories were unraveling like dreams, crashing and contradicting — if only contradictions existed in death. The Spirit Realm only had two laws: the first one was that, sooner or later, you would fade. Like it or not, you would fade into nothing, into the Spirit Realm, melding into its collective consciousness. And the second law? Once you were down here, there was no going back.

Unless, of course, you were Rowland.

Rowland had been sent back to the Living Realm once before, but not this time. Definitely not this time.

He was, however, determined not to fade— not to give himself over to the Spirit Realm.

It was beckoning him now, as it had been for some time. For all the millions of stories unfolding in the darkness, Rowland's was the one to watch. He could feel the Spirit Realm trailing him with its overarching gaze. The Spirit Realm would say that it didn't take things personally, but Rowland knew better. After three centuries, it had finally gotten him— the one that got away.

Until now, of course. Presently, his only move — the only way he could still spite the Spirit Realm — came in the form of spurning its advances, which even he was growing tired of. The

Spirit Realm wanted to talk, and frankly Rowland had absolutely nothing better to do. Not anymore.

He'd been moseying around the darkness for a while now, passing through glimmering fantasies and grim nightmares. The mind was either a kingdom or a prison, and the Spirit Realm was a patchwork of both. Though fellow spirits rarely acknowledged his presence. Perhaps they couldn't be bothered— perhaps they were simply too far gone.

Except that one: a young boy, nine or ten by the looks of him. He was bald and gaunt, black bags beneath his eyes. Rowland found him curled over crying in the middle of a long, forgotten road. The path wound through an endless forest of dark, jagged crystals, and Rowland could tell they were once beautiful, the crystals, once clear blue, once full of magic. But black lines ran through them now, like cuts below the surface — cuts you couldn't reach or remedy — branching out further and further, each new limb giving birth to two more, until the lines took over and the crystals grew dull and hopeless.

The boy tripped over his own feet scrambling toward Rowland. "Daddy." He picked himself up. "I don't want to die." He was wearing a hospital gown. "Don't leave me, daddy."

Before long, the boy was hugging Rowland's ankles. Rowland said nothing, but he waited until the boy let go, waited until the kid stopped sobbing.

It bothered him still, that boy in the forest of crystals, even though Rowland had grown used to suffering, immune even. Then finally it struck him, the reason he was so unsettled. He couldn't be sure he hadn't imagined the whole damn thing, boy and all. And that more than anything — more than death itself — scared the hell out of him.

The trick was not to lose track of time, Rowland regularly reminded himself. He knew that was the first step to fading: losing your internal clock. He'd already lost his hours, but perhaps he could hold onto his days. He was pretty sure it had been a week since he'd died. A week that the Spirit Realm had been pestering him, weighing over him like a poison cloud.

At last, Rowland was ready to give in.

After all, it didn't matter what the Spirit Realm had to say because he had no intention of listening. Might as well get the sanctimonious spiel over with.

Rowland found his way through the darkness with ease, transporting himself to the bottom of a tall, steep staircase, red light lining the edge of each step. Through the archway above, his host undoubtedly awaited him. Rowland took his time walking up.

As he reached the top, he couldn't help but notice how easy the stairs were; he would have been out of breath had this been the Living Realm. Death had at least one perk, he supposed.

And there, at the other end of its great hall, the Spirit Realm was waiting for Rowland, its eternally emotionless eyes trailing his every movement. Rowland wondered if its attention was divided; the Spirit Realm maintained an aura of omnipotence and omniscience, as if it could be in all places at all times. The Spirit Realm never professed godhood, but it did like to show off its endlessly tall pillars. They were see-through, glimmering columns spinning slowly on either side of Rowland, row after row of them, infinite in number and size. It was a bit much.

"Rowland," it spoke.

The Spirit Realm's enormous face melted into the body of no one in particular: just the anatomy of a human being, if humans were eight feet tall and looked like sculptures made of mercury. A person without the personification. Its sunken chest was a maelstrom of silver, subtle waves rolling outward and down the Spirit Realm's long limbs. Purity incarnate, the Spirit Realm was, unblemished by its endless existence. After three centuries, Rowland was a skeletal mess of scars and veins, even down here. The Spirit Realm was everything he was not and never would be— that, at least, was the message, and Rowland got it loud and clear.

"I am glad you have finally come to see us." The Spirit Realm spoke with no hostility. "How are you?"

Rowland looked dumbfound and then angry. "How am I?"

"Yes," it said. "How are you?"

"Fuck you." It wasn't a phrase Rowland used often. "You assassinated me. You sent that… *child* to kill me."

"We did what was necessary," the Spirit Realm replied. "It brought us no pleasure. Even through our collective wisdom, we could not see the future, could not see what you would become. It was our fault for returning you to the Living Realm. We should not have sent you back. In a normal life, you would not have become the man you are now. For some, time tempers their tendencies. For others, the opposite. Time did not temper you,

Rowland. Your anger, cynicism, and sense of isolation festered for decades, centuries, longer than any other human's before you. You grew more extreme, more powerful— too powerful.

"It was our responsibility," the Spirit Realm said, "to close the door that we had opened, to stop you from wreaking havoc on the world. We wronged you, Rowland, but not last week. We wronged you three hundred years ago."

"And yet," replied Rowland, crimson with rage, "you admit you cannot see the future. You have no idea what I might have accomplished. You simply assumed you knew better, as you always do. You are not as wise as you think. Your so-called collective wisdom is as much your weakness as it is your strength. All the brilliant minds you have absorbed are weighed down by the masses of fools who have faded too."

"My mind is pure," said Rowland.

"Your mind," the Spirit Realm replied, "is corrupt. And we are sorry for that. Perhaps you will learn to see things differently here. Either way, Rowland, you will fade."

Rowland stared into its eyes, or rather where its eyes should have been; the vacant mercury gaps in their place revealed nothing. "We will see about that," he said.

And for a moment, the room became utterly soundless. True silence didn't exist on Earth, but here, as Rowland and the Spirit Realm stood facing one another, it was deafening.

"We have said our apology."

Slowly, the Spirit Realm began morphing again, this time into a silver globe, rising over Rowland into the black sky like an ascending planet. Its white light colored the peaks of the necromancer's creviced face as he stared upward, illuminating his contemptuous glare, his hate.

His hate, which no longer mattered now— because he no longer mattered.

Rowland flew from the hall as fast and as far as he could. Distance was only a feeling in the Spirit Realm, so he settled for the furthest emotion he could find. Rowland found himself back in the black sea that had welcomed him here, deep under water where nothing could be seen or heard.

So, that was that: the last chapter in his relationship with the Spirit Realm. And in a way, the last chapter in his relationship with Uilliam, for he was in there somewhere— the collective consciousness that called itself the Spirit Realm. Unlike Rowland,

Uilliam had faded willingly. And though Rowland still loved him the only way he knew how, he was beginning to realize how far he'd come. Uilliam had been wise, and Rowland had needed him once, but that was then.

No one had reached the heights Rowland had. Not Uilliam, and he'd be damned before he let Mason Cross surpass him. Well, that first part had happened, he supposed — the Spirit Realm had just damned him — but, no, Rowland wouldn't be held back by colloquialisms.

Rowland had lived longer than all of the greats, learned more than any man or woman before him, and from now on, he would follow only his own philosophy. His, he realized, was that humanity had only scratched the surface of greatness. They were stuck in their cycles, but Rowland had broken free. He'd fallen back into the darkness, tumbled down into the cave— but a man was his mind, and Rowland still had his. Even here, in the middle of literal nowhere, it was all he would need.

The philosopher Friedrich Nietzsche birthed a famous saying: *That which does not kill us makes us stronger*. But that old quote was younger than Rowland, and he had already proven once before that, sometimes, the opposite was true.

Bonus

PREVIEW OF WINTER'S END

WHILE INCREDIBLY RARE, *soul stealing spells may be the most heinous, most unforgivable known to necromancy. For victims, the outcome is worse than death.*
—Samuel Benedict, *Advanced Necromancy*

Kyle McDonald knew that tonight was inevitable. Everything was inevitable.

Dragging his razor over his Adam's apple up to his chin, Kyle cut against the grain of his stubble, once, twice, then again, shaving until his skin was perfectly smooth. Bleeding in two spots but smooth. He washed the blood away, splashing his face with handfuls of tap water, then pulled a white towel off its rack. The metal bar twirled and squeaked. He patted his cheeks, eyeing the curved corners of his round face, as soft and slippery as a wet melon— as inoffensively bland too. Thirty years to the day, Kyle was, but people often told him he looked twenty. Looked innocent, cordial, unremarkable. Looked like a Kyle.

Kyle, however, was none of these things, though that was hardly his fault. The universe was clockwork, he had learned. Every moment, every birth, every death, every human being the consequence of what came before them. Cause and effect. Kyle was who he was, what he was, and nothing could change that. His future was already written, his victims already chosen.

Next came his hair. With his flat black comb, Kyle meticulously parted each thin brown strand to one side. Finally, he brushed his teeth, and he was ready.

Kyle used to resent his illness. Psychopath— it sounded more like an accusation. People didn't understand. Then one day he had a life-changing epiphany: it didn't matter. Nothing did. Free will was a facade, he realized. Humans were mere products of nature, and his nature compelled him to consume, to grow. You can't blame a tornado for destroying a few trailers.

Or a psychopathic necromancer for stealing spirits.

The first one had been the hardest. First times usually were, but it wasn't just the chant that proved difficult. More, it was the price: not only a person's life but their afterlife too. A stolen spirit couldn't enter the Spirit Realm, couldn't fade peacefully into nothing. It remained a prisoner within its captor, within Kyle McDonald. It went against everything his parents, talented necromancers in their own right, had taught him. But each time he grew more powerful, albeit increasingly less so. The returns were diminishing. Though not his desire. Nor the voices in his head, dozens of them now, screaming and begging for release— for a real death.

What's more, everyday spirits no longer satiated Kyle's appetite. These days, he had to kill his fellow necromancers. It was the difference between gruel and steak. Necromancers had a special connection to the Spirit Realm, and each spirit was unique. "Like a fine wine," he often said. Thing was, he could only tap into that special connection if he consumed it, and Kyle needed to grow. That was simply a fact. Simply his nature.

He flicked off the bathroom light and stepped into the living room, a simple space, clean and overwhelmingly beige. It looked like every other $100 hotel room. Kyle had stayed in a lot of them over the years. There were only so many necromancers out there, after all, and a bit of traveling was required. Kyle liked to think of himself as a sort of hunter-gatherer, roaming to survive.

He grabbed his blazer off the bed before sliding it over top his freshly ironed dress shirt — appearances were important — then fetched his collar stays from the nightstand. Kyle pushed them in one at a time, checking himself out in the small oak mirror above the dresser. "Your name is Leonard Sutton," he said aloud and then walked out the front door, locking it behind him.

Kyle made his way to the elevator, politely nodding to an old woman passing him in the hallway, a smile stretched across his plain face, ready as ever to face the inevitable.

"You must be Leonard." The man was in his late forties but youthfully groomed. His suit looked new — silver, sharp at the edges, and a pretty good fit save for the waist. A modest gut poured over his belt and under a skinny black tie that matched his thick-rimmed glasses. Untailored, his suit, but meticulously chosen. Diego Castillo wasn't quite as wealthy as he appeared from a distance, but then Kyle wasn't here for his money.

Diego leaned forward to shake hands. His was rough and tan, but his grip was soft and warm. He smiled then reclined back into his seat. Kyle joined him, grinning as he sunk into the leather upholstery. It was a small, intimate table, a candle and two cocktails all that lay between them.

"I hope you don't mind," said Diego. Kyle could feel his breath. "I got you an old fashioned. It's my favorite, so if you don't want it… " He trailed off teasingly.

"You shouldn't have." Kyle took a small sip. "I'm not much of a drinker, but I think I can make an exception tonight. Cheers."

"Cheers," said Diego. "To exceptions."

"To exceptions."

"It's not often I meet a fellow, shall we say, hobbyist in Salt Lake City." Diego eyed the room around them, but the dim hotel bar was mostly deserted.

"It's my first time," replied Kyle. "I wish I could stay a little longer."

Diego looked incredulous. "You wish you could stay longer," he said, eyebrows raised, "in Salt Lake fucking City?"

"Hah, hah, hah." When Kyle laughed, he spoke each "hah."

"Don't get me wrong," added Diego. "I grew up here and all that. But let me tell you, boy, as soon as my kids — whom I love to bits." He took a deep, melodramatic breath. "As soon as those wonderful bastards go off to college, I am out of here. And I mean for good. Being a gay man in Salt Lake City is like being a butterfly in a hornet's nest."

"Lucky for me, I found the butterfly." Kyle feigned a sip of his old fashioned.

Diego rolled back in his chair, guffawing, his whole body rocking as his cheeks grew redder and redder. His laugh was everything Kyle's was not. "Oh God, Leonard." Diego wiped both eyes with the back of his hand, one after the other. "You are too goddamn cute."

"Hah, hah, hah."

Diego let out a satisfied sigh. "So, you're in sales, are you? How do you like that?"

"It suits me. I like people. Heck, I even like small talk." Kyle hated small talk.

"Well, you're very good at it." Diego drank down the last of his old fashioned as if it were a shot and then signaled the server for another.

"Your profile said you're a lawyer." Kyle was referring to the dating website the two had met on three weeks earlier. For a baby-faced millennial like Kyle, meeting men was hardly a challenge. Meeting necromancers, on the other hand— now that was trickier.

Kyle's dating profile said nothing of necromancy. It was spotless, cheerful, almost abnormally innocent. He was a fun-loving salesman from Seattle who traveled a lot— "for work AND pleasure." Leonard Sutton was a cliché. Unless, of course, you knew what to look for. Unless you were a fellow necromancer.

A single line gave him away: "People say I have a lot of spirit— realms of it!" To most readers, an awkward phrase (Leonard was no master wordsmith). But to necromancers, the words spirit and realm side-by-side stuck out like a blot of blood on white canvas. And sometimes, on those rare occasions, one of them would reach out.

If there was one hole in Kyle's plot, it was the possibility of drawing unwanted attention, of attracting inquisitors— the religious fanatics who hunted and killed his kind for a living. They were always searching for subtle clues that might lead them to their next target. But Kyle didn't fear inquisitors. There seemed to be fewer of them these days, and he'd already killed a couple. He was the real predator, after all, the tornado— and he'd swallow up anyone who crossed him.

Diego, on the other hand, was a gentle soul. Kyle could sense that much. He harboured no ill will toward the man, but then he rarely did. It wasn't about who deserved what, because in Kyle's universe, no one deserved anything. If people were snowflakes, as they say, then humanity was an avalanche, each individual barreling down the mountainside, a prisoner to physics. And here, in this hotel bar, Diego had hit ground.

Soon, he would melt into Kyle.

"Sad to say it." Diego rolled his eyes. "I am indeed a lawyer." He leaned forward on one elbow. "Did you know that seventy-five percent of lawyers regret becoming lawyers?" He poked the table with his index finger. "Seventy-five percent."

"Wow, really?" Kyle pretended to look surprised, to care.

"Actually, I have no idea." Diego chuckled. "I think I read that somewhere. Could be true."

"Hah." Kyle tried not to overdo it this time. He sometimes wondered what it felt like, having a good laugh. He heard once that some women went their whole lives without ever experiencing an orgasm, mistaking ripples of pleasure for the real thing. Kyle wondered if he was like those women, smirking and chuckling but never truly laughing— never knowing how hilarious life could be.

"You know what I don't regret, though," said Diego. Then, under his breath: "Becoming a necromancer."

A grin spread across Kyle's face, and for the first time that night, it was authentic. "That," he said, "makes two of us."

Once more, they clinked glasses.

◆❖◆

"Make yourself at home."

They were back in Kyle's hotel room. Diego kicked off his shoes and went straight for the bed, unfurling onto his back, arms outstretched. "Mmm. Comfy."

Kyle locked the door then headed to the bathroom. "To freshen up."

"I haven't been this drunk in some time," said Diego.

Kyle could see him reflected in the bathroom mirror, rolling and giggling, crinkling his crisp sheets. "Nothing wrong with having a little fun," he replied. "You've earned it."

"Have I, now?"

"Sure," said Kyle, splashing water on his face— he liked to stay clean. "We all deserve to have what we want. To do what we want."

"Is that so?" Diego could see Kyle's reflection too; he was staring back at him, lust in his eyes. "I don't always know what

I want, Leonard — lovely, lovely Leonard — but right now... I am dead certain of it."

Kyle flicked off the bathroom light and stepped out from behind the doorframe. "That makes two of us," he said.

Diego sat upright with renewed energy, downplaying his drunken demeanor. He watched every step Kyle took toward the bed like a cat trailing a fly.

Kyle sat down beside him, close enough that their hips touched. Diego lifted his hand from the bed, tracing Kyle's spine, up and down, then in swirls. He leaned in, inhaling Kyle's neck and cheek before kissing him.

Truth be told, Kyle had never figured out his sexually. Though he generally preferred women, gender mattered less than the act itself. They were all just bodies, after all, some more pleasurable than others. In a sense, his psychopathy freed him: he felt no remorse, no pressure to be straight or gay. He simply wanted what he wanted when he wanted it— and he would take it without hesitation.

But Kyle did not desire Diego, at least not sexually— he was too old, too drunk. All the same, he was a necromancer. Not a particularly gifted one, granted, but that would only make him easier to consume, to contain. And Kyle was hungry.

"You smell like soap." Diego chuckled, his hand crawling down Kyle's stomach, making its way to his belt.

Kyle said nothing, nor did his eyes. His hand, however, moved up to Diego's throat. Kyle had learned the hard way that if you're going to attack another necromancer, you best stop them from chanting— stop their ability to reflect your spells, to strike back. So Kyle squeezed.

For a second, Diego seemed to think he was just playing rough. It wasn't until the air in his throat was cut off like a closed valve that he noticed Kyle chanting. That his eyes were no longer unassuming and kind but a venomous crimson.

Diego took a swing at him, but his fist struck Kyle's cheek like a pillow, his strength diminished to a child's. The younger necromancer remained unblemished and unfazed, staring through him with his red eyes, through a man who was vanishing by the second. The spell had already taken hold. The air between them was a veritable strainer, Diego's spirit being pulled through as Kyle consumed its mangled remains.

Once Diego could no longer move his body, he knew it was over. His gaze said as much, but now Kyle could hear his thoughts. The thoughts of a dying man, because though Diego wouldn't truly die — held prisoner in the Living Realm, in Kyle — the very thing that made life worth living in his view, his autonomy, would be left behind like his corpse. If Diego had possessed free will, it was evaporating in the space between them.

Kyle, of course, did not believe in such things.

The two men fell to the carpet. Diego's body landed on its side, Kyle on his ass. He gasped for air, sweat streaming down his pale, round face. Consuming another man's spirit was like swallowing an apple whole— getting it down was the hardest, if not seemingly impossible, part.

But Kyle had done this many times before and knew that pain was just part of the process. He crawled off the floor onto his bed, clinging to the sheets, his fingers curled into claws.

Sometimes Kyle passed out afterward. But not today. He was getting better at this, growing stronger. His body was adapting, evolving, transforming into an impossible creature.

Impossible— if only Kyle McDonald were not inevitable.

♦❖♦

**Our titles are available at major book stores
and local independent resellers who support
Science Fiction and Fantasy readers like you.**

EDGE Science Fiction
and Fantasy Publishing

www.edgewebsite.com

Our titles are available at major book stores and local independent resellers who support Science Fiction and Fantasy readers like you.

Alphanauts by J. Brian Clarke (tp) - ISBN: 978-1-894063-14-2
Apparition Trail, The by Lisa Smedman (tp) - ISBN: 978-1-894063-22-7
As Fate Decrees by Denysé Bridger (tp) - ISBN: 978-1-894063-41-8

Bad City by Matt Mayr (ebk) - e-ISBN: 978-1-77053-093-5
Bedlam Lost by Jack Castle (ebk) - e-ISBN: 978-1-77053-105-5
Black Chalice, The by Marie Jakober (hb) - ISBN: 978-1-894063-00-7
Blood Matters by Aviva Bel'Harold (tp) - ISBN: 978-1-77053-073-7
Blue Apes by Phyllis Gotlieb (pb) - ISBN: 978-1-895836-13-4
　　Blue Apes by Phyllis Gotlieb (hb) - ISBN: 978-1-895836-14-1
Braided Path, The by Donna Glee Williams (tp) - ISBN: 978-1-77053-058-4

Captives by Barbara Galler-Smith and Josh Langston (tp) - ISBN: 978-1-894063-53-1
Children of Atwar, The by Heather Spears (pb) - ISBN: 978-0-88878-335-6
Chilling Tales: Evil Did I Dwell; Lewd I Did Live edited by Michael Kelly (tp)
　　- ISBN: 978-1-894063-52-4
Chilling Tales: In Words, Alas, Drown I edited by Michael Kelly (tp)
　　- ISBN: 978-1-77053-024-9
Cinco de Mayo by Michael J. Martineck (tp) - ISBN: 978-1-894063-39-5
Cinkarion - The Heart of Fire (Part Two of The Chronicles of the Karionin) by J. A. Cullum - (tp) - ISBN: 978-1-894063-21-0
Circle Tide by Rebecca K. Rowe (tp) - ISBN: 978-1-894063-59-3
Clan of the Dung-Sniffers by Lee Danielle Hubbard (tp) - ISBN: 978-1-894063-05-0
Claus Effect, The by David Nickle & Karl Schroeder (pb) - ISBN: 978-1-895836-34-9
　　Claus Effect, The by David Nickle & Karl Schroeder (hb)
　　- ISBN: 978-1-895836-35-6
Clockwork Heart by Dru Pagliassotti (tp) - ISBN: 978-1-77053-026-3
Clockwork Lies: Iron Wind by Dru Pagliassotti (tp) - ISBN: 978-1-77053-050-8
Clockwork Secrets: Heavy Fire by Dru Pagliassotti (tp) - ISBN: 978-1-77053-054-6
Clockwork Trilogy Boxed Set by Dru Pagliassotti - **COMING IN SPRING 2015**
Coins of Chaos edited by Jennifer Brozak (tp) - ISBN: 978-1-77053-048-5

Danse Macabre: Close Encounters With the Reaper edited by Nancy Kilpatrick (tp)
　　- ISBN: 978-1-894063-96-8
Dark Earth Dreams by Candas Dorsey & Roger Deegan (Audio CD with booklet)
　　- ISBN: 978-1-895836-05-9
Darkness of the God (Children of the Panther Part Two) by Amber Hayward (tp)
　　- ISBN: 978-1-894063-44-9
Demon Left Behind, The by Marie Jakober (tp) - ISBN: 978-1-894063-49-4
Distant Signals by Andrew Weiner (tp) - ISBN: 978-0-88878-284-7
Dreams of an Unseen Planet by Teresa Plowright (tp) - ISBN: 978-0-88878-282-3
Dreams of the Sea (Part 1 of Tyranaël) by Élisabeth Vonarburg (tp)
　　- ISBN: 978-1-895836-96-7
　　Dreams of the Sea (Part 1 of Tyranaël) by Élisabeth Vonarburg (hb)
　　- ISBN: 978-1-895836-98-1
Druids by Barbara Galler-Smith and Josh Langston (tp) - ISBN: 978-1-894063-29-6

Eclipse by K. A. Bedford (tp) - ISBN: 978-1-894063-30-2
Elements by Suzanne Church (tp) - ISBN: 978-1-77053-042-3
Europa Journal by Jack Castle (tp) - ISBN: 978-1-77053-104-8
Even The Stones by Marie Jakober (tp) - ISBN: 978-1-894063-18-0
Evolve: Vampire Stories of the New Undead edited by Nancy Kilpatrick (tp)
 - ISBN: 978-1-894063-33-3
Evolve Two: Vampire Stories of the Future Undead edited by Nancy Kilpatrick (tp)
 -ISBN: 978-1-894063-62-3
Expiration Date edited by Nancy Kilpatrick (tp) - ISBN: 978-1-77053-062-1

Fires of the Kindred by Robin Skelton (tp) - ISBN: 978-0-88878-271-7
Forbidden Cargo by Rebecca Rowe (tp) - ISBN: 978-1-894063-16-6

Game of Perfection, A (Part 2 of Tyranaël) by Élisabeth Vonarburg (tp) - ISBN: 978-1-894063-32-6
Gaslight Arcanum: Uncanny Tales of Sherlock Holmes edited by Jeff Campbell & Charles Prepolec (tp) - ISBN: 978-1-8964063-60-9
Gaslight Grimoire: Fantastic Tales of Sherlock Holmes edited by Jeff Campbell & Charles Prepolec (tp) - ISBN: 978-1-8964063-17-3
Gaslight Grotesque: Nightmare Tales of Sherlock Holmes edited by Jeff Campbell & Charles Prepolec (tp) - ISBN: 978-1-8964063-31-9
Green Music by Ursula Pflug (tp) - ISBN: 978-1-895836-75-2
 Green Music by Ursula Pflug (hb) - ISBN: 978-1-895836-77-6

Healer, The (Children of the Panther Part One) by Amber Hayward (tp)
 - ISBN: 978-1-895836-89-9
 Healer, The (Children of the Panther Part One) by Amber Hayward (hb)
 - ISBN: 978-1-895836-91-2
Hell Can Wait by Theodore Judson (tp) - ISBN: 978-1-978-1-894063-23-4
Hounds of Ash and other tales of Fool Wolf, The by Greg Keyes (tp)
 - ISBN: 978-1-894063-09-8
Hydrogen Steel by K. A. Bedford (tp) - ISBN: 978-1-894063-20-3

i-ROBOT Poetry by Jason Christie (tp) - ISBN: 978-1-894063-24-1
Immortal Quest by Alexandra MacKenzie (tp) - ISBN: 978-1-894063-46-3

Jackal Bird by Michael Barley (pb) - ISBN: 978-1-895836-07-3
 Jackal Bird by Michael Barley (hb) - ISBN: 978-1-895836-11-0
JEMMA7729 by Phoebe Wray (tp) - ISBN: 978-1-894063-40-1

Keaen by Till Noever (tp) - ISBN: 978-1-894063-08-1
Keeper's Child by Leslie Davis (tp) - ISBN: 978-1-894063-01-2

Land/Space edited by Candas Jane Dorsey and Judy McCrosky (tp)
 - ISBN: 978-1-895836-90-5
 Land/Space edited by Candas Jane Dorsey and Judy McCrosky (hb)
 - ISBN: 978-1-895836-92-9
Lyskarion: The Song of the Wind (Part One of The Chronicles of the Karionin) by
 J.A. Cullum (tp) - ISBN: 978-1-894063-02-9

Machine Sex and other stories by Candas Jane Dorsey (tp)
 - ISBN: 978-0-88878-278-6
Maërlande Chronicles, The by Élisabeth Vonarburg (pb) - ISBN: 978-0-88878-294-6

Milkman, The by Michael J. Martineck (tp) - ISBN: 978-1-77053-060-7
Milky Way Repo by Michael Prelee (ebk) - e-ISBN: 978-1-77053-092-8
Moonfall by Heather Spears (pb) - ISBN: 978-0-88878-306-6

Necromancer Candle, The by Randy McCharles (tp) - ISBN: 978-1-77053-066-9
nEvermore: Tales of Murder, Mystery and the Macabre
    edited by Nancy Kilpatrick and Caro Soles (tp) - ISBN: 978-1-77053-085-0

Occasional Diamond Thief, The by J. A. McLachlan (tp) - ISBN: 978-1-77053-075-1
Of Wind and Sand by Sylvie Bérard (translated by Sheryl Curtis) (tp)
    - ISBN: 978-1-894063-19-7
On Spec: The First Five Years edited by On Spec (pb) - ISBN: 978-1-895836-08-0
    On Spec: The First Five Years edited by On Spec (hb)
    - ISBN: 978-1-895836-12-7
Orbital Burn by K. A. Bedford (tp) - ISBN: 978-1-894063-10-4
    Orbital Burn by K. A. Bedford (hb) - ISBN: 978-1-894063-12-8

Pallahaxi Tide by Michael Coney (pb) - ISBN: 978-0-88878-293-9
Paradox Resolution by K. A. Bedford (tp) - ISBN:978-1-894063-88-3
Passion Play by Sean Stewart (pb) - ISBN: 978-0-88878-314-1
Professor Challenger: New Worlds, Lost Places edited by Jeff Campbell &
    Charles Prepolec (tp) - ISBN: 978-1-77053-052-2
Plague Saint, The by Rita Donovan (tp) - ISBN: 978-1-895836-28-8
    Plague Saint, The by Rita Donovan (hb) - ISBN: 978-1-895836-29-5
Pock's World by Dave Duncan (tp) - ISBN: 978-1-894063-47-0
Puzzle Box, The by The Apocalyptic Four (tp) - ISBN: 978-1-77053-040-9

Railroad Rising: The Black Powder Rebellion by J. P. Wagner (ebk)
    - e-ISBN: 978-1-77053-098-0
Red Wraith, The by Nick Wisseman (ebk) - e-ISBN: 978-1-77053-095-9
Reluctant Voyagers by Élisabeth Vonarburg (pb) - ISBN: 978-1-895836-09-7
    Reluctant Voyagers by Élisabeth Vonarburg (hb) - ISBN: 978-1-895836-15-8
Resisting Adonis by Timothy J. Anderson (tp) - ISBN: 978-1-895836-84-4
    Resisting Adonis by Timothy J. Anderson (hb) - ISBN: 978-1-895836-83-7
Rigor Amortis edited by Jaym Gates and Erika Holt (tp)
    - ISBN: 978-1-894063-63-0
Rosetta Man, The by Claire McCague (ebk) - e-ISBN: 978-1-77053-094-2

Shadow Academy, The by Adrian Cole (tp) - ISBN: 978-1-77053-064-5
Silent City, The by Élisabeth Vonarburg (tp) - ISBN: 978-1-894063-07-4
Slow Engines of Time, The by Élisabeth Vonarburg (tp) - ISBN: 978-1-895836-30-1
    Slow Engines of Time, The by Élisabeth Vonarburg (hb)
    - ISBN: 978-1-895836-31-8
Stealing Magic by Tanya Huff (tp) - ISBN: 978-1-894063-34-0
Stolen Children (Children of the Panther Part Three) by Amber Hayward (tp)
    - ISBN: 978-1-894063-66-1
Strange Attractors by Tom Henighan (pb) - ISBN: 978-0-88878-312-7

Taming, The by Heather Spears (pb) - ISBN: 978-1-895836-23-3
Taming, The by Heather Spears (hb) - ISBN: 978-1-895836-24-0
Technicolor Ultra Mall by Ryan Oakley (tp) - ISBN: 978-1-894063-54-8
Ten Monkeys, Ten Minutes by Peter Watts (tp) - ISBN: 978-1-895836-74-5
    Ten Monkeys, Ten Minutes by Peter Watts (hb) - ISBN: 978-1-895836-76-9
Terminal City by Trevor Melanson (tp) - ISBN: 978-1-77053-083-6
Tesseracts 1 edited by Judith Merril (pb) - ISBN: 978-0-88878-279-3

Tesseracts 2 edited by Phyllis Gotlieb & Douglas Barbour (pb)
 - ISBN: 978-0-88878-270-0
Tesseracts 3 edited by Candas Jane Dorsey & Gerry Truscott (pb)
 - ISBN: 978-0-88878-290-8
Tesseracts 4 edited by Lorna Toolis & Michael Skeet (pb)
 - ISBN: 978-0-88878-322-6
Tesseracts 5 edited by Robert Runté & Yves Maynard (pb)
 - ISBN: 978-1-895836-25-7
  Tesseracts 5 edited by Robert Runté & Yves Maynard (hb)
  - ISBN: 978-1-895836-26-4
Tesseracts 6 edited by Robert J. Sawyer & Carolyn Clink (pb)
 - ISBN: 978-1-895836-32-5
  Tesseracts 6 edited by Robert J. Sawyer & Carolyn Clink (hb)
  - ISBN: 978-1-895836-33-2
Tesseracts 7 edited by Paula Johanson & Jean-Louis Trudel (tp)
 - ISBN: 978-1-895836-58-5
  Tesseracts 7 edited by Paula Johanson & Jean-Louis Trudel (hb)
  - ISBN: 978-1-895836-59-2
Tesseracts 8 edited by John Clute & Candas Jane Dorsey (tp)
 - ISBN: 978-1-895836-61-5
  Tesseracts 8 edited by John Clute & Candas Jane Dorsey (hb)
  - ISBN: 978-1-895836-62-2
Tesseracts Nine edited by Nalo Hopkinson and Geoff Ryman (tp)
 - ISBN: 978-1-894063-26-5
Tesseracts Ten: A Celebration of New Canadian Specuative Fiction
 edited by R.C. Wilson and E. van Belkom (tp)
 - ISBN: 978-1-894063-36-4
Tesseracts Eleven: Amazing Canadian Speulative Fiction
 edited by Cory Doctorow and Holly Phillips (tp)
 - ISBN: 978-1-894063-03-6
Tesseracts Twelve: New Novellas of Canadian Fantastic Fiction
 edited by Claude Lalumière (tp)
 - ISBN: 978-1-894063-15-9
Tesseracts Thirteen: Chilling Tales from the Great White North
 edited by Nancy Kilpatrick and David Morrell (tp)
 - ISBN: 978-1-894063-25-8
Tesseracts 14: Strange Canadian Stories
 edited by John Robert Colombo and Brett Alexander Savory (tp)
 - ISBN: 978-1-894063-37-1
Tesseracts Fifteen: A Case of Quite Curious Tales
 edited by Julie Czerneda and Susan MacGregor (tp)
 - ISBN: 978-1-894063-58-6
Tesseracts Sixteen: Parnassus Unbound edited by Mark Leslie (tp)
 - ISBN: 978-1-894063-92-0
Tesseracts Seventeen: Speculating Canada from Coast to Coast to Coast
 edited by C. Anderson and S. Vernon (tp)
 -ISBN: 978-1-77053-044-7
Tesseracts Eighteen: Wrestling With Gods
 edited by Liana Kerzner and Jerome Stueart (tp)
 - ISBN: 978-1-77053-068-3
Tesseracts Nineteen: Superhero Universe
 edited by edited by Claude Lalumière & Mark Shainblum (tp)
 - ISBN: 978-1-770530-87-4

Tesseracts Q edited by Élisabeth Vonarburg and Jane Brierley (pb)
   - ISBN: 978-1-895836-21-9
   Tesseracts Q edited by Élisabeth Vonarburg and Jane Brierley (hb)
   - ISBN: 978-1-895836-22-6
Those Who Fight Monsters: Tales of Occult Detectives
   edited by Justin Gustainis (pb) - ISBN: 978-1-894063-48-7
Time Machines Repaired Whie-U-Wait by K. A. Bedford (tp)
   - ISBN: 978-1-894063-42-5
Triforium, The (The Haunting of Westminster Abbey) by Mark Patton (ebk)
   - e-ISBN: 978-1-77053-097-3
Trillionist, The by Sagan Jeffries (tp) - ISBN: 978-1-894063-98-2

Urban Green Man edited by Adria Laycraft and Janice Blaine (tp)
   - ISBN: 978-1-77053-038-6

Vampyric Variations by Nancy Kilpatrick (tp) - ISBN: 978-1-894063-94-4
Vyrkarion: The Talisman of Anor (Part Three of The Chronicles of the Karionin)
   by J. A. Cullum (tp) - ISBN: 978-1-77053-028-7

Warriors by Barbara Galler-Smith and Josh Langston (tp)
   - ISBN: 978-1-77053-030-0
Wildcatter by Dave Duncan (tp) - ISBN: 978-1-894063-90-6